The Covenant of Blood

J.S. Living

Published by J.S. Living, 2022.

THE COVENANT OF BLOOD

First paperback edition November 2022

Book design by Giulia Calligola
Photos by Alejandro Smith

ISBN 978-0-5783-6677-7 (Paperback)
ISBN 979-8-9857-0010-7 (eBook)

www.thejsliving.com

To those who don't believe they have a choice in what they do, and to those who need a little extra guidance in regards to their decisions, this book is for you.

Part 1: The Blood Quest
A Letter to Mother

Dear Elizabeth Bathory,

My name is Elizabeth Mina Bathory-Tepés, daughter of Vladimir Tepés, also known as the daughter of Dracula. I know how my father gained his horrid nickname, which has never been an issue for me. He did, after all, impale all those men and, in some cases, women. I rather enjoy having that part of history. Especially since it keeps the males within the region from courting me. Even though my father wishes for me to find a husband, I am glad his legend has deterred the men in this country from doing anything untoward. I was cursed with beauty.

I am not writing this letter to discuss the antics of young men or my father's outdated notion that women exist to serve—although my father does wish for me to find love, it is just that love is to come after duty. No, I am writing this letter to you, Elizabeth Bathory, because we share a name.

As far as I know, my father was only ever interested in courting two women. The first whose name I do not know, and the second Jusztina Szilágyi. I was told I am the daughter of Jusztina and that my mother died after giving birth to me. However, my father has always kept me hidden from my relatives, and aside from those who take care of the establishment and my father, I do not have company. The idea that my mother would be Jusztina seems preposterous. If I were her daughter, would not I have been raised with my family instead of being carted off from country to country to learn about history and geography and the state of affairs?

What I believe happened, Ms. Bathory, with whom I share a name, is that you are either the mysterious first woman that my father wanted to court, or you are a mysterious third woman no one has heard of. Regardless of which, I implore you to write me back.

As a young, impressionable woman, I have many thoughts, ideas, and needs that should be addressed and explained by someone who is, perhaps, my mother.

I have been aching for such a connection, and from the letters you and my father have exchanged, I can only assume the two of you were enamored with each other. Which begs the question, why did you stop writing him? The last letter was sent in 1573, and it is now 1593. The only conclusion I can come to is that you stopped writing him after my birth.

How could you do this to me? To us? Did you not want to know your daughter? Did you not want to hold her in your arms and sing her sweet lullabies like most mothers do? Did you not want to see her grow into a fine young woman? If you are indeed my mother, then I would think you would at least have the decency to check on us, your family.

Although I am sure you have your own affairs to deal with, considering the love you once held for my father, I thought you might want to know that he spends a significant amount of time outside at night and only wants to sleep in the day. He is increasingly agitated, and I am told the last time this happened, he impaled people left and right. I am not sure what ails him, but I would hate for the locals to find out what we are.

I also fear if nothing is done, if it is not explained, then I might end up the same.

Miss Bathory (or are you a missus?), if you care for me at all, or at the very least my father, I implore you to write back so that I may know how and why Father is like this.

He will not admit it—as a matter of fact, he discourages me from reaching out—but I believe you are the great love of my father. He never speaks of loving anyone, and the women he brings home from time to time are simply here to entertain him or sate his hunger, one way or another. If what you wrote in your previous letters is true, I must believe you feel the same.

Come back to us, or at the very least, respond to this letter. Godspeed and bless you.

Yours truly,

Elizabeth Mina Bathory-Tepés

Chapter One

The letter was sent back with nothing on it but a red lipstick mark. I kept it as a reminder that my mother is out there, somewhere.

When Father found his and Mother's correspondence sitting on my desk, he was furious. Once he calmed down, I finally found the courage to ask why he was so upset. He sighed and explained that my mother did not want to be found and that he had tried so hard to keep the correspondence away from me.

As an incorrigible child, I asked more questions. Where he would usually brush me off and send me away to learn things such as sewing and knitting, this time, he indulged me. He told me the family secrets. At least some of them. It would be years before I learned the whole truth.

At ten years old, I discovered that I am a Dhampir, one of few vampires that can procreate. Ten years later, during a training exercise at the age of twenty, I learned the truth of what my mother was and why my father had insisted that I not look for her.

I am not only Dhampir, but human and Sluagh too. A tribrid.

It was then that I wrote her this letter.

Over four hundred years have passed since then, yet, I am still looking for her.

It is pathetic.

I pack the letter into my bag and toss it over my shoulder. Mississippi is nothing like I remember it from when I visited in my youth. The trip was short, only a few days, but I remember the dirt roads and small cottages. Now everything is covered in concrete and the houses are large.

Mother is nowhere to be found.

I sigh, peer into the mirror, and apply a new coat of rouge onto my full lips. I smack them together to be sure that the matte stays in place. The last thing I need while I am out for a food run is my makeup smearing.

I leave out the door and begin my hunt.

I DAB AT THE CORNER of my mouth with a napkin as the jukebox plays a tinny tune. People can say what they want about the South, but there is no better place to get fried chicken and blood. The small but plump Black cook from the diner is slumped in her seat across from me. She was kind enough to give me extra helpings of her signature fried chicken, mashed potatoes, and collard greens.

My lithe frame suggests I have not had a proper meal in a while. In truth, I just have not had regular human food for the past few months. Instead, I have been subsisting on cooked rodents and deer and the bare amount of human blood I needed to survive until I situated myself.

When she handed me the biscuit drizzled with honey, I could not stop myself from downing the meal in a hurried frenzy. When she asked if I was still hungry, I realized regular food was not the only thing I wanted. The sweetness of cinnamon, honey, and grace wafted from her body, and her delicious, sugary blood was hard to resist.

Once everyone cleared the diner, I made my way over to her and struck up a conversation. Moments later, I extended my teeth, bit into her vein, and licked the blood with my tongue.

I had been right. Her sweet disposition hummed to the very core of her body. Even her soul smelled saccharine. It was difficult to avoid grabbing it, caressing it, and licking it until it filled me to the brim with an ecstasy I have not had since my first soul tasting.

But only those who were truly evil deserved to be damned to this earth.

This woman, this beautiful, brown-skinned woman, did not deserve that. But her blood? Well, that was fair game.

Instead of guzzling the blood like I would normally do, I took my time. I spoke to her and assured her that everything would be fine. I made sure every drop I tasted was in reverence. Once I finished, I licked the wound to close it and kissed the spot.

I look at the woman one last time before leaving a large tip in her pocket. I hate the idea of owing someone. Plus, I have made it my mission to leave a little something in the human lives I disturb.

I check my smartwatch for the time, but the flashing message on the screen distracts me. I dial the person who sent the text. Finally, he answers.

"Andrei." I wait for his response. There are muffled noises in the background, but I cannot make out what is being said.

When he does not say anything, I call his name again, yelling, "Andrei!"

"Oh, yes. Sorry, Elizabeth. I'm here."

"Is it true?" I ask. "And call me Lizzy. I miss the nickname you gave me."

"Your father says I shouldn't call you that since you are my superior."

"And like I always tell the both of you, it is all right to have a nickname for the person you raised. Father does not get a say."

"Bu—"

"If you are about to comment with, 'But I must obey my orders,' please remember that I am ordering you to call me Lizzy. Besides, you deserve to call me that more than he ever did." The words come out heavier and more bitter than I meant them to, but Andrei's response is swift.

"Yes, ma'am."

"'Yes, ma'am' you will call me Lizzy or 'Yes, ma'am' to it being true?"

"Both," he says calmly.

"Excellent. Are you sure this private investigator will be helpful? The last one you sent..." I do not finish the sentence. Andrei does not like to be reminded of that incident.

"Yes, he'll be helpful."

"And my father?"

"He doesn't know."

"Excellent." I grin. If this private investigator is anything like his profile suggests, he will be able to locate my mother in no time. "Where shall I meet him?" I hold back my excitement. If he thinks I am eager, he will not give me what I want.

"Just outside of Oxford. I'll text you the address."

"Great. I will look out for it." I am ready to hang up, but he says something. "Come again?"

"It's nothing."

"Andrei, I have known you forever. Spit it out."

His footsteps clomp through the receiver as he walks across the stone floor. He sighs and then confesses, "I said be careful. When you look how you do in the South... Well, things can become difficult."

"You mean because I am beautiful?" I say, hoping to get a chuckle.

"No," he says seriously. "Because you're dark-skinned, and Mississippi..." He lets the statement die.

"I get it."

I was not let out of the house much as a child, and even as an adult, I would spend more time inside than out. Because of what

I am, whenever skin color was an issue, I would use my powers on the individual who questioned me to smooth things over. If it were anyone else, Andrei's warning would be valid. But I am a tribrid. Racism is the least of my worries.

"Thank you, Andrei," I say. The man can be sweet when he wants to be.

"You're welcome," he mumbles before hanging up.

I look at the address he sent. It's not too far from where I am, so I head there immediately.

THE GPS LEADS TO A remote cabin in the woods. I get out of the car and stretch my legs while surveying the surrounding greenery. Limelight Hydrangeas, Frost Proof Gardenias, and knockout roses catch my eye.

A whiff of baked goods indicates someone enjoys sweets.

The moon's bright light bathes the dark cabin in a white glow that calms my nerves.

I check my watch again. He should be here soon if he is not already. I walk toward the cabin, but a sultry voice stops me.

"Can I help you?"

"That depends," I say. "What is your name?"

The corners of his mouth tug up when I turn around and stop myself from gasping.

His skin is a gorgeous sepia, and with his gangling height and athletic build, the man looks familiar. Like someone from my younger years. A servant, perhaps? But that would be... Well, nothing short of impossible.

We hired him to help me find my mother, but that does not mean I cannot check up on him and his credentials. "Well," I say, "are you going to answer?"

He takes a moment to reply, but his next words surprise me. "I don't think I want to tell you." He walks closer and whispers in my ear, "I should keep it to myself." Then, he smiles and pulls back before I can swat him for his insolence.

"That's fine," I say coolly, crossing my arms over my chest. "You are entitled to your privacy. But," I look him over with my amber eyes, "I shall remind you, you took this job on your own." I raise one of my brows and wait for his response.

"That I did. But now, after seeing you, I think I'll pass." He turns and begins to walk away.

I gawk at him, dumbfounded and irritated. "You do know who I am, who my father is?"

He stops. "Yes."

One word. But he seems like a man who enjoys conveying what he wants with that one word.

"And yet you're walking away?" I tilt my head and move closer to him.

"Yes." He scratches his dark hair as he turns to face me. "I've decided my time would be better spent elsewhere."

This is a disappointment. Andrei had spoken highly of this man. His online profile listed him as "The PI," but many immortals have hired him, so he must know about our predicament. I was excited when Andrei had made this meeting happen, especially since Mother's trail had gone cold until now.

But this guy—this man—made this decision on a whim. I am not amused.

"My name is Elizabeth Mina Bathory-Tepés, and you will give me the information I want." This man was not going to impede me from reaching my goals.

"What information do you seek, Elizabeth?" He pronounces my name in an insulting manner, accentuating each letter in my name.

I interpret his comment to mean that he wants a fight, and if that is the case, I refuse to disappoint. He has riled me up, but I will get what I want.

I pull out my miniature weapon, a chainsaw of sorts intended to kill immortal humans but only slightly scratches regular humans.

"My mother," I say. "You will take me to her."

He laughs. "And who is your mother?"

"Elizabeth Bathory. But you knew that. Now, stop with this nonsense and tell me where I can find her. I know you know." My finger moves to turn on the tiny contraption.

"I don't. I haven't seen her in years. Sorry." He shrugs. "You'll have to find a new lead." His smile is smug, which only annoys me more.

I pull my hair into a high ponytail and walk toward my car.

I have had enough.

I stop, whip around, and punch at the PI, aiming for his kneecaps, but he dodges.

I am unrivaled in combat, and hitting the kneecaps tends to immobilize my opponents immediately, so the miss unsettles me.

I take in his body and movements as we fight. There is something familiar about his stance, his countenance, his entire being, but I cannot put my finger on it. His sweat is akin to aftershave, his blood tastes of strawberries, and his soul hums of love and loss, making it difficult to concentrate.

He reminds me of a day I have been trying to forget for an eternity. The day I destroyed my home. The day I accidentally killed all the servants, including the man I loved.

The PI looks just like him, smells just like him, and even has some of the same quirks. But it cannot be him. It would be nice to think he was a descendant of the family, a brother or cousin, but that would be hard to conceive and even harder to believe.

This man's combat skills are impressive, but not impressive enough that I am willing to lose to him.

I stop the train of thought before I drive myself crazy. I come after him, my attack aimed at his neck this time. If I can bite him, then I can compel him, or vice versa. I grab at him with my hands, my nails extended like a cat to give me extra leverage, but he swiftly sidesteps, which should be impossible. I try again, and he sidesteps me once more. It becomes a game of me trying to corner and pounce on him and him dodging me by ducking or sidestepping.

Eventually, I grow tired of the game.

He must have, too, because he stops for a moment, backs up, and then rushes toward me. Then, he disappears for a moment before reappearing behind me. He puts his hand out and taps me on the back. The motion almost causes me to double over, the force within the simple touch shocking me to my core. I laugh to shake off the uncomfortable moment, and then I do the same to him, but with double the impact.

He falls over.

"How did you—" he begins, but I do not give him time to finish the statement. I climb on top of him and press the miniature chainsaw against his neck. I use my legs and my free arm to pin him under me.

"Do not worry about that," I say.

"How is your speech so proper right now?" It comes out muffled.

"I spent a lot of time in the United Kingdom. I might as well be British." I roll my eyes and push my weapon into his flesh a little harder. "Now, are you going to give me what I want?" I raise my eyebrows. "Or are you going to become bait for the night creatures around here?"

"First—" He coughs again, his face turning red from the pressure I have put on his lungs. I cannot get an answer out of him, or help, if he cannot breathe. I ease the chainsaw up enough for him to speak but not enough for him to overpower me and turn the tables. "How were you able to defeat me? ...No one's been able to do that in an extremely long time."

"Practice," I say. Really, it was luck. The tap he gave me could have brought me down if this fight had happened a few months ago, but I have been training in case the need arose to destroy another immortal.

"The next thing you say," I snarl, "better be an answer to my question, lest you find yourself headless."

"But if I have no head, how would I be able to see?"

"I never said you'd be dead." I grin, letting my fangs glisten in the moonlight.

"True."

His eyes are the same dark brown with flecks of amber as my former lover's eyes. My body is on top of his, and his breathing steadies as I try not to imagine what it would be like to take off his dark blue jeans and black t-shirt. I try not to imagine the lines and curves on his body matching those of someone I once cared about. I try not to like him at all.

But, although it is insane and makes no sense, although I have not even spent a full day with this man, I sense we are linked. Somehow, his soul is connected to mine. I almost forget we are in the middle of something when he says, "I don't know where your mother is."

The spell is broken.

I change my mind, and I yearn to kill him.

"But," he continues, "I know where she'll be."

I pause. Most likely he is lying, but I take the bait. "Continue." It comes out as a warning.

"Elizabeth Bathory is typically in this area around this time, but she hides away. A woman like that can't stay in one place too long."

I look at him quizzically.

"You shouldn't be here in Mississippi but in Georgia."

"Georgia?" My eyes widen and my nose wrinkles. "Why would she be there? It is not nearly as remote as the cities and towns in this state."

"Depends on what part of Georgia you're talking about."

"And what part of Georgia are we talking about?"

"I'd show you, but I'm kind of preoccupied right now." He gestures toward my body on top of his. My cheeks warm, and I pray I am not blushing. The last thing I need is for him to discern that I have been thinking about his body.

"Right." I disentangle myself from him and help him up. "Then come along. You will be my guide." I pause, then for good measure, say, "And if I catch you staring at my bosom again, I will throw you so far you will find yourself in space. Understood?"

"Yes, ma'am," he says with an awkward salute.

I hold back a smirk. "Very well. Let us be on our way."

I lead him to my parked vehicle and wait for him to get in. Finally, I am one step closer to finding Mother and that much closer to discovering the truth behind Father's madness.

Chapter Two

I try my hardest to avoid punching the PI in the face, who still refuses to tell me his name. His incessant chatter about his exploits border on asinine, and I wish I was in a car with anybody but him. Unfortunately, I cannot ditch him. I check the GPS to see how far we are from the hotel. The ride from the airport to Midtown is taking much longer than I expected, and my need to feed is wearing on me.

"Will we be stopping soon?" I ask.

"We're not even halfway to the hotel. Why would we stop?" He keeps his eyes on the road as he speaks. Though I am not sure why since we are barely moving.

"Because if we do not stop, I might end up taking a bite out of your neck." I would have added that I was kidding, but it would have been a lie. The hunger within me spreads like a weed. I am not sure how long I can go.

"Maybe," he turns to smile at me for just a moment before turning back to the road, "but then you wouldn't have anyone to help you with your current predicament."

"Do you have a quip for everything I say?" I hold back a small chuckle. He has been doing this for the entire trip. I try not to be amused by what he says, but his humor is very fetching.

"I think that it's just a you thing."

I shake my head. "You are annoying. Do you know that?"

"I've been told that my whole life."

"Good, because it is true." We are silent for a moment, but the hunger in my body breaks it. "So, about feeding me?"

"Don't worry. I know who, well, what I'm dealing with," he says. He stretches his arm behind my seat and pulls a bag to the front. "This should hold you." He sets the bag in my lap and gestures for me to open it.

I unzip the container, and my jaw drops at the sight of the bags of blood. Each one is neatly packaged and labeled. I touch it, expecting it to be cold, but it is not.

"How did you...?"

"I've been doing this for a while. Most of my clients are vamps, so..."

"So, you just have bags of blood stashed in your car in case of emergency?"

"Not exactly."

"And why is it not cold? Blood has to be refrigerated after leaving the human body if it is to last."

"This blood is special."

I look at him skeptically.

"Trust me, it's fine for you to drink. Besides, I wouldn't dare think of harming the daughter of Dracula." He says my father's name as though he is a cheesy cartoon character.

"As if he cares." I snort and examine the contents of the bag once more. I sniff the blood, and sure enough, it smells fresh.

The car slowly moves toward our exit.

How did he get fresh blood into this car without it spoiling? I do not recall seeing this bag on the plane or at any point during our trip. I wonder if this is the reason the paranormal community trusts him with their affairs. Regardless, I cannot stave off the hunger any longer. I extend my teeth and bite into the plastic the way I would a human neck. The experience is still awkward. It is not as though this is the first time I have drank from a blood bag, but it is not something I do often. I am a Dhampir of the olden times, when blood bags did not exist and the only way to get what I needed was through biting flesh. When blood bags and blood banks became more normalized, I found it difficult to adapt. I reserve the use of them for times like these when I am starved and trapped in a place I do not have access to the source. Luckily, this is the only supernatural meal I am forced to consume regularly. I limit my consumption of souls to once a month. Sometimes being a tribrid can be taxing.

"You're mighty quiet," the PI says.

I pull the drained bag off my teeth. "It is rude to speak while one is eating."

"Technically, you were drinking." He glances at me with a wry expression on his face.

"Eating, drinking, it does not matter how you look at it. It is still rude." I put the second bag on my fangs before he can comment.

By the time I finish draining the bags, we have arrived at a hotel. We get out of the car, and he loads our things while I go inside. The hotel is lavish, with its thousand-dollar plush seats and artwork, and it was just cleaned with bleach, lavender, and water. Thankfully, the smell of the bleach is not too strong for my sensitive nose. The smell could be worse, I remind myself.

The PI walks in with our things and checks us into our room.

We use the elevator to go to the penthouse floor. It has a window, so I take a moment to look at the scenery. I would talk, but based on the scowl on his face, the PI is not interested in mundane conversation. Finally, the doors open. When we walk inside, the first thing I notice is that there is only one bed.

"You are kidding, right?" I ask, staring at him in disbelief. "We are not sharing a bed."

"Wouldn't dream of it, princess." He motions to the couch. "This room was just bigger."

"If you could not afford it—"

He cuts me off. "I can afford anything. I just thought you would appreciate having a larger bed." He shrugs. "But, if you want me to go back..."

"No, no, it will be fine. Just remember that this was your decision when you wake up with back pains."

He nods. "Will do."

We spend the next few minutes unloading our bags and looking up places we can eat at for lunch. The blood was enough to satiate my darker nature, but my human side needs nourishment too. After a while, we finally decide on a burger joint.

"I'M JUST SAYING," THE PI talks around his food as though he lacks intelligence, "how is it that you enjoy drinking the blood of humans, but red meat freaks you out?"

"Shh, you are speaking too loud," I say as a few people glance our way. I lower my voice, "It is not as though the irony is lost on me. But you must understand," I take a sip of my drink, "human blood and animal blood tastes different. So, yes, I prefer my meat well-done. I would go vegetarian, but I enjoy eating meat."

"Then why did you get a veggie burger?"

"Because I also enjoy the creativity of vegetables pounded into the shape of a burger." I sigh, exasperated that my food choices are this fascinating to him. "Why do you care?"

"Just getting to know you. If we're going to be working together, then I need to know everything I can about you."

"Yet you refuse to tell me your real name. Explain to me how that is fair?"

"I'm human. If I give you my real name, you'd be able to find me anytime you wanted. The violence within the supernatural community isn't lost on me." He pauses, and his eyes turn serious. "I don't want any of my clients looking up my information and coming back to threaten my life because I know too much."

I let that sink in. A part of me had assumed he was supernatural too. But for him to be human and still want to help, that is shocking. "I guess it would be difficult to fault you for that. However, I cannot continue to call you the PI. I need some way to reference you."

"Names have power. The PI will do."

Exasperated again by his unwillingness to cooperate, I groan. "Fine. Suit yourself." We finish our meal in silence, and I let my thoughts wander. How did he get to this point? How does a human become a premier PI for the supernatural community? Is it because of the money? Does a part of him like the danger? I have all these questions and more but cannot seem to bring myself to ask any of them.

He pays for the food and grumbles at me to come on.

"Where are we going?" I ask as I get out of the booth. "Do you have a lead?"

"Yeah, I do."

We walk several blocks after leaving the restaurant, and by the time we stop, I am out of breath.

"This is my lead." He gestures to the massive building in front of us.

"The Georgia World Congress Center? How is this a lead?"

All sorts of people are milling about. Some are in everyday clothes, but others wear elaborate costumes—groups of maids, popular superheroes, people with tentacles, robots, and many others.

"What is this place?" The aroma, colors, and sounds are so immense that my senses become overloaded. "I think I am going to be sick."

The PI just chuckles. "You'll be fine," he says. "Besides, your crowd is over there."

I follow his finger to a group of people shrouded in dark clothes. They wear capes, black nail polish, and dark lipstick. They hold rosaries and vials of blood. "You have got to be kidding me." I roll my eyes at him.

"What? That's not what vampires look like?" He appraises my wardrobe. "It seems you're the one out of place wearing dark jeans and that frilly top. Oh, and not to mention the sandals."

It takes everything within my being not to punch him with all my might. Instead, I give him a little shove, and he stumbles backward. "Seriously, PI, why are we here?"

"Because you need to let loose. You've never been to an anime convention, right? Don't you want to see what nerd culture thinks of you?"

"Not particularly."

"Oh, come on. It'll be fun. Besides, I've been dying to come to this convention for a while. I even have passes for two."

"And if I say no?"

"Then I'll go by myself. Though it would mean I wasted a few hundred dollars." He looks at me earnestly. When I do not reply, he continues, "Okay. Suit yourself. I'm going to register."

He walks off and leaves me staring dumbfounded. I swear and then walk toward him.

"I knew you'd change your mind." He smirks.

I blench at him and direct all my anger and frustration his way. "We are supposed to be searching for my mother!" I scream at him. I am not sure where the rage comes from. Perhaps it is his easygoing nature. Or, maybe, it is attraction. Maybe the idea that I am beginning to like him, even though we have only spent one day together, is getting to me.

People stop talking and stare in our direction. If this were the first time that people stared at me this way, it would be unnerving.

I glare at the onlookers until they return to their former activities. Then, I eyeball him, stone-faced. "I am paying you for a service. Dropping by a hotel, eating lunch out, attending a convention, these are all vacation things. This is not a vacation. It is a job." I take a deep breath, which helps me feel better.

"You done yet?"

I hold back my scream of frustration. I do not want people staring at us again. "Yes. I am finished."

"Good. First, we must sleep somewhere. So, getting a hotel was a good idea." He huffs and waves his hands around as he continues. "We can't traipse around the city all day."

I try to interject, but he shushes me.

"Second, we were both hungry, albeit for different things, but we have to eat. It's one of the first things you should do before starting on any case."

I fold my arms across my chest and try to get another word in, but he stops me again.

"Last, you'd be surprised how many supernaturals come through for this event. Anime conventions are like an ode to your kind. If there is a clue to finding your mother, this is as good a place as any to start. Plus, I had these plans long before I accepted this job. I told you I didn't want to take the job, but you insisted. So, you're on my schedule."

I raise my hand, but he ignores it.

"So, either you come along and watch the magic or go back to the hotel and let me work alone. You're the one who insisted on coming along even though I told you that I work better by myself. What's it going to be?"

Honestly, he could have stopped a while ago, but perhaps he felt the need to vent as well. "Fine." I kick at air. "We can do it your way."

"Great, then let's go."

"But I am not wearing one of those ridiculous costumes."

"Noted," he says, dragging me into the building. He looks at me and smiles. "We're going to find your mom, so relax. You've waited over four hundred years, a few more days won't hurt."

And with that, we head into my first anime convention.

A FEW HOURS LATER, I am destroying some red-headed youth in a video game. It is not as though I have never played them before, I have, it is just that they have never garnered my attention for long. Today, after spending time with the PI, that has changed.

"In your face!" I squeal at him. Apparently, I am well-versed in the multiplayer game Mario Kart. "I win again." I stick my tongue out at him as though I am one hundred years old again.

The boy, and everyone else around us, grunts and walks away.

"Was it something I did?" I chuckle innocently.

The PI's heavy hand touches my shoulder.

"Oh, there you are," I say. "I have just realized that this game is quite enjoyable."

He raises an eyebrow and drags me away.

I try to protest, but it is of no use. "What?" I ask.

He eyes me for a second too long before whispering in my ear, "I told you I was good at my job."

I crook my head to the side and raise my brow at him. "How do you figure that?"

"Because guess who just found a clue to where Elizabeth Bathory is staying?"

It takes a moment for his words to register. "What?" I gasp. "Wait, what? What?" I try not to let my excitement take over, but it is too late. A smile spreads across my face, and the energy of my happiness is about to burst and take control. I grasp the PI into a tight hug. "Really?" I ask, looking up at his face. "When can we go?"

He shakes his head in amusement. "As soon as you're ready. Did you, you know?" He bares nonexistent fangs and mimes biting into someone's neck.

"Of course not," I say. "Although now that you mention it, I am sort of peckish."

"Hurry up then. We don't want the trail to go cold."

I nod and scout for the person whose blood calls out to me the most. When I get a whiff of blood with a faint hint of cinnamon, I walk around the area to find out where it is coming from. The closer I get, the more I inhale. The scent is more than just cinnamon. It is also infused with honey, apple, and a touch of an herb I cannot place. Like apple pie on steroids. After a few minutes of searching, I finally place the scent coming from the red-headed boy from earlier. Strange how this scent did not waft from him then. I walk close to him and sniff again as he bumps into me.

"Hey, watch it," he says. Then, "Oh, it's you. Have you come to ruin this game too?" His freckled and boyish face does not wear the expression of menacing very well.

"No. I was just wondering if we could have a chat." I size him up, feigning interest.

He smiles and says something to the guy next to him. The only words I catch are "hot" and "brb."

"Okay," he says, "where to?"

I smile. Young boys like him are so easy to catch. "This way," I say as I grab his hand.

I pull him toward the supply closet I saw earlier. Since there are not any quiet or private places here, this is the best I can do. I use my nails to unlock the door and am happy to see it is a spacious closet.

"What are we doing here?" he asks in a panic. He clears his throat. "Not that I mind, you're pretty and all, it's just that..."

"Shh," I command him. He stops speaking, and I pull his face to mine as though I am about to kiss him. Instead, I push his head to the side and plunge my teeth deep into his neck. His life force seeps out of him and into me.

I see myself through the boy. My eyes are wide and amber with black flecks, the color that marks me as a Dhampir. He is ecstatic I picked him, and euphoria accompanies his loss of blood.

The blood. My god, the blood tastes impeccable. I continue to drink, more and more. A small voice in my head tells me I need to stop, but I ignore it and continue drinking.

The boy goes limp in my arms. I should stop, but I keep going until there is a knock on the supply closet door, interrupting my trance. I blink and take in my surroundings.

"Shit." I stare at the boy in my arms. He looks like he might be dead. I try measuring his pulse, but it is not present. I use my abilities to search for a presence of a soul and find it. It is minuscule and hiding in a small section in the center of his chest, but it is there. I coax it out and appraise it. The soul is timid and shy, much like the boy, but at least it is existent. I search for a pulse again. If the soul is there, then he cannot be dead. This time, I find it.

"What's going on in there?" a loud, masculine voice booms. "Open the door!"

I am at a loss as to what to do. If they come in here and see this boy like this, they will know I did it. But if I do not let them in, then they will still consider me suspicious. I weigh my options. I have no choice but to use my powers on them. I brace myself and open the door.

There is no one there except the PI. He stands in the doorway, a confused look on his face, and crosses his arm.

"Where did the person go?" I ask, the panic present in my voice.

"I sent them away." He peers into the supply closet and raises an eyebrow. "Mind explaining this?" He waves at the situation before him.

"Later," I say. "Right now, I need your blood."

"Oh no, you don't need my blood," he says. "From the looks of this mess, you just had an entire meal."

"The blood is not for me, you imbecile. It is for him." I gesture to the child.

"My blood is not good for that either."

I sigh. "Then what are you good for?" I pace the area, and then decide. "Fine. I guess I will break Rule 579 then."

"What's Rule 579?"

"Never feed a human your blood," I quote, "even if it can save them." It is an arbitrary rule from before blood banks existed, but since this is an emergency, I do not mind. I just pray the child will not have side effects. I go toward the boy and use my nail to cut a slit on my wrist, then feed him a few drops. Not too much and not too little. He sputters and coughs, then sits up.

"What happened?" he asks.

"Do not worry," I say. "You will be fine." I compel him to forget the incident and send him back to his friends. The smell of his luscious blood disappears in an instant, as though it never existed. Now his blood stinks of strong metals.

"That is odd."

"What's odd?" the PI asks.

"I could have sworn... Never mind. Let us go." I motion for him to move out of my way. We exit the supply closet and head out of the convention. "So, are we going to follow this clue of yours or what?"

The PI gives me a hesitant smile and then leads the way.

I get a prickling sensation, like we are being watched, but I let it go. "The convention hall is just large," I whisper. But the sensation of eyes following me lingers.

Chapter Three

I frown at our destination. The venue stinks of dried blood, urine, and feces. The building in front of us is dilapidated and covered with graffiti. And, although it is dark, my eyes can make out the brown patches of grass on the ground.

"This place is disgusting," I say, covering my nose and mouth with a handkerchief.

The PI shrugs and continues to walk forward.

"How are you not disturbed by this?" I mumble around the cloth in my hand.

"I've been to worse places," he says as he opens the door. "Ladies first."

The inside of the building is not as bad. The further we go in, the better it looks. The dirty and worn marble becomes shiny and pristine. The old, ragged, and discolored pews transform into beautiful shades of red and gold. The ancient and tattered paintings are fresh and current renderings of angels, demons, and God.

The PI leans in. "You're not going to burst into flames, right? I mean, I don't want to be held responsible for that happening."

"Why must you always joke?" This time, I do not hide my grin.

He beams back. "Because I was waiting to see that. You haven't given me a real smile since I met you."

"Shut up. I have so."

"You have not," he says, mimicking me.

"Your accent is horrible."

"I think it's impeccable." He looks down at me and brushes a piece of hair behind my ear. "And you're pulchritudinous."

26

"You think I am beautiful?" I scoff. *I can see I am beautiful. I have been told so by many people before him.* But, when he says it, it is different. Like it is a truth that must be kept so secret that nobody is willing to say it.

"Inside and out," he says.

This makes me blush. "How do you know? It has barely been a day."

"I just do," he says. "Plus, those eyes don't lie." His eyes soften, smolder even.

"What—"

Another voice cuts me off. "So nice to meet you," the voice says from somewhere deep in the building.

"Who are you," I ask.

Several moments go by without an answer. But then I see him. Or, rather, I see his black soul. The man himself has vibrant, white skin. Usually nothing in this world scares me, but in this moment, I huddle closer to the PI. He gives me a quizzical look, but I ignore him and gawp at the man who has just presented himself to us.

"My name is Anton," he says in a deep voice that does not match his boyish face. "How can I be of assistance to you?"

I take in a sharp breath. Anton. That name is familiar for so many reasons. So familiar, it causes the hair on my arms to raise, and it takes everything I have not to let my fangs protrude or my instincts to take over.

Anton is one of the oldest Dhampir vampires. The only Dhampir that compares is my father, and according to the rumors, he may be older than my father. The legends say he was the first of the Dhampir born into this world to emit nothing but strife and chaos. They say he was born with blood, of blood, and in blood. It is also said that he feeds until his victims are near dead. Then he pumps them full of blood through transfusions and repeats the process until their bodies can no longer be used.

But what is he doing in the States? Anton was rumored to be on the run ever since the Dhampir Council was established. He had been banned from most major countries, including the United States and the United Kingdom.

I stare in part awe, part shock, and part dread.

"We were told you may be able to help us find a missing person," the PI says, unaware of who he is speaking to. "Her name is Elizabeth Bathory. Perhaps you've heard of her?"

"Oh, my darling Elizabeth," Anton says with feigned delight. "I love her." He appraises me before looking back at the PI. "Has she gone missing?"

This time I speak up. "No." The sound comes out tiny and small. I clear my throat and try again. "No, she is not missing in the sense you think."

"Oh, then how is she missing?" he asks, amusement playing across his face.

"Well, Sir Anton, she is my mother."

Anton's mouth hangs open.

Before he can say anything, I continue, "Yet, I have never met her. I wrote her a letter once, but the only thing I received back was a rouge lipstick mark in the corner by my name." I take the letter out of my knapsack and show it to him.

"Ah," he says, "so it is true."

"What is true?" It is my turn to be confused and to wonder about things I should not have to worry about.

"That Elizabeth birthed a secret child before marrying her husband. Does this mean you were raised by the church?"

"No. I was raised by my father. Why would you ask such a question?"

Anton ignores me and paces around the room. "Then who is your father?" It is more of a demand than a question.

I flinch and answer immediately, "Vladimir Tepés, but you know that already." The words slipped out of my mouth before I had a chance to stop them. I gauge Anton's response, but he is muttering to himself as he walks ten paces up the aisle, five paces to the left, and then ten paces down. He continues this madness until we break him out of it.

"Anton." The PI touches him softly.

Anton's eyes turn red and his face contorts. "DO NOT TOUCH ME," he yells at the PI. His voice reverberates through the chambers of the church.

The PI steps back and holds his hands up as if surrendering.

Anton clears his throat. "I apologize." He runs his hands through his sunlit blond hair. "We old ones, we do not like to be touched."

The silence stretches as we look at each other, all of us wondering who will speak next. "Anton," I say, my voice small and soft, "do you have the information we seek?" After his episode a few minutes ago, I do not want to alarm him.

Anton smiles. "Of course I do."

"Will you tell us where we can find her then?" I could add that my father would be grateful for the information as well, but Anton would be able to tell that I was lying. The old ones are good for that.

"I can, but it will come at a cost."

"What is it? I will pay anything to locate her." I sound too eager, but the idea that someone, somewhere, finally knows where she is causes joy to bubble up within my entire being.

"Don't be so hasty," the PI whispers. "You don't know what he'll ask for."

I thought he would be happy this little adventure was coming to an end, especially since it took only one day. "I know what I am doing," I whisper back. "Do not worry about me. Just make sure you leave here without making Anton angry."

The PI opens his mouth to say something else, but this time it is Anton who clears his throat.

"Elizabeth," he says.

I look at him. "Yes?"

"What I want from you is simple." He looks at me with a gleam in his piercing green eyes. "I just want a favor."

"A...favor?" I wait for the punchline. One of the oldest Dhampir in the world wants a favor from me. I do not understand why. "What kind of a favor?" I ask, hoping to gain some clarity as to what I might be getting myself into.

"I haven't decided yet," he replies. He moves in close and whispers in my ear, "It will be decided at a later date. I have to iron out the details of this favor. I have an idea of what I want, but I have to make sure it is the right decision before I ask it."

"Do I have to answer now, or can I decide on this favor once you have given me the details?"

"Where would the fun in that be?" Anton says with a devilish smile, his mouth wide and teeth showing like an imp.

The PI's words of caution linger in the back of my mind. "Then, can I think about it?"

"You have twenty-four hours. After that, my information and I disappear." He turns to leave.

"Do I come back here to give you an answer?" I call after him.

"You will know where to find me," his voice echoes from somewhere within the building.

The PI and I shiver uncomfortably. I check my phone for the time. It is already past midnight and the fatigue of the day begins to settle over me.

As we make our way back to the car and eventually to the hotel, my mind wanders. What type of favor would Anton want of me? Does he want me to kill someone? Or perhaps do something forbidden by the Dhampir Council? Does he want loyalty or for me to do his bidding whenever he calls? These options seem beneath him. If he has been ignoring the Council's orders for centuries and has made the States his home, then surely there is no one who can stop him from achieving whatever his goals might be.

"You're awfully quiet," the PI says.

"A lot to think about," I reply.

We enter the hotel room, and I make my way to the shower. The PI bumps into me, and I become aware of his entire being. His breathing, the smell of his body and blood, the depth of his soul.

"Excuse me," he says. "I didn't realize—"

"It is quite all right," I say. In my worries about Anton, I had forgotten how attractive the PI had become. This trip was more of a day-long date than anything else. If his purpose had been to woo me, or even to bed me, then it succeeded. I search his eyes to determine whether I should move, but he decides for me.

"I'm just going to..." He scoots me aside and goes into the bathroom.

I stand outside the door, wondering how I could be so stupid. Of course the attraction is all in my head. He just looks and acts and is so much like...

But they are not the same person, and I cannot expect them to be. Whatever I thought had been blooming today, whether it was infatuation, love, or lust, clearly it was not.

The toilet flushes and water from the sink runs before he steps out of the bathroom. "All yours," he says.

I nod and go inside. I turn on the hot water and watch as the mirror is covered in steam. I pull my hair out of its ponytail, and my long brown locks rest on my shoulder. I step into the shower and let the water wash away the frustration and longevity of the day.

When I am finished, I step out of the shower and don my nightgown and robe. I detangle and dry my hair and gaze into the mirror. I check my eyes for any indication I might need to feed, but they are their normal color. I check my complexion next. There is nothing out of the ordinary there either.

When I open the door, I am startled to see the PI in front of it. His eyes bore straight into mine. He comes closer and brushes a piece of my still-damp hair behind my ear. He leans in and kisses me. His lips are soft and hold the redolence of Green Apple Jolly Rancher, my favorite flavor.

When it is over, I look back at him, but he says nothing. He just stands there. I wave my hand in front of his face, but it is as though he does not see it. I walk around him, but I still do not get a response.

He is sleepwalking.

I do not know how to proceed, and I am disappointed. What does it mean when someone sleep kisses you? I am not sure. So, I give him a peck on his cheek and then snuggle into the bed, leaving him standing in the doorway to the bathroom.

THOUGHTS OF ANTON KILLING me if I refuse his offer plague my dreams. When I finally wake, my body is soaked in sweat and I am panting. I do not need twenty-four hours to mull over this choice. I will grant Anton his favor, consequences be damned. I look at the pull-out couch to see if the PI is still there, but he is not. I assume this means he has gone down to breakfast and use the opportunity to take another shower. Once I am dressed, I head downstairs as well. The PI is nowhere to be found. I try to call him, but he does not pick up. Unsure how to proceed, I call Andrei. He picks up on the second ring.

"Hello?" his deep voice reverberates through the phone.

"Hi, Andrei," I say. "Do you have a moment?"

"I always have a moment for you, Eli—"

I scowl at the phone.

"Lizzy," he corrects quickly.

I smile. "I just wanted to update you."

"And?"

"And I am getting closer to finding Mother."

"So, this PI was worth the hype?"

"You could say that." I walk outside of the hotel. The heat is blistering, and I am thankful that my human and Fae sides keep me from burning to death. Most Dhampir must have witches perform a special ritual on them to keep them from turning into a fiery pit of pain, but hybrids do not have that issue. Apparently, tribrids do not either. "I have a dilemma."

"What is your dilemma?"

"To find Mother, I have to promise a favor to someone."

"Who?"

"What is with the third degree?" I shake my head as he muffles a chuckle. "I would rather not say."

"Lizzy..." He waits for a response.

I take my time to reply. Andrei has been there for me since I was born. So much so that I wish I were his child instead of the daughter of the famed Vladimir Tepés. Andrei has always been supportive of my dreams, and he taught me the essentials of my existence. "The favor is to Anton," I whisper, almost hoping he does not hear me.

But the silence on the other end is so stark, I could hear a pin drop. And then, "Elizabeth Mina Bathory-Tepés. Please tell me that I misheard you." Andrei's voice is serious and deadly, making me feel like a small child. It has been a long time since he has used my full name.

"I-I have not. Not yet anyway." I try to remain calm. "But I think I will take him up on his offer. It is the first solid clue we have found, and I cannot ignore that."

His disapproval radiates through the phone. "If you do this, I'll have to—"

"You will have to what?" I ask, daring him to threaten me. "Tell my father?"

"Well—"

"Keep in mind, Andrei, if you tell my father what we have been doing, he will not only be angry with me but with you as well. And the consequences—"

"You don't have to remind me," he says sharply. "I was going to say that I will have to prepare in case things go wrong. You're always quick to assume you know what other people are going to say. One day, it's going to be your downfall."

I roll my eyes as I head back inside. "Fine. I will keep that in mind." Shuffling footsteps grab my attention as the PI comes into the hotel lobby. "I have to go, Andrei." Before he can say anything, I hang up the phone.

The PI looks terrible, as though he just got into a fight. His clothes are ruffled, his face and arms are bruised, and he reeks of sweat and anger. I approach him, but he passes by with a mumbled, "I'll be right back." I consider following him up to check on him but figure it is better to give him space and wait for him to come back down.

Half an hour later, he gets off the elevator and walks toward me. "Okay," he says in a cheerful voice, "are you ready to go?"

I observe him. "So, are we going to ignore what just happened, or..." I let the question linger.

"Oh, that?" He laughs, but it is humorless. "It was just a tiff. I left early to spend some time at the con and things got a little out of hand." He shrugs. "But I took care of it, so we're all good."

He is lying, but I do not press the issue. "Okay," I say with confidence even though I am anything but, "let us go to Anton. I have made my decision."

"What did you decide?"

"I am going to do it."

"Okay. Then let's go."

"What?" I ask with a wry smile. "You have no objections?"

"Nope. It's not my life. Do what you want. I'm just here to help you find your leads. The rest of the decisions are all you."

On one hand, I like that he is more preoccupied with making sure I do this in a way that best suits me. On the other hand, I was hoping he would protest out of concern for my safety. But I cannot dwell on these feelings. I came here for a reason, and I must not get distracted.

WE LEAVE THE HOTEL and head back to the church. It looks different in the daylight. The sun casts light onto the windows making the room sparkle—it is almost beautiful, save for the cracks and the old cushions on the pews. I wonder why Anton and his group would make their home here when there are much better options in the world—like a house, a hotel, a condo. It never made sense to follow the old ways when we can have the luxuries of the modern world.

Anton appears as soon as we enter the church. This time, he is in regular, everyday clothing instead of a cloak. His body is built like a teenage boy, and the extensive tattoos on his arms depict the Dhampir vampire crest and his family crest from the old days. I cannot make out the other intricate designs from where I stand.

"Well." He clasps his hands together in front of his sleeveless band t-shirt. The tight-fitted jeans and black tennis shoes help sell the teenage boy idea. "I see you have decided. What is your answer?"

I hesitate to consider whether I should say what I am thinking, but the words tumble out of my mouth before I can stop myself. "We have a deal. Give me the information."

Anton's blank expression transforms into a smirk and then a full-on grin. He flashes his teeth and says in joyous celebration, "Excellent. Let us seal it with a Blood Pact. That way, it cannot be undone."

"Aren't those frowned upon?" the PI asks.

"No," Anton says, "not when it's with another supernatural being, vampire, or," he looks around slyly, "otherwise."

The PI looks at Anton skeptically and then turns to me.

"He is correct," I say. "It is only frowned upon when we enter the contract with humans." The PI mumbles something, but I ignore him and turn to Anton. "If that is what is necessary."

"Then come to me, young Elizabeth."

I do as he says and walk toward him. We bite into the flesh of our hands. The blood wells to the top of our wounds and we press them together. The pain of our blood mixing is almost unbearable, like being branded with a hot iron. I clench my fists and lock my jaw, but I do not close my eyes. I endure it. Once the pain subsides, I make my pledge. "I, Elizabeth Mina Bathory-Tepés, promise to uphold my end of this bargain and agree to complete the favor asked of me by Anton..." His full name is a mystery, and I cannot finish the pledge. But he bows his head to indicate it is fine.

He then repeats the pledge. "I, Anton, promise to uphold my end of this bargain and agree to tell Elizabeth Mina Bathory-Tepés where she can find her mother."

When he finishes, the blood boils and burns. It is fiery and painful, like when hot water is run over ice-cold hands, and when it is over, I hold back my tears because Anton is not a person to appear weak in front of.

Once I have swallowed my screams of pain, I nod toward Anton. "Now, about my mother."

Anton grins sheepishly before responding, "Ah, yes. Your mother. She is here in Atlanta."

I grit my teeth—we already knew that. If this was the only information he had, then this was for nothing.

But he continues, "More specifically, she has made this her home base for the past four hundred years or so. She has homes in other areas, as we supernaturals must migrate, but her main home is here."

It is not the clue I was hoping for, but it is something.

"Let me see." He puts one hand on his hip and the other on his chin as though he is thinking hard about it. "Oh, right. You can most likely find her at Piedmont Park." He snaps his fingers and a man in a black robe appears. "Here's a map. I am certain that he," Anton points toward the PI, "can find his way around, but you should probably take this just in case."

The robed man hands me what seems to be a normal map, but when I open it, little dots move on it. "What are these?"

"Do not mind those," Anton says. "They are of no importance to you."

I find it difficult to believe him. I would not have thought to look for Mother in a park, but Father did say their first encounter, or unveiling of each other, took place in one, so it is not a stretch to think she would visit one. Why she would go in this unpleasant, hot, sticky weather is beyond me, but she has always been an enigma. Perhaps fairy hosts do not mind the heat.

"Thank you for this." I bow toward Anton to show him my respect.

"So long as you keep your promise, no thanks are needed." He grins.

I shudder to think what those words are supposed to mean. Once he allows us to leave—because, with Anton, you cannot simply bid adieu, you must wait until he dismisses you—we make our way to the parking lot.

I turn to the PI, awaiting a snide remark, but his drooping tired eyes, which are red from rubbing too much, and low breathing and heart rate indicate he does not have it in him right now.

Chapter Four

For the next two weeks, I sit at the park, hoping to see her. I wait in the morning. I wait in the evening. I wait at night. She never appears.

Today, I sit on a bench shaded by one large oak tree. The heat from the beating sun has me sweating profusely. After making sure no one is watching, I sniff under my arm. Luckily, there is no stench.

As birds chirp, lawnmowers hum, and people walk by, I breathe in the aroma of the flowers and trees. Nature has always had a calming effect on me. I roll my shoulders and stretch, but there is still no sign of her, so I reach into my bag and pull out the one picture I have of my mother. On the back, in a scrawled handwriting, are the words *Love is fleeting, love is forever, love is you, and you are mine.* I run my fingers over the jagged edges, caressing the tears and rips from the paper being swaddled in the hands of a lover longing for a personal touch.

The painted image of my mother has lost its coloring and is almost nothing but a blur, but I hold it close to my heart.

Across the park is a family of three eating their lunch. I wonder what it would be like to have that moment with Father, Elizabeth, myself, and maybe even a sibling. I picture Father outside in his cloak, to protect him from being severely sunburned, a long-sleeved workout shirt, and jeans. Elizabeth would wear a dress that shows off her curves. Based on Father's descriptions, I can only picture her in that or a Victorian dress. I would be in jeans and a peasant top with a corset. I imagine us laughing and smiling, sharing some inside joke about something that happened earlier in the day. We are doing

39

what families do on a picnic: bird watching, enjoying a meal, playing a game of tag.

A hand taps my shoulder, waking me from my daydream. It takes me a few moments, but I blink and look up at the older, Black gentleman. The essence of his soul, a mix of Irish Spring soap and purified lake water, shows he will be dying soon.

His eyes are wide, and he is staring at me as though he has just seen a ghost.

"Yes?" I ask curiously. "Can I help you?"

He bends down and picks up the picture of my mother. It must have flown out of my hands while I was daydreaming. He hands it to me.

"Thank you," I say. I place the photo in my backpack, but his eyes are still on me.

Finally, he speaks. "Liza, is that you?" His voice is deep and gravelly. "That can't be you. Except it is."

"Excuse me?" I am unsure why this man is calling me Liza.

"Liza, I've missed you so much," he continues.

He comes closer. Aftershave and mint leaves permeate my nose as he hugs me. Unsure what to do, I hug him back. The rough, cotton texture of his blue shirt is pleasant to the touch.

"But how is this possible?" he asks, "I saw..." His eyes bulge out. He looks as though he is about to fall, so I shift over and help him sit next to me. "It's been ten years, Liza. You said—" He coughs, and the spittle gets stuck in his throat. I pat his back, but he continues speaking, "I wasn't supposed to see you for a few more months. You told me I had time."

"I am sorry," I say. "My name is not Liza. I am not sure what you mean." As the words leave my mouth, his body shifts. Even though I have never seen this man, he clearly seems to think he recognizes me. There is only one explanation. "I am sorry, what did you say your name was again?"

He points at himself and laughs. "Oh, silly me, Liza. I guess my age isn't sitting as well with me as yours is." He coughs again, but this time he seems okay. I do not have to worry about him dying on me yet. "It's Calvin. Calvin Carter. If nothing else, you should at least remember my name." He winks at me, giving me the feeling he means that I remember him in the biblical sense.

"I am afraid I am not who you think I am, Mr. Carter."

He squints his eyes and looks at me closer, as though inspecting me.

"My name is Elizabeth. Elizabeth Mina Bathory-Tepés."

"You got married?" he asks, and his mouth makes a wide O.

"No," I say, frustrated he does not understand I am not who he thinks I am. "I was given my name at birth."

His eyes wrinkle in confusion and his heart rate increases. I remind him to breathe, and he follows my instructions. "Liza, I mean, Elizabeth, you really don't recognize me?"

I shake my head. "Sorry. I do not."

"But you're the spitting image of her..." He hands me his oak cane and reaches into the pocket of his tan slacks, pulling out a wallet and searching for something. His feeble fingers brush against the leather as he struggles to take it out.

When he shows it to me, I gasp. In his hand is a color picture of a woman who looks exactly like me. He trades the picture for his cane, and I hold the photo close to my face. I trace every inch of the photo, but it is the expression in the eyes that reveals this woman and I are different. While we share some facial features and a similar body structure, her lips are slightly fuller than mine, her nose wider, and her eyes hold a darkness I have only seen in two other people: my father and Andrei.

"Where..." I hiccup, and the corners of my eyes well up with tears. "Where did you get this?"

"You gave it to me, Liza. See the back, that's your handwriting."

I turn the picture over and cannot believe what I see. I take my picture back out of my bag and compare the two. The exact same message, almost the exact same handwriting, the exact same woman. "It is not my handwriting," I tell Calvin. "It is my mother's."

Calvin nods. "That makes more sense." He lets out a slight chuckle. "You'll have to forgive me. I can be a bit out of it sometimes." He sits back on the bench and looks at me again. "But my, the likeness is uncanny. I am glad though."

"Glad about what?"

"That she was able to find happiness."

"What do you mean?"

"You don't know?" he asks cryptically. "Well, it's not my job to tell you. You should ask her yourself."

"I cannot," I say.

He frowns. "Why not? Unless..."

I can tell what he is thinking, and even though I know I should not do it, even though I know it is wrong, I need answers. So, I nod my head solemnly. "Yes. She passed. A year or so ago."

He closes his eyes, and the wrinkles on his face crease and become deeper. This man has led a hard life, and I think I just made it explode. He takes a handkerchief out of his pocket and wipes his face with it, making sure to dab at his eyes.

I use the opportunity to hit the nail in the coffin, for lack of a better phrase. "She never talked much about her history. I would have asked her, but she told me that she would tell me one day. One day never came." I stare at him intently, willing him to believe me while holding back my urge to make him tell me. I do not have control over my Sluagh abilities, and since the soul-sucking incident, I have been trying to train myself not to go into people's minds or use compulsion to get what I want.

Psychology is fair game.

"Could you tell me about her?" I ask softly.

It does not take much for him to talk.

"Liza, rest her soul," he makes the symbol of the cross on his chest. "Liza was one of the most beautiful women I had ever seen." As he talks, images play across my mind. The era, the fashion, it all comes to life. "I was surprised when she asked me out. I had never met a woman so forward. It was the '60s, so you can imagine..." His voice becomes a gentle lull as he recounts meeting Mother for the first time, their first date, and the first time they kissed. Throughout the stories, his eyes shine and his younger self, his younger soul, bursts out of the seams. It is as though the story did not just transport me into the past, but him as well. When he begins to talk about the first time they made love, I tell him he can skip to the next day. I may be over four hundred years old, but I do not need to picture a young Calvin Carter and someone who looks like me copulating.

When he gets to the part about her personality change, I pay close attention. "She would go into these fits," he says, shaking his head, "and I couldn't stop them. One time, oh, I remember it clearly. One time, she went on a rampage. Destroyed everything around her. She hospitalized a man and almost killed another one." It sounds like the fit I had before Father had Andrei teach me some self-control.

"After that," he continues, "she told me she had to leave but that she would be back in fifty-five years to say hi to me." He smiles without pleasure. "I thought it was weird at the time, but when I saw you, I thought..."

I finish his sentence, "That you had passed on to Heaven?"

He nods. "But obviously that's not the case." He cracks his knuckles. "Still, she only had one more year. Why didn't she come see me? Was she too sick or something?"

I do not want to tell him any more lies, but I cannot tell him the truth either. I settle on a half-truth. "I am not sure. Maybe she thought it would be odd to come sooner?" I ask more than tell him.

He chuckles. "That's just like her. Always on schedule. Every five or ten years, she drops by here and checks on me."

"Then why did you think I was her? Besides the fact that we look alike, I mean." If he has another reason for thinking I am my mother, then I need to be prepared. It might be another clue as to where I can find her.

He sighs. "I guess she really didn't tell you nothing, huh?" He frowns. "Your mother never did age like me. Every five or ten years, on the exact same day, she would come and sit in this park." He winks at me. "She would wait for me and catch me up on her life. Never mentioned she had a daughter, though." He gives me the side-eye as though it is my fault for existing. Perhaps he is blaming me for her supposed death. "I asked her about the aging once, but she told me it was a five-hundred-year-old secret that had to do with blood." This time his laugh has humor to it. "I told her if she didn't want to tell me the truth, that was fine. And she said—"

He coughs and spittle flies everywhere. I pat his back. "Thank you," he says. "She told me she was a Sluagh. I thought it was funny until she showed me the truth." He closes his eyes and shakes his head as though warding off a bad memory. "And then she told me something I didn't want to hear. That was the last time I saw her. That was ten years ago."

I leaned closer to him, drawn in by his story and how my mother had blatantly ignored the rules of the supernatural. "What did she tell you?" I am intrigued by this man and his tales of my mother but also embarrassed about how little I know about her. Honestly, this is the most that anyone has ever told me about her.

"She told me that the next time I saw her, it would be my time. But, if she's gone..." His eyes shine, filled with a sparkle of hope.

"I am sorry," I blurt. It is out of my mouth before I can stop it.

He looks at me with confusion, and suspicion settles on his face. "Sorry about what?"

"She is not...she is...she is not dead." I clear my throat and try to explain, but his anger is so apparent in his soul, it hurts. I take a deep breath and try again. "I did not know you knew. What she is, I mean. I..." I sigh. "I have never met her, and I was not sure who you were at first. I...I apologize." I close my eyes and breathe, hoping the flare of his anger will vanish like a whisper in the night. When I open my eyes, he is looking past me, staring at nothing. He looks at me how Father does when he is disappointed in me. It stings. But then, he looks me in the eyes.

"I'm not angry at you, child," he says. "I'm angry at myself for thinking..."

And it hits me. The shining of his eyes. "If she was gone, then you might live." I sigh again. "Mr. Carter..."

"Call me Calvin, young Elizabeth."

"Calvin," I correct myself, "even if she were gone, that would not mean that you get to live. Another being, perhaps dæmons, would have come to take you."

"Demons, huh. So, there are no good choices in the afterlife."

"Hmm?" It takes me a moment to figure out what he means. "No, not demons. Dæmons. They are like guardian angels. They guide the good spirits to where they are supposed to go."

"Unlike fairy hosts who damn you to walk the Earth." This time his cough is more violent, and I worry he may be going sooner than Mother predicted.

"Exactly," I say, looking for the telltale blue-green light that appears when a soul is close to death. He will die soon, but he has at least a few more months. "So, you were saying?" I prod him, but his eyes are glazed over with tiredness. There is not much left he can tell me, and the sun is setting. "When does she come here, Calvin?" I ask.

"Typically, every five years. Sometimes ten if someone or something is after her. Multiples of five have always been a favorite of hers." He smiles at this small detail. "And on the same day."

"What day is that?"

"The winter solstice. This is the wrong month, but you have the correct year." He gets up and stretches. "But I do hope you find her." As he yawns, a woman in her thirties with curly dark brown hair and an empty wheelchair jogs up to him.

"Daddy," she pants, "is this where you've been the whole time?" Her southern accent is thick with worry. "Sit down in this chair. You know you can't be on your feet for too long." She looks at me. "Who's this?" she asks him.

"That's Liza's daughter," he says, winking at me.

The young woman looks at me. "*The* Liza?"

"*The* Liza," he says.

"Nice to meet you," I say. "Mr. Carter..."

"I told you to call me Calvin."

I hide a smirk. He sounds like me when I correct Andrei. "Calvin," I correct myself, "you almost forgot your photo of my mother."

"Keep it," he says. "And remember, the solstice is on the 21st of December." He turns to his daughter, "Let's go," he says. She begins to roll him away.

"But—" I try to hand the photo to him.

He waves it away. "I have another one," he calls back. "You keep that one. Yours looks worn."

As they roll off into the distance, I look at the photo with a sort of emptiness in my heart. "Yours is worn too," I whisper.

That feeling is soon replaced by rage as I gather my things. Anton lied. Well, lied might be a strong word. He coerced me. Told a half-truth. Pulled a *Fae*, as we like to call it in the supernatural community. He was smart when he made the Blood Pact. The only thing he promised was that he would uphold his end of the bargain, which was to tell me where I could find Mother. He was cunning with his word choice. He did not specify he would tell me *when* I could find her, which means he did not have to tell me the year, the month, the day, the time, or any other helpful information. Had I not run into Calvin, I never would have figured it out.

I ball my fists and try to do my breathing exercises. If I let the anger out, everyone around me could be in danger. I need to find a secluded spot. An area away from civilians, away from animals, and away from buildings. I look for such a place, and my breathing becomes more frantic. I have fucked up—and fucked up is not a term I use lightly. I have royally screwed myself by entering into a Blood Pact, with Anton of all people. Of course he would pull something like this. It is one of the reasons why they call him the Fae Whisperer. He is the only being on earth that can compete with and decipher how they work. As such, he uses that knowledge on humans, vampires, werewolves, and the Fae themselves.

I am so stupid.

It is as though I am a kettle and the steam from the pot is about to burst out of me. My face is clammy and hot. My nostrils flare, and my hands clench. My head begins to hurt, and I cry out in pain. I must hurry. If the anger boils over, if I let it out in the wrong place, the madness will take over. Just like then. I double over in pain, and then I spot it. A condemned building. It is perfect for what is about to happen. I run over to it as fast as I can. Once I am inside, I let it out.

My screams fill the air. The building begins to crumble. The rubble and debris fall around me, but not on me.

My power is unleashed.

The paroxysm has surfaced.

AN HOUR LATER, I LEAVE the condemned building, which has been reduced to nothing but ash, and make my way back to the hotel. When we first got this information from Anton, the PI would accompany me to the park and help me watch for Mother. But by the fourth day, he said that his time would be better spent doing other things. When I asked him what he could do, he pointed out that we had not searched the area to see where she might work. Whenever I come back to the room, he is either working on his laptop or sleeping. Today is no different.

"Hey," he says. "How's it going?"

I try not to let him see my eyes. I did not feed after the tantrum, and if he notices them, he will do nothing but worry and force blood bags down my throat. I am not in the mood for an argument, so I do my best to shuffle into the room.

"Today was better," I say as I walk into the bathroom and strip down to take a shower.

"Yeah? How so?"

I step into the hot water before answering. "I met one of Mother's acquaintances." A rush of cold air hits me as the shower curtain opens.

"Really?" he asks, his face beaming.

I am flattered when he looks everywhere but below my neck. "Really," I say. "Do you mind closing that?"

"Oh, uh, right." He closes the curtain and sits on what I can only assume is the toilet or the counter. "So, do you, I don't know, want to tell me about it?"

I contemplate for a moment, but if I tell him now, it will only trigger another tantrum. "I...can we talk about it tomorrow? I am beyond exhausted."

"That's fine."

When I step out of the shower, he hands me a towel, practically wrapping it around me. Then he pulls out a blood bag. "Your eyes," he mumbles.

I sigh and take the bag from him, but I cannot be mad. He is only looking out for me.

Today he's wearing a muscle shirt and basketball shorts. His hair is frizzy, but his eyes are as beautiful as ever. If it were possible to bite your lip while drinking a bag of blood, then I would be doing exactly that right now.

"So...while you're drinking that," he begins.

I cock my head and raise an eyebrow. It sounds like he is about to give me bad news.

"I, uh, I wanted to ask you." He wipes his palms on his shorts and looks everywhere but at my face. "Would it be okay if I, uh..."

I finish the bag and toss it in the trash. "Spit it out already," I say, walking toward the sink to get my toothbrush.

"Right," he says but still hesitates. He takes a deep breath, and I catch him puffing up his chest in the mirror. "You're going to say I told you so, but can we please share the bed?"

I blink a few times and brush my teeth. The air fills with silence. There are a million things I thought he would ask me, and this was not one of them.

On the one hand, I would love to share a bed with him. There are plenty of things I would love to do to his body. That has not changed. On the other hand, I told him to get a two-bed room so that this would not have to be a conversation, and I am just sadist enough to make him sleep on that uncomfortable pull-out couch until we go to our next destination, whenever that is.

I spit into the sink and rinse out my mouth, then grin at him.

"Oh no," he says. "That's your 'I win' grin. What do you want?"

I smile even wider, making sure that he can see my sharp fangs. "You can sleep in the bed," I say. He sighs in relief, but I hold up a finger. "On one condition."

"What, are you Anton now?"

By the way he backs up, I imagine my eyes flashed at the mention of Anton. I shake my head to show him that I mean no harm. "No," I say, "but I do like the idea of you having to do something for me in exchange for me letting you sleep in the bed and not telling you I told you so."

"But you just did," he mutters.

I laugh. "Do not worry," I say. "It is a simple task."

"Fine. What?"

I raise my eyebrow. "Do you want to make a Blood Pact first?" I try to make it sound like a joke, but the pain in my head tells me it was not a good idea.

"Ha-ha," he says, "very funny."

I shrug. "Tell me your name."

"Nope." He does not even think twice about it. "I will sleep on this lumpy-ass makeshift bed before I do that."

This is the response I thought I would get from him. But that is all right because I will likely get what I actually want. "Fine," I say. "Then kiss me."

It is his turn to stop and survey me.

I shrug and wait to see what he will do.

"You have to be kidding me." He scratches his head. "I can't do that. You're paying me. You're practically my boss..."

"But you are asking to sleep in a bed with me, so..." I tilt my head. "I feel like we have already crossed the lines that you speak of." I inch ever so slightly toward him to see what he will do. "What? Do you think I will bite you? Turn you into a vampire?"

"No." He hesitates before saying more. The beat of his heart sounds like a jackhammer, and I recognize the scent of stress sweat. "I... Why?"

"Because. I like you. It has been two weeks, and you are one of the few men I have met who actually gets me." I look down because I have never told anyone this next part. "I seldom have people like you in my life, and of all my partners, I have only kissed a handful of them."

My cheeks are hot, and I cannot remember the last time I was embarrassed like this or wore my heart on a sleeve. It is not a feeling I am used to, nor is it a feeling I like.

"I..."

He stops me before I can say another word. His lips are soft and warm. They taste like Green Apple Jolly Rancher and lime-flavored Kool-Aid. The scent of his body is intoxicating, and I press closer to him. His hands wrap around me like a warm blanket, and I am transported into my teenage years, as though I am with him again. I tug at the PI's hair with one hand and use the other to nestle the back of his head in my fingers. As our lips move together and our tongues intertwine, the mood shifts and bliss envelops me.

And then it stops.

"Which side of the bed should I take?" he asks, pulling away. His voice is rough and slightly raspy.

"What?" I ask, dazed. "Oh...the bed." The disappointment in my voice is evident, but he does not comment. I turn to face the headboard. "You can take the right, I guess."

When I walk toward the closet to grab my clothes, he grabs my hand, spins me toward him, and sits me on his lap on the bed. His eyes bore into mine. "I didn't say we had to stop."

It takes a moment for his words to register, and when they do, I am not sure what to do next.

THE SMELL OF EGGS, pancakes, waffles, fruit, yogurt, bagels, cereal, milk, orange juice, and other foods wakes me up in the morning. I open my eyes and wipe the sleep from them. Based on the absence of a warm body next to me and the array of foods scattered on the table, the PI has woken up, gotten dressed, and went to do whatever he does in the morning. Blood, a newspaper, and the novel I have been reading at the park sit on the table as well. I wave my hand over the food to find it piping hot. My stomach growls, and I do not think twice before digging into the meal set before me.

I am halfway through my second plate when a voice behind me says, "You didn't waste any time."

I roll my eyes. "What do you expect me to do when you leave a meal like this in front of me?"

"I'm not sure. Wait for the person who got it for you so that you can eat with them?" He sits on the seat across from me and slouches in it. "Did you at least save some for me?"

I gesture to the massive amount of food left in front of me. "Does it look as though I have eaten it all?"

We stare at each other with serious facial expressions and then laugh.

He makes a plate for himself and takes it to the pull-out couch. Before biting into his meal, he takes out the map that Anton gave us. "So, it's been bugging me for a while now. What do you think the dots on this map represent?"

I raise my brows at him. "Anton said not to worry about the dots."

"That's exactly why I'm worried about them though." He traces his hands across the white and gold border. "Anton strikes me as the kind of person we shouldn't trust, wouldn't you agree?"

He is, of course, correct. The stories I heard of Anton growing up are unsavory, to put it mildly, and if any of them are true, he is definitely someone to steer clear of, and that is not including his most recent stunt of deceiving me.

I bite my lip before answering the PI. "Well, we do not have to trust him. But if he says to leave the dots alone..." I shrug and go back to eating my meal.

"Well, what are they about? Wait, first you have to tell me about your mom's acquaintance."

I finish the blood bag he had set aside for me and take a swig of orange juice. I should have known he would remember we were supposed to talk about this. I sigh. "Right, so, his name is Calvin Carter," I begin. I tell him everything that happened, from me sitting in the park to Calvin giving me the picture of Mother. The only thing I do not tell him is what happened between me leaving the park and coming back here. Luckily, he does not bother to ask.

As he muses over the information, I pack up the breakfast items on the table and put them in the refrigerator. Growing up, Father always said, "Waste not, want not," which meant if it came into the house, it was used or eaten. This especially applied to food sources. I smile as I recall the time I killed my first deer and brought it home. He had the cooks prepare deer stew for us, but I did not want to eat it because it was not prepared with the broth I preferred. Father looked me straight in the eye before taking a spoon and shoving it into my mouth. I tried to spit it out, but he gently held my mouth closed until I swallowed it. Some would call this violent, but for Father, it was normal.

It turned out that the stew was rich in flavor, and it became one of my favorite meals. He told me, "Everything we are given in this world lasts only for a moment. We must appreciate everything we are given because the moment we do not, we could lose it all. Do you understand, my little trefoil?" I nodded because I did. It was the one lesson Father taught me that I held on to.

"So, what do you want to do?" the PI asks, breaking me out of my thoughts.

"I am sorry. What were you saying?" I wipe my eye as a few tears drip down. God, I miss those moments with Father. I turn to the PI. "I was distracted."

"I was saying that it sounds like the information Anton gave you was only partially useful. If you hadn't run into Calvin, you would have spent another few weeks waiting for her to show up. Now that it's confirmed she won't be here until the solstice, there are only a few options left to go forward."

"And those would be?" I grab my clothes from the suitcase and change in the bathroom. I hear him stand up and shift toward the bathroom door. "You know I can hear you from where you were, right?" I ask.

"Yes, but sometimes I like to pretend you're human too." A moment of silence passes before he speaks again. "We have three options. We can sit and twiddle our thumbs until the winter solstice, check to see if there are any other clues Calvin can give us, or explore this map."

I step out of the bathroom and gauge his response as I say, "And I am guessing you would like to explore the map." It is more of a statement than a question.

"Uh, um, yeah," he stutters, trying to get his answer out. Then he squints at me. "Are you sure you want to wear that?"

I chose a magenta crop top with high-waisted, tight-fitting skinny jeans, a magenta belt with loops for a holster, and black combat boots. My hair is in its natural state, a mess of long, dark brown curls, and I put in all five of my ear piercings, my nose ring, and my belly piercing. "What is wrong with what I am wearing?"

"Nothing, it's just..." He clears his throat.

"It is 'just' what?" I lean closer to him.

He shakes his head. "I mean...the way you look right now and the way you speak...it's a bit..." He stops talking, and I assume it is because he knows if he whispers it, I will be able to hear.

I frown. "It is a bit what?" I rather like my modern-day look. Say what you will about modern-day fashion, but it is a lot more doable than the time of petticoats and skirts.

"Disconcerting," he finally says. "If you're going to dress like that, which you look really good by the way, then you should at least adjust your mannerisms to match."

"Why?" I ask. "Because if I speak properly, then I cannot possibly look this way?"

"Well, I didn't say that."

"You did not have to." I close my eyes, take a deep breath, and push past him. Hundreds of years in this world, and people are still stupid enough to make assumptions, even the ones who look like you. It truly is a shame.

I change the subject before my irritation can take over. "If you want to explore the map, then let us explore the map."

We spend the next few hours working. The silence between us thickens, and any moment of sweetness we may have shared is now tinged with the awkwardness of his earlier comments. Around 2:00 p.m., I finally break down and speak to him. "Did you find anything?"

"No," he says as he looks at the dots on the map moving around.

I stand over his shoulder and look closer at the map. "The colors changed."

"What do you mean they changed?"

"Just what I said. Look." I point at what are now a mix of white, black, and sparkly rainbow dots. "They were all black when Anton gave it to us. Now it is a mix of colors."

He picks the map up and watches as the dots move around like gnats in a field. Then, he puts on his shoes and walks out of the hotel room.

I roll my eyes and follow him.

He dashes down the stairs and out the door, heading toward a small grocery store.

I run at the pace of a human. There are too many people milling about for me to risk my speed. When I finally catch up to him, he is glancing frantically from the map to the surrounding area. He takes fifteen paces forward and goes five to the left. Then he moves twenty paces forward and ten to the right.

I follow his movements for about five minutes before I can no longer contain my curiosity.

"Okay, this is strange," I say. I touch his shoulder. "What are you doing?"

His eyes glisten, his nose crinkles, and his mouth widens into a bright smile. "I know what the dots are."

Chapter Five

"**Y**ou figured out what the dots are?" I repeat, jumping up and down on the hard cobbled road. "Well, do not hesitate. Spit it out!" I am excited and curious to hear what he thinks. All my senses heighten in anticipation. The cool wind becomes crisp against my face. The colors of the small shops and eateries around us become sharper. The PI's soul becomes three times more potent. And my body tingles.

"Well, it's just a theory, but..."

"But what?" I swear if he continues to hold out on me, I will punch him in the face.

"Okay. Well, you see these two dots here?" He points to a white dot with an orange center and a black, white, and orange dot with sparkles on it.

"Yes, I see them."

"Those two dots are ours."

"How do you know?"

"Because... Watch closely." He holds out the map and places my arm on his. The two dots move closer to each other. We take a few steps forward. The two dots move forward as well. We move to the left, the dots move to the left. This pattern continues until we've made a large circle.

This time, my eyes are the ones bulging. "Those two dots are ours!" I scream.

"Shh," he admonishes. "Now, look at the other dots." He points to the dots close to ours. "What do you see on the map and near us?"

I inspect the map and then study my surroundings. There are about four people in front of us and two to our left. The map shows three white dots and one black dot in front of our two dots. On the left side of our dots are two white dots. I mirror the excitement on his face. "This map shows us the people around us."

He nods, and we lock eyes. "I never thought I'd see something like this," he whispers in awe.

I say nothing. Instead, I take out my phone. When the PI looks at me, I tell him that I will just be a moment. I take the map from him, lean against the wall of a nearby shop, and dial Andrei. He picks up on the third ring.

"Hello?" Andrei's deep, husky voice penetrates through the phone.

"Andrei," I reply. "How are things at home?"

"They're getting worse. Are you any closer?"

I squeeze my eyes tightly and massage my temples. "Yes, but I wanted to ask you something."

"Well, you will have to hurry. I don't have a lot of time."

"Yes, well, have you ever heard of a map that shows you and the people around you?"

A loud clang and the sound of items breaking in the background startles me. There is the shuffling of footsteps and yelling as well. "Andrei?"

"I'm sorry, Lizzy. It's just a bit hectic here." He pauses and muffles a yell. "Get it out of here now!" Then he comes back. "A map that shows people? Yes. I remember one."

"Excellent. Where does it come from?"

"Where does anything magical come from?" he asks sarcastically. There are more sounds of destruction on his end of the line. "Is it something that's going to help you find your mother?"

"Yes," I say. "Andrei, is everything—"

"Then hurry. Your father is—"

The phone cuts out. I try calling again, but it is useless. The connection will not go through. I try texting Andrei next, but the text comes back as failed.

"What was that about?" the PI asks.

I wish to answer him. To tell him of Father's condition and the full truth as to why I began this search for my mother. To tell him about the problems back home. To confide in him about everything. But the words are stuck in my throat and there is no way to force them out. "Nothing." I hand the map back to him. "Andrei was not of any help. I am not sure what we should do next."

In the end, we decide that the library is our best shot at discovering more about the map. There is nothing definitive that makes me believe this map is the key, but I can see no other reason Anton would give it to me. It is not as though GPS and other maps do not exist. This map is special. It may be a red herring, but I think there is more to it.

When we arrive at the library the next day, the PI suggests we test the map's radius. If it is ever moving with the person who holds it, then there must be a point you can no longer see other people. Which is why I am now sitting on the steps, holding the map, while the PI walks toward the parking lot. The farther away he walks, the farther his dot appears on the map.

Eventually the entire thing bores me. I take the edges of the map in my hand and trace my fingers over them. The map is thick, considering its age, in every part but one. A small piece on the top left corner is paper-thin. I let my finger caress the soft, smooth edge, but the material feels the same as the rest. I check to see how far the PI's dot has moved and shake my head, but I can still see him. I hope whatever he has been using to gauge the distance works how he said it would. Otherwise, this entire experiment is for naught.

The sun beats down on my head and rivulets of sweat drip down my face. I have never been so glad to be adorned in breathable workout clothes. The sweat absorbent feature on this outfit makes me happy since Georgia is so hot. I watch as my sweat hits the stone steps of the library. One of them splashes onto the map, and I check to make sure there are no negative effects.

That is when I notice it. The map was in the perfect spot for my sweat to drop, and the sun is bright enough that I notice something that was not there before. In the corner is an insignia. An insignia I would not have seen otherwise. I pick up the map and inspect it further. It is in the shape of a pentagram, a witch's symbol that represents the elements and protection. It is faint and would only be noticeable in the sun. I peer closer at the spot where my sweat dropped. It has landed directly in the middle of the symbol, turning it navy blue. This gives me an idea.

As gross as it is, I wipe the sweat from my head and cover the paper-thin corner of the map with it. As I suspected, the intricate symbol becomes colorful. The outside circle is now an ombré of colors, beginning with white, shifting into reds, oranges, yellows, greens, blues, indigos, and violet. It finishes in black. The inside circle follows the same ombré pattern but in reverse. The five outside triangles that make up the star shape are different colors as well. One is white, one is brown, and one is orange. Two sparkle as though someone tossed a large amount of glitter on them. The first one is sparkly rainbow-colored and the second one is orange. Between the outer and inner circles, in scripted handwriting, is the name Mira Morian. This is another clue and not just any clue. It is the clue that will help us figure out why this map was created. My cell phone rings, bringing me out of this realization. The caller ID shows it is the PI, so I pick it up.

"Did I travel far enough?" He sounds out of breath.

His dot is on the edge of the map. "Yes, if you take a few more steps, you should be completely out of range."

"Right," he breathes heavily, "doing it now."

I watch as his dot slowly moves out of view. "Okay, stop," I say once he is no longer visible. "I cannot see you on the map now." He sighs in relief, so I ask, "How far out are you? You have had me out here twiddling my thumbs for about three and a half hours."

"Surprisingly, I'm about fifteen miles out. Do you know how long that would take a normal person?"

"Are you saying that you are not normal?" It would make sense if he were not. After all, what kind of human would willingly put himself in danger regularly by helping out the supernatural?

"I assure you, Elizabeth, I am nothing but." The way he emphasizes my name sends tingles down my spine.

"Well, are you walking back, or—"

"Hell no. I'm getting a ride. I'll be back in about fifteen to twenty minutes."

"Okay, well, I have found something, so I will be in the library when you come back."

"What did you—"

"Bye." I hang up the phone. It is necessary to investigate this before he makes it back. I fold the map up and put it back into my bag. I marvel at the tall, two-hundred-year-old building in front of me. Its steps are cracked and worn, and the large, ornate wooden door is heavier than it looks. I step inside and gawk at its vastness.

"Hello, Elizabeth," a voice chimes. I turn to look behind me and am met with a familiar face.

"Idabelle," I say.

"Hello, old friend."

We spend the next few minutes catching each other up on our lives since 1895, the last time we saw each other. We are trying desperately to avoid making a raucous in the library when the PI finds us.

"Ida," I say using her nickname, "this is the PI. PI, this is Idabelle. Ida for short."

Ida smiles at the PI and bats her eyelashes. "Pleased to meet you," she says in her sweet, southern belle accent.

"You too," the PI replies. To me he says, "So, what did you find out?"

"Keep a hold of your britches," I say to him. "I am speaking with Ida right now."

"Yeah, but—"

I shush him and turn back to Ida. "So, you were saying?"

She smiles and looks at the PI. "I was just telling Lizzy here about the time I stole a car in the 1950s." She turns to me. "Lizzy Bear, you should have seen it. There I was in one of those old, billowy skirts. I hopped in the car and sped away like there was no tomorrow." The two of us laugh as she takes us through the rest of that day. We swap stories about the '60s, '70s, and the decades leading to the present when the PI clears his throat.

"What?" I ask him. He points at the clock. Is that how much time has passed? "Oh. Um, Ida," I begin.

"Yes, Lizzy?"

"I am sorry to cut you off, but we have to start looking for what we came here to get."

"The information about your mother, right?" she asks.

"Yes. Can we catch up another time?"

"Of course." She reaches into her pale pink purse and takes out a business card. "That's my cell phone number up there. I work here in the library, so if you need anything..."

"Thanks, Ida."

"You're welcome. Will you be here tomorrow?"

"Most likely. Why?"

"So that we can grab lunch, silly." She looks at me knowingly. "Unless you're already covered?" She eyes the PI as though he is a tasty piece of steak.

I narrow my eyes at her and respond sweetly, "I am afraid I do not have anything of the sort ready. We will have to go much farther out for a decent meal." I smile at her to ensure my subtext is very clear.

She nods. "Very well. What time?"

"I shall call you," I say.

She nods again and waves goodbye. "It was nice meeting you, Mr. PI," she calls back.

He does not respond. Instead, he turns to me, "It's one o'clock."

"Yes, captain obvious, it is. I am sorry that I spent three hours speaking to my friend. Had I known she was here, I could have spoken to her while you were testing the distance of the map."

"Testing the distance of the map was important."

"Yes, but you did not have to walk the entire way. You could have gotten into a car."

He furrows his brows. "I wanted it to be as accurate as possible."

"I bet you did." I shake my head. "I found this." I take him to the water fountain and douse the left-hand corner of the map with it. He starts to open his mouth, but I shush him. Once it is covered in water, I show him the insignia.

He inhales sharply.

"You recognize it?"

"Yes." His eyebrows raise, the skin below his brow stretches, and his eyes widen. His face freezes like this for a moment. If his face had not given it away, his one-word answer did.

Sometimes I swear he believes that elaborating will be the death of him. "Where do you recognize it from?" I prod.

"Long story." He studies the insignia further. His fingers softly brush against the symbol and linger on Mira's name.

"So," I try to push for one more answer. "Do you know her?" I point to Mira's scrawled handwriting, whoever that might be.

"No, I-I don't. Excuse me." He walks into the men's bathroom, and I am tempted to follow him in, but I do not. I believe he needs his privacy, and while I could search for the information myself in the library's catalogue, I do not. I sit outside of the restroom and wait for him.

And wait for him.

Ten minutes later, I barge into the men's restroom and get ready to yell at him. Except he is sitting on the sink counter with his head between his legs. I hop onto the counter next to him, but he does not do or say anything. I gently touch his shoulder, and he looks up at me. His eyes are rimmed with red and snot is dripping down his face. I hand him some tissue from my bag.

"Thanks," he mumbles.

"You are welcome," I say.

I do not know what is going on. He said he has not met this Mira person, but his reaction tells me otherwise. I wonder what happened. Why did his heart quicken at the sound of her name? Why were his hands sweaty when he spoke of her? How does he know about the insignia? I do not ask him the questions because it would only cause him pain. I told him I would respect his privacy and I meant it. But it nags at me. He is lying, but I do not press the issue. Instead, I shove the worries away and lean my head against his.

Once the PI is finished wallowing, he tells me about his connection to the insignia. He still does not mention Mira's name, but I get the feeling time will tell me what happened there. For now, I listen.

"The insignia definitely belongs to a witch coven," he says. "Specifically, the Morian Coven."

"How do you know it is from a coven and not just that one person?" I should have the answers to questions like these, but since Father kept me locked in a castle and then boarding schools for most of my life, my knowledge of the supernatural world and what it contains is more limited than others.

"This Mira may have been the one who put it on here, but individuals don't have crests. Only covens. If it was just her, she only would have signed her name."

I nod even though it does not make sense, but he need not know that. "So, how do we find this coven?"

He finally smiles, and that makes me happy inside. "Yeah, I know where to look."

"So, what are we doing here then?" We've moved from the men's restroom to get more privacy, but we are still in the library.

"Because witches are scary, and we want to be prepared when we meet up with them."

"Witches are just humans with powers, correct?" I ask.

"Yeah, but... Never mind. Just read these." He hands me a few books, and I flip through them. They are filled with runes, symbols, and spells from all over the world. One page that stands out warns to never see a witch without a protective charm.

"Is this what you wanted me to read?" I ask.

He nods.

"Do not worry," I say. "I have one." And I do. The necklace I wear is a protective charm given to me by my mother. Since she was half human and half Sluagh at birth, her parents wanted to ensure she would be safe. When she had me, she did the same and gifted me with the talisman that hangs at my neck: a black-and-red rosary with the Bathory name carved on the back. If this cannot keep me safe from a witch, nothing can.

Chapter Six

The PI drives us to our next destination: the Morian Coven. I ask him how he knows where to go, but he refuses to answer. He only tells me the coven resides in Augusta, Georgia, which is a two- to three-hour drive, depending on traffic. I settle in our rental car and use my candy straw to suck up the remaining blood from my bag. As usual, it is warm as though it has come fresh from the source. I wonder if the magic blood bag came from witches as well, and if so, why did I not know about it? It could have saved a lot of trouble for me over the years. The PI plays soft jazz music for the entire ride, and I fall asleep.

The dream I have is more of an exaggerated memory.

It is the year 1600, on the day of my twenty-seventh birthday. I am excited about my lover's plans. I spend the day primping and prepping myself to be presentable. Today is the day he and Father meet. After nine years, my boyfriend—a servant of the castle—has finally saved up enough money to be thought of as respectable. There is no way Father can refuse him.

In the dream, the day whirls by, and soon it is night. Everything is set up, and I introduce them. But it does not go as planned. Father and I get into a heated argument. My insides twist and turn, and then I black out.

When I come to, everything has been destroyed. The guards, the servants, everyone within a five-mile radius of the castle have been blown to smithereens. I step through the carnage, but there is nothing except bodies burnt to a crisp. The pungent odor of sulfur and smoke rises above me, and the sight before me is abhorrent. I dig and dig, praying it is not true. In the rubble is the leather band I gifted to my once-formidable sweetheart.

I cry and cry until there is only emptiness. When I look up, my father is glaring at me from above. But I am too numb to feel anything. When I can finally move, there is only a long, dark corridor in front of me. The faster I walk, the longer it becomes.

But then I see it. A light at the end, and someone waving at me. When I get there, the PI is the person in front of me. He embraces me and pulls me away from the darkness that is my mind.

A light tapping on my shoulder startles me awake. My hand instinctively forms a fist and punches the person next to me.

"Ow," the PI yelps, "that's some hook you've got there."

"What?" I ask. "Oh, sorry." I try to find a marking on him, but there is no bruising on his shoulder. "In my defense, I have told you to be careful when you wake me."

"Yeah, yeah," he says. "Rise and shine. We're here."

I try to see where exactly "here" is. We are at a house between Augusta Levee Road and Lovers' Lane. A sign reads that some place titled Phinizy Swamp is nearby. "They live near a swamp?" I ask.

The PI shrugs and opens my door. I follow him out of the car and into the unknown. The answers to my questions will not find themselves. The dirt road in front of us is long, and I contemplate asking him to drive up, but then I notice the charms hanging every few feet or so. "What are the dolls about?"

The PI looks at me and smirks. "You're the one who's four-hundred-some-odd years old, and you don't even know about poppets?"

"I know about poppets," I mutter. "I just do not have much experience with them."

"Whatever you say. Come on." He jogs farther up the driveway, and we finally reach the door. He knocks on it three times and then steps back.

An old woman opens the door. She smells of chamomile, passionflower, valerian, and lemon balm. Herbs meant to evoke calmness and serenity. Even her soul has an herb-like aroma. She eyes us warily and then opens the door and gestures for us to come in. Unsure if we should speak, since everyone has been silent up to this point, I keep my mouth shut and say nothing.

She guides us to her living room, and the scent of earth becomes stronger. I take in the tiny bobbles and trinkets on the wooden shelves. The floor is made of the same redwood as them. She walks to her kitchen and puts a kettle on the stove. Though the house itself seems to be centuries old, the kitchen is filled with modern appliances and cookware.

The melding of the old and new is a nice change from what I normally see when we visit people. As the kettle boils, she takes out some tea leaves and places them in small, metal diffusers. When the water is ready, she takes her time to pour the piping hot liquid over them. She sets sugar cubes, spoons, and teacups on a tray and places them on the coffee table in front of us. She nods toward the cups, and we oblige. There is no use being rude to someone who has invited you into their home.

I place a few sugar cubes in my tea before stirring it with the spoon and smile with delight. The tea is passionfruit, one of my favorites. We sit and sip our tea for what feels like hours before the woman finally speaks. "Let me see the map," she says in her gravelly voice.

The PI hands it over to her without any objection. She looks at it and nods. "Yes. I can answer your questions about this one." She looks directly at the PI. "Though I am not sure why you have brought her with you. You realize what this means for you?"

I look between them, not understanding.

"I haven't told her anything, so I didn't break any rules."

The woman's wrinkles deepen as she frowns. "Just because you and Mira—"

He cuts her off, "Are you going to help us or not?" He glowers at her until she finally acquiesces.

"I already told you that I would help."

They are speaking around me, and I have no idea why. Did he think I did not notice she said the name Mira? He told me that he did not know her, but was he lying? And what was this about him not being able to tell me anything? I begin to use my influence but then remember I am supposed to be exercising caution and restraint, so I hold back and listen.

"Moira," the PI says, "what do the colors of the dots mean?"

She appraises the map, paying special attention to the insignia on the top left corner before answering him. "First," she says, "do you know why the map was created?"

"No."

She turns to me, and I expect to see hostility. Instead, what I see is pity. "Do you?" she asks.

"No," I say. She shakes her head, and something tells me that I have given her the wrong answer. "Should I?"

She takes a deep breath and sighs. "You are a tribrid, no?"

"Yes. That is correct." I wait for her to continue.

"Your father calls you 'little trefoil' because you are vampire, human, and Fae."

I narrow my eyes and bore directly into hers. "How do you know that?"

She rolls her shoulders back and leans into me. "Witches hear all, know all, and see all, dear," she says with a grimace. She taps the insignia. "Do either of you know what these represent?"

We both shake our heads.

"Then this is going to be a long night." She stands, stretches, and walks toward a tiny phone hanging on the wall. It is an older phone hooked to a landline via a cord as opposed to being wireless. "I'm calling the girls and telling them to bring home some dinner. It will only take a moment." She speaks on the phone for all of five minutes before hanging up and walking back toward us. "Now, where were we?"

"You were just about to tell us about this lovely map," the PI says.

She scowls at him but relays the history to us without preamble. "This symbol represents all the beings that currently exist in the world," she says, pointing to the colored insignia. She explains how each species received their colors and why they represent those groups. "As for the map itself," she says, "who did you get it from?"

"I thought you said witches hear, see, and know all?" It comes out of my mouth before I can consider the ramifications.

"In the greater scheme of things, yes, but this," she traces the edges of the map and then holds it up, "this should not even be in front of me right now."

"Why?" the PI and I ask in unison.

When she rolls her eyes and clicks her tongue, I can tell she is becoming irritated with us. So, when the door opens and a small voice calls, "Grandma, we're back," I am glad. I turn around, and behind me stands a little girl. Her small, pudgy, beige body radiates all that is good and pure in the world. Her mother, who looks exactly like her, just taller and bustier, greets us with a simple "yo" before setting her overstuffed grocery bags onto the counter. She and the little girl wash their hands and prepare dinner while the rest of us continue our conversation.

"This map belongs to the Bathory's," the old woman says.

"I am a—"

"Yes. You are. But your map, unlike the others, was not passed down to you. So, I ask you again, where did it come from?"

The PI and I exchange a look before answering. "A man named Anton," I tell her.

Her nostrils turn up and the muscles around her mouth contort like there is a stench in the room. She recognizes the name. "You shouldn't interact with that man."

"That's what everyone keeps telling me," I say, "and yet he was the only one willing to give me the information I seek."

She scoffs. "It's your funeral."

I am about to respond, but the little girl shouts. "Dinner's ready!" she trots over to us with a spread of food that makes my mouth water.

Moira smiles and invites us to eat with them. As we dine, she tells us the origin story of the map, how a long time ago—around the year 1100 BCE—the fairy hosts were persecuted. Since they were able to consume the souls of any creature, every race rose against them and pushed them out of the Fae communities. With nowhere to go and everyone after them, they had no choice but to go into hiding. "There was only one coven willing to help them: the Morian Coven. But their witches were not strong enough, so they had to wait until the next Crone, the leader of the coven, was born. Apparently, that did not occur until 1565, when Mira was born. "Once she was able to control her powers—as a prodigy, it only took her until the age of five—they got to work. For the five Sluagh clans, they created five maps." She takes a sip of her vegetable soup.

"Who were the five clans?" I ask.

"The Bathory Clan, who you are descended from," she answers, "along with the Arvay, Morici, Vados, and Zambo clans."

The name Morici stands out. "I thought the Moricis were witches. My friend Idabelle—"

"The Moricis were originally fairy hosts," she says before I can finish my statement. "They married into a witch family and the line became diluted until their offspring were witches."

"But that is at least seven generations." I count it again in my head to be sure.

"There was some magic involved," she says. "The five maps were made for two reasons. The first, so that they could find viable food sources. The second was to avoid detection. That is why humans and almost all supernatural beings are identified by different colors. When there were more species, shapes played a role as well. But, as you can see, the only shape left is the circle."

Once she points this out, the answer is obvious. Had we paid more attention while at Anton's lair, we would have realized this sooner.

"Is there some type of key? You know, to tell us what the colors mean?" the PI asks.

Moira ponders his question for a moment. She slowly stirs her soup before sipping the broth. Her wrinkled hands look fragile as she repeats the motion. "There was a key, but we decided it would be better if those who possessed them memorized the shapes and colors. Less likely to be caught that way."

This makes sense. If I were on the run, I would not want the enemy to decipher any hidden messages or codes I might have with me. The only options are to burn or eat the evidence. But, if you never have it with you, then it is a moot point.

Moira points to me. "Before your mother died in 1614, she was supposed to send the map to your father so that you would have it. Instead, she allowed it to be stolen from the Castle of Čachtice. That's why I wanted to know how you had gotten it."

I look at her, confused. "1614? Mother died in 1573."

Moira shakes her head. "No, she didn't. Your mother was killed, or at least her human side was killed, in 1614. She faked being dead so that others wouldn't pursue her."

"Huh," I say. I do not have the luxury to inquire about this right now, so I put the information aside for later. However, Moira's other comment strikes a chord within me. If the map was stolen from my mother, then how did Anton get it? Clearly, she is acquainted with

Anton, but she did not know he had the map. What would cause her to overlook, forget, or not notice something like this? And what about Anton? He is conscious enough of my mother to prevent me from finding her. Why would he do that? But then, if that were his goal, why would he leave the map for me? None of it makes sense, and thinking about it too long is giving me a headache.

But, if I can put together the pieces, it may be easier to find Mother. And I must find her soon because if I do not, I will never have my answers and Father's condition will get worse.

He did not want me to look for her because his soul is missing, and he does not want to be perceived as weak. But his condition—his need to feed recklessly and without caution, biting off the heads of anyone he meets when hungry, draining humans of their blood completely—well, the Dhampir Council will not have that.

I sigh. The man is stubborn. Has he ever considered, if Andrei and I do not handle it, there will be more at stake than the family fortune? Luckily, Andrei and I have found a way to subdue him for now, but he has come a long way since 1650, and he regains strength every day. It will not be long before he breaks free.

I stuff another dumpling in my mouth and chew thoughtfully. Andrei and I found out that if they are someone with a connection to souls—such as a Sluagh or witch—the lover of a Dhampir can locate a missing soul. I thought it would be simple. Unfortunately, it has been anything but.

I finish the remainder of my food and help Mina and Misha with the dishes. When we are finished, the PI and I thank Moira for the information.

Before we leave, she grabs my hand. Her grip is iron-tight for an old, wrinkly woman. "I know why you're looking for her," she says. "Word of advice, what you seek may not be what you actually want." Her eyes bore into mine, and I detect her attempt to enter my mind.

I snatch my hand from her and say, "Thank you for the advice. But I do not need it."

She places her hands up in surrender and backs away.

As the PI and I make our way back to the car, he asks, "What was that about?"

"Nothing," I say. Something about Moira does not sit right with me. She was helpful, and I am grateful for that, but why would she try to enter my mind without my permission? Granted, I have done it before as well, but only when necessary. I do not go around perusing in people's minds for the fun of it.

"It sure looked like something," he says.

"Then why not ask her?" I sneer. His voice is grating now, and I do not want to talk about it.

"Well, I would, but she isn't the one keeping secrets."

I stop walking and turn toward him, "OH!" I yell. "You want to talk secrets now. That is rich coming from you."

"Okay. Chill."

"Do not tell me to 'chill,' Mr. PI. Speaking of, what *is* your real name? Huh? Moira seems to know. This Mira person probably knew. Hell, the whole damn coven probably knows." This anger is not like me, but I cannot rein it in.

"Well, you never told me why you're looking for the great Elizabeth Bathory. You understand your mom's a serial killer, right? A grade A nut job. Why would you want that in your life?"

"Do not presume you know anything about my mother or father."

"I don't! And that's why this," he points between us, "was never going to work."

"This?" I ask. "What is this even? We've spent about two months together, and every time I try to get close to you, you push me away. Then you ask to sleep in my bed and we almost—" I stop because I do not want to finish the statement. I take a deep breath. "Just take me back to Atlanta and you can be released from your duties of helping me. But do not worry, I will make sure Andrei pays the rest of your retainer in full."

"We almost did that because the apple doesn't fall from the tree," he retorts.

"What is that supposed to mean?"

"Don't play stupid. You were trying to seduce me. And guess what, it worked. And I can't even—" He exhales. "Forget it. Let's do what you just suggested."

By this point we have reached the rental car. We get in and drive back to Atlanta in silence. When we arrive, we do not speak to each other.

BEFORE WE HAD LEFT for Augusta, we had extended our hotel stay for two more weeks. Neither of us knew what would happen, so it made sense at the time. I would have left regardless, but unfortunately, when I asked Andrei about bringing me home, he said that it would take at least two weeks for him to have enough time to pick me up from the airport and that he did not trust anyone else to do the job. And, while I am old enough to make my own arrangements, I know that going over Andrei's head would be like defying Father, pointless and messy. But why the PI chose to stay in the room with me, I do not know. What I do know is that we both regret the decision. For the past two weeks our conversations have been limited to good morning, good afternoon, and goodnight.

I assumed he would want to sleep in the bed, but upon our arrival from Augusta, he extended the pull-out couch and slept there.

From that night on, his sleepwalking has become worse. This time when it happened, I knew what was going on. Not that I would ever tell him this, but every night, I pull him by the hand and lead him back to the couch. He mumbles and murmurs in his sleep, and had I been paying attention before we slept in the same bed, I would have known earlier that he was suffering from a Blood Pact. He never outright said it, but when you hear phrases and words like "Why are you doing this to me?" or "I promise to uphold this pact," and "I want to tell her the truth," you can put pieces together. Especially when it is in conjunction with your name being said a million times over. It is possible the secrets he is holding on to so tightly are a result of a dire consequence. It does not change the fact that I am also entitled to my secrecy, but it does put it into perspective.

When I receive a call from Andrei the day before our two weeks are up, I am more than happy to pick up. "Hello," I say as I ogle the PI, who is paying me absolutely no attention.

"Lizzy," Andrei says. His voice sounds serious. "Have you found your mother yet?"

"No, Andrei, I have not. And things here have been..."

The PI looks up from whatever he is doing.

"Awkward," I finish. "I would have called if anything had changed." I flip the page of the book I have been looking at. There is nothing about a Sluagh being able to replace a soul in this one either. Another dead end. "What do you need?"

He hesitates before answering, "Would it be possible for you to come home then? Just for a little while?"

I cast a skeptical eye even though he cannot see. "Well, according to Calvin—"

"Who is Calvin?"

I had forgotten I did not tell him about Calvin Carter yet. "I will tell you another time. The point is Calvin said that Mother will not be here until December. So, yes, I can come home." I try not to notice the PI risking a glance at me before typing away on his laptop. Maybe he does care. But if he does, he does not express it. "Our stay ends tomorrow, and I purchased a ticket just in case you called me early."

"Good. Then that means I will see you tomorrow. Send me your flight information."

"Okay." We say goodbye, and I hang up the phone. I think about telling the PI, but I am sure he overheard the conversation, so I do not explain. I send Andrei my flight information before it slips my mind. The next day, we pack our things, pay for the hotel room, and leave.

I try to muster up the courage to say something, but I cannot. When we arrive at the airport, I gather my luggage and exit the car. There are no hugs, no goodbyes, and no words between us.

I make my way inside, call Andrei, and tell him that I am on my way home.

WHEN I ENTER THE AIRPORT, the first thing I do is look for Andrei. After searching for a few moments, I find him holding a sign that reads Lizzy. I try not to chuckle as people attempt to avoid his bulky six-foot frame and wide shoulders to no avail. His dark brown eyes follow every person in the crowd until they land on me. I run toward him and envelop him in a hug.

"Andrei," I say, but it comes out muffled and sounds more like "Hanray."

He hugs me tightly before saying, "Elizabeth."

I let the nickname thing slide because I am truly happy to see him. We begin walking, and Andrei manages to bump into at least five different people. "I see you have not become any better at walking," I jest.

"Ha-ha," he says. "Make fun of me all you want, but my size has served me well. Case in point..." A football comes out of nowhere, and he catches it. He spots the person who threw it, an eleven-year-old boy, as far as I can tell, and tosses it back with a scowl. The boy catches it and hurries to catch up with his family.

"Well," I say, "it has to count for something." He glowers at me and takes my bag. "How are things? How is Father?" I ask.

"Things are...fine, and your father is doing all right." The small hiccup in his voice tells me he is lying.

"When you say fine..." I raise my brow at him while he gets the door for me and leads me to the black, armored, seven-passenger SUV.

"He decided to come out of isolation."

I stop walking and gawk at him.

He nudges me forward, and we get into the car. He gives the driver the address, and we are off.

I sink back into the plush leather chair and cogitate over what he has just said. The odor of sweat and Cheetos from the previous trip made in this car lingers, and I wrinkle my nose in disgust. If Father has come out of isolation, then all hell must have broken loose. "Well, I will have to convince him it isn't time. After all, he has not been the same since—"

"Good luck with that." Andrei snickers. When I give him a questioning look, he replies, "You'll see what I mean when you get there."

I roll my eyes and look out the window. My home looks as beautiful as ever. As we make our way through the main parts of London and through the roads and hills that lead to our secluded mansion near Epping Forest, I think about the events that led me to search for Mother. The letters Father had hidden from me, my existence as a tribrid, the death of the love of my life, and the subsequent destruction of my childhood home. Father's decree that I was not under any circumstances to search for or attempt to locate my mother with no explanation.

From that first lie to the moment he demanded I give up one of the few joys in my life, I decided he did not deserve to call me daughter. Especially since Andrei picked up the pieces and comforted me.

My feelings were solidified when he tried to hold me captive on our many family estates from 1615 to 1650. I grimace at the memories of those days. Carted from city to city like cargo. I was never able to make friends, never able to form relationships, and every new place was a challenge. Plus, he refused to let me go to America, the only place I wanted to visit.

But now I know it is because Mother was there, and he knew at some point I would find out. Not that it did him much good.

When he became sick and rampaged the surrounding areas, he decided to isolate himself. During those years, Andrei and I had searched for two things: what Father's ailment was and a way to heal him, even though he did not deserve it. The former was found easily. Father kept journals upon journals of his life and travels, including the day his soul was stolen. Shortly after that, he met Mother, but their life fell apart right after she had me. One of his last letters to her explained that he knew how to fix everything. He just needed his soul returned to him. But she never responded.

Andrei and I spent months researching lost Dhampir souls and came across a text that said the blood of a Fae, specifically one born of human and Sluagh or human and witch, could return souls to anyone. As Mother is the only person we know of born of human and Sluagh, we assumed she was the key and that we needed to locate her without Father finding out. It was a folly journey, or so I thought, because we had only one clue. Every time I got closer, she would move on to the next place. That is how I ended up in Mississippi. Meanwhile, Andrei was tracking the PI. It was sheer luck he was there at the same time as me.

I gulp and hold back tears. The PI. I should have kept myself in check. If I had not been attracted to him, or if I had found someone else to track Mother down, I would still be in America right now.

I stop myself from forming these pointless ideas and catch Andrei up on what he missed. By the time I finish talking, I can see my home. The view is breathtaking and gives me some reprieve from thoughts of the PI. I smile as I take in the forestry and wildlife around us. The only people who know about the estate are those who live here and the witches who hide it from the view of the public. This home was built to withstand my bursts of rage after I burned down our family castle in 1600.

As we pull into the driveway, I hug myself. When the car stops and my door is opened, I take off my shoes and run into the forest. The air has a tang of fresh rain, and dark grey clouds are still present in the sky. I let my feet sink into the muddy ground. The feeling is so pleasant that I curl my toes and play in it as though I am a child again. A ladybug crawls across my foot, and I laugh as its little legs tickle my feet. The birds chirp, the bugs buzz and zip around me, and the animals purr and make tiny noises. It is good to be home.

When I come back, I look as though I have just come from a monster truck fight. My white dress is covered in mud and I reek of outside.

"Do you have to do that every time?" Andrei asks.

I smirk at him. "Yes. It has become tradition."

He just laughs and pushes me inside.

Chapter Seven

They say home is where the heart is, but that is not how it feels for me. Every room is dusted and pristine, but it is devoid of anything one would consider living. Well, apart from specific humans in on the secret. I make my way to the corridor that leads to Father's isolation room. If he insists on coming out into the real world, I at least need to assess the situation. But when I reach his domain, he is not there. The entire wing of the house is empty. I go to the largest meeting room we have, spot Andrei, and wave him over to me. He gestures to the people seated at the table, but I gesture to him that it is important.

"Excuse me," he says, walking out of the room. "What?" he asks. "Can't you see I'm busy?"

"Yes, I see you are busy speaking to a group of humans—one of whom is checking you out as we speak, by the way—while Father is out of the castle."

He gets ready to dismiss me but then stops. "Oh, so you finally noticed?"

"That one of the humans is checking you out?"

"No," he says in a serious tone, "the other part."

"Oh, right," I say, feigning innocence, "Do you mean to tell me that Father is running amuck?"

"Bingo."

"You told me that he came out of isolation. Not that he left."

He raises an eyebrow, "Are you mad?"

"What do you think?"

"Shit," he looks back at the humans within the meeting room. The group of three women and four men seem to be studying something in front of them. The fragrance of their souls, cinnamon rolls with a tinge of darkness, is magnificent. Some will be turned to fairy hosts, while the others are teetering between that and paradise. "So, you're not okay with this?"

"I hope that was a rhetorical question."

"Come on, Lizzy." He saunters back to the meeting room and pushes the door open a bit. "It's time for you to do your job."

"What about his illness?"

Andrei stands his full six-foot height and straightens his tie. "There won't be an illness for us to fix if we don't get his affairs in order. I let you go on this goose chase because you convinced me it would be best to go against your father's wishes."

I try to interrupt, but he does not give me an opening.

"Now that he knows and is gone, it's time for you to own up to your position."

I cross my arms and tap my foot as my fangs come out. "Who do you think you are?" I ask in a cold voice. "The only master of this house is Vladimir Dracula Tepés, and he seems to be out right now."

Andrei walks toward me and looks me in the eyes. His are no longer a sky-blue but red as fire, likely mimicking mine. "I have six-hundred-plus years on you, little girl. Do you really want to chance a battle of authority?"

I hold my breath and consider the situation. Andrei never gets angry at me. For him to become Cold Andrei, my nickname for when he unleashes his full power, there must be a lot more going on here than I initially thought. I swallow the lump in my throat. "No," it comes out as a hiss.

Andrei reverts to his normal, kind, sweet self. "Good. Then get your ass in this meeting."

FROM THE END OF JULY to October, I help Andrei get the affairs of the house and our many businesses in order. The daily drudgery of waking up and being dragged from one place to another wears on me. It is an endless loop of misery. You would think the sunlight would deter a one-thousand-plus-year-old vampire from going into the world during the day, but you would be wrong. He takes pleasure in torturing me by discussing fiduciary and fiscal responsibilities. If I must go over one more budget, I might end up taking a stake to my heart and praying I do not come back as a fully-fledged fairy host. That would be everyone's worst nightmare.

I draw on the notepad in front of me as we talk about what to do with our income from the blood banks, art depots, and charities we own. The drawing displays a world with no supernatural beings in it, a world with no Draculas, no Blood Countesses, and no Fae Whisperers. It is a peaceful world.

A hand slaps the part of the desk in front of me, and I jump. Andrei is scowling at me, a face I have grown used to over the past few months.

"Yes?" I ask.

"Are you paying attention, future president of this company?"

I feign innocence. "Of course. We were just discussing the importance of Dhampir-human relationships in the workplace."

Andrei is displeased with my answer. "That was last week's topic." He sighs. "Come on," he says and pulls me into the hallway. "Really? Of all the things you could have said?"

I slouch against the wall. "I have explained to you that I am not cut out for this world. I make the art. I donate to the charities. I drink the blood. Managing it all is not my cup of tea. Why force me to do it?"

He balls his hands up and curses at the ceiling. "Elizabeth..."

"Lizzy," I correct him.

"Elizabeth Mina Bathory-Tepés," he says in a disparaged voice, "what happens to everything if your father dies?"

"We celebrate?"

"What happens if I die?"

"I get another you."

"Damn it, Lizzy, why are you always so sarcastic?"

I shrug. "It is how I deal with all of this." I wave my hands around me. "Father does not care about this empire. It is your empire. You built it. Mother is who-knows-where and probably does not know about it. And I—" I look him in the eye. "Andrei, these companies, they are your babies. You built them to take care of the supernatural world, specifically the vampires. Why are you trying to pawn it off on me?"

"I'm not 'pawning it off.' I am leaving it to you."

"Why?"

"Because I owe it to this family. I owe it to you."

"No, you do not."

"Yes, I do."

We are at an impasse, and we both slide down to the floor. Andrei fidgets with his wallet and pulls something out. "Here," he says, handing it to me.

I take the crumpled paper. "What is it?" I ask.

"It explains a lot of things. But you won't be able to read it until I'm gone."

"Why?"

"Because this family has a lot of secrets. This empire, as you call it, is built on the backs of those secrets."

"What does that have to do with me?"

He smiles sadly. "You'll see. In the meantime, go home."

I study his expression to see if he is being genuine. I sense no subterfuge on his part, so I take the bait. Later he sends me a text message saying that I am relieved of most of my obligations but that I am still required to attend the morning meetings. I take it as a win. Then, I get an idea. I look for Ida's phone number and call her. I do not worry about the time because Ida is the type of person who is always awake. She picks up on the third ring, and I put my plan into motion.

WHEN IDA ARRIVES AT the estate, I squeal and hug her. "I am so glad you are here," I gush. I am not typically a woman who enjoys frills and girlish things, but with Ida, I cannot help but to indulge.

"I'm glad I could make it," she replies while taking in our home. "This is funny, but I do not believe I have ever had the pleasure of staying here with you." Her thick, southern accent makes me smile.

"That is because I do not invite many people here. For obvious reasons."

"Right." She glances around. "Mind if I take a few pictures? The folks would love to see it."

"They are still alive?"

"Unfortunately." We laugh at our inside joke. Ida's parents are two centuries older than us, but they do not feed how we do. We always joke that their method will be the death of them, but it has not happened yet.

I tell her she can take as many pictures as she wants and lead her to her room.

Thankfully, Andrei leaves me alone.

"So," Ida says, "tell me about the PI."

I snort, "What about him?"

"Did you two..."

"No. Of course not."

"Really? Because with a body like that, I am certain he could rock this world and the next."

"No. Besides, no one has been able to compare to—"

"Yes, you have told me a million times and then some. But eventually, you will have to settle for someone."

"I am not settling," I say. "I will simply die alone in this house with Andrei watching over me."

"If that's not the saddest thing I've ever heard."

I shrug.

Ida continues to ask me questions about the PI, and I answer as best as I can. In reality, I have tried to forget about him and everything else. There is no point in this if Father is out and about, Mother is unreachable, and Andrei is sulking. Besides, the PI was just a means to an end. Anything else was pity.

IDA STAYS WITH US FOR the entire month of November. Since she has spent a lot of time in the South, she makes us a traditional Thanksgiving meal of turkey, ham, macaroni and cheese, collard greens, cornbread, cranberry sauce, and other foods we rarely eat in our household. The Dhampir's enjoy every bite, while the made vampires complain there is not enough flavor to excite them. The difference in their physiology makes me wonder what it would be like to experience life like them.

Later that night, Ida and I are discussing the areas we live in when her phone rings.

"One minute, Lizzy Bear," she says. She steps outside of my room and into the hallway.

Generally, I try not to listen to other people's conversations, but when Ida has been out in the hall for almost an hour, I check to see if everything is all right.

I open the door and catch her saying, "Yes, I did... Yes, but if I continue... No. I can't do that to her—she's my friend... What do you mean not anymore? I... Yes. I understand. And this is all because of her... But isn't she innocent? ...Yes, of course I love you... I... Okay. Bye."

I scurry into the room and pray she did not hear me.

The look on her face says otherwise. "Lizzy Bear?"

"Yes?"

"Were you listening to my conversation?"

"Depends on what you consider listening." I squint my eyes at her.

She does not say a word, she just broods for a moment.

"Well, then I have no choice."

"Ida, what is wrong?"

She smiles, but something is off about it. "Nothing. I just realized I am done here."

"Done? But—"

"Let's not fight, Lizzy Bear. We'll see each other soon. But," she walks toward her room, "word of advice, you shouldn't listen in on other people's conversations. It could be dangerous."

I AM UNSURE WHAT HAPPENED, but I am convinced that Ida and I just had a fight. This is confirmed when the only thing she leaves behind is a note that reads "Tsk-tsk." I try to call her, but the line is out of service. I am bewildered, and at the same time, I understand it. Idabelle was talking about me in that conversation, and whomever she was speaking with wanted something. I massage my temples, wishing the answer would come. And when the phone rings, it does.

Chapter Eight

I do not pick up when the PI calls the first time. The area code reads 404, so it must be him. The only other person who lives in that area is Anton, and he does not seem like the phone call type.

The second time the phone rings, I deliberate answering, but then I remind myself what a jerk he was and how I have blocked out every memory and dream I shared with him. I debate whether I am being foolish. I do not want to admit that our argument was as much my fault as it was his, if not more so.

As I read through messages from Andrei about upcoming meetings, the phone chimes a third, fourth, and fifth time, but I still refuse to answer. He attempted to communicate via text every month, but I never responded. When he tried texting from a different number, I blocked it so that I would not have to see the messages. It hurt too much to read them. But today, the calls from this new number are an annoyance.

One of the servants knocks on my door and hands me Andrei's phone. I frown and take it from her.

"Hello?" I say into the device.

"Hello."

The PI's deep voice causes my cheeks to warm, and my heart flutters.

"Why are you calling?" My reply comes out tired, as though I cannot be bothered by him.

"I thought it was time we spoke," he says.

His footsteps patter as he walks across a tiled floor, and I imagine him at home and half-naked. This is why I did not want to talk to him. My mind always goes places it should not.

"What is there for us to speak about?"

"We never finished talking that night, and..." He pauses for just a moment, and I swear his heartbeat quickens. "Well, I wanted to apologize."

I wait before responding. This is my chance to make it right, and I long to make it right, but as usual, the words are stuck in my throat, so I say nothing.

"It's okay if you don't want to apologize. I mean, I get it, I was a real jerk." He laughs. "That being said," he continues, "I called to give you a message."

"A message? From whom?" I doubt he has found my mother.

"It's from Idabelle," he says. "More accurately, Anton told Idabelle to give me the message."

This surprises me. After Idabelle left, I did not think she would want to speak to me again. But if she wanted to give me a message, why ask the PI to call? "Well, why would Ida not just contact me directly? She has my number. And why would she give you a message from Anton?"

"That's the thing..." He takes a deep breath, and I wait for him to explain further. "I never stopped looking for Elizabeth."

He never stopped looking. But why? It has been over three months. I pace in my room and ponder what this means. If he never stopped looking, then that could mean...

"And while I was digging, I found out that Idabelle and Anton have an interesting history."

"What kind of history?"

"Put simply, they're lovers."

"What?" I ask half shouting, half laughing. "You are joking, right? She was just here, and she never mentioned—"

He cuts me off. "She was spying on you."

I smile wryly. "And I am supposed to believe you?"

"No, I'm telling you to believe her. To believe that she didn't want you to figure it out."

"But that does not make any logical sense. Ida was so kind when she came here. We talked about all sorts of things. Until—"

"Until she picked a fight with you and left in a hurry?"

"How do you know about that?"

"She told me when she gave me the message."

"And what exactly did she want you to tell me?"

"You are required to be in Anton's presence before the winter solstice." He clears his throat. "More specifically, three days before the winter solstice."

The winter solstice. That is when Elizabeth is supposed to be in Atlanta. Anton knows I plan on going back to Atlanta. "Do I have a choice in the matter?"

"Do pigs fly?"

"Point taken." There is silence for a moment, and I wish I could stare him in the eyes as I speak. "Thank you for passing the message along to me."

"You're welcome," he says.

I start to hang up, but then I speak into the receiver again, "PI."

"Yes?"

"I am, uh." I scratch my head and take a deep breath. "I am sorry as well. I...have an idea why you would not tell me anything. And the fight..."

His breathing shifts as he waits for me to speak, indicating he is listening.

"What I mean is that you were not the one who needed to apologize. It was my fault. And there does not have to be an *us*." When he does not say anything, I get ready to hang up, but then he speaks.

"I want there to be an *us*. It's just that we were moving at two different paces. I mean..."

Neither of us speak for a while. "So, you knew?"

"That you were one of those 'love at first sight' people? Yes. I think you built me up in your head. As though you knew—" He cries out in pain.

My heart drops. "PI? PI?" I yell while fighting back tears, "Are you okay? What's—"

"Nothing. I just, I said too much."

"What does that mean?"

"Read those texts you've been ignoring."

"But—"

"I'll see you three days before the winter solstice." He hangs up the phone.

I pull up the blocked messages on my phone and am astonished to see I have over one hundred messages from the PI. I groan. This will take forever to get through.

Instead of starting right away, I check my schedule for any last-minute things to do for Andrei. Once I complete the tasks set aside for me, I tell Andrei that I am not setting foot in a meeting room until I finish reading through the messages. When he protests, I remind him that I can be scary too.

Once I am given my time off, I slink into my room, lay on my bed, and read through every text message the PI has sent me over these past few months. Some make me angry, some make me cry, and some have me jumping up with excitement. When I get to the last one, I notice something strange. The message has a rune inscribed on its background. I go through all the messages again and notice that a different rune is inscribed on every five messages.

I draw the symbols on a piece of paper and go to the massive library in the furthest reaches of the house.

It takes me a few days, but eventually, I piece together the message. The runes do not give me a direct translation, but they tell the story of a coven of witches and a vampire conspiring to keep two lovers apart through a magical curse. The message is obvious. I would have to be an idiot to not understand. I call him immediately.

"I'll be on the next plane out," I tell him. "Wait for me." I hang up the phone, pack my bags, and tell Andrei I am going on a trip.

"But—" he begins.

I hold up my hand. "Andrei, this life is not for me. Besides, it is not only important that I find Mother now, but I must find Father as well. You cannot keep me holed up in this place, doing everything except what I have been trying to do this whole time."

"And I don't want to see the last functioning member of this family go bat-shit crazy." He throws his hands up in frustration.

"I will if I am stuck here!" I shift my weight from one leg to another and sigh. "Andrei, you have to let me go."

He gives me a hard stare and then hugs me. "The last time I let a Tepés out of my sight, people were impaled. The last time I let a Bathory out of my sight, you were almost killed," he shakes his head and places a hand on my shoulder. "There are reasons the rules are in place."

"I understand, but I am not them." I look him in the eyes and smile. "I am going to find them. Among other things..."

Andrei sighs and opens the door. "As you wish, Lizzy. Just come back safe. Okay?"

"Okay." I smile at him and walk out.

The way he was talking, you would think he was sending me off to war or something. Then, it clicks. I hurry to the car and have the driver take me to the airport.

It is time for me to see the PI.

I AM READY TO RUN INTO the PI's arms, but I stop myself because I must know. "It has been bothering me all along. Our souls, they are connected."

"Connected, you say?" He moves closer. "I guess you want to get right to it then?"

"Yes."

"Yes?" He raises his right eyebrow.

"Yes, I am jumping into this, and yes, our souls are connected."

"Okay. I'll play."

"During our fight, I told you that I know you from somewhere."

"You did," he responds as he steps even closer.

"But you left before I could ask."

He grins as though he knows what I am thinking. "If you ask now, I'll tell you the truth."

This encourages me. From the time I met him to when the witches explained what the colors of the dots on the map represented, I had wondered if the PI was someone I had met before. The likeness was too uncanny. Not just his physical appearance or that I felt our souls were connected. His mannerisms, how he snores in his sleep. The way his eyes light up the room. The way he eats and drinks. It is all reminiscent of the one man I could never get over. And now, he is finally willing to tell me if my suspicions are correct. I wanted to ask him while we were with the coven, but he kept avoiding it. But now I know about Mira and his past and everything else. So, if I am right, and if he is willing to tell me the truth, then maybe, finally, we can be together. "What is your name?"

He grabs me by my waist, pulls me close, and whispers, "Dmitri Kovács."

I try to contain my emotions, but it is impossible. I cry and hit and curse at him. Once I am finished, I embrace him. "Stupid," I say. "Why did you refuse to tell me?"

He takes some tissue from his pocket and wipes the tears and snot from my face. "I couldn't," he says. "At least, not without permission from the Morian Coven. And I didn't get that until—"

"I figured out the text messages," I finish.

"Yeah, and by the time I was released from my pact, we were arguing, and I didn't know how to talk to you, so..." he looks at me longingly, and his mouth turns up in a half smile. "But you know now."

I fixate on his brown eyes and take in the beautiful amber flecks. God, I have always loved his eyes. I search them for the truth and find it is the only thing reflected there. Satisfied, I lean into him. "Do not ever do that again," I tell him.

"Which part?"

I punch him lightly in the chest. "Lie to me."

"I won't."

"Promise?"

"Promise."

"Good," I say. "Now, can you get me some blood? I am starving."

He hands me the magical bag of blood and takes me to his rental car. From there, we drive to the hotel, and I ask him to catch me up on everything in his life.

After our tête-à-tête, everything around me is crystal clear. I can make out the tiniest of dust specks. My hands and feet can feel every living thing within a one-hundred-mile radius, in every direction, from the sound of boots on the pavement to the smallest whimper of a cat. I get a whiff of the Mexican restaurant located one hundred fifty miles away and the blood of all the humans within it. I can sense the souls of the depraved from the underworld.

And it is all glorious.

I brush my teeth and take a shower. The hot water relaxes my muscles, and the aroma helps transport me into my own little world. When Dmitri jumps in with me, I lay back into his arms. He massages every inch of my body. His kisses begin on my forehead, but it does not take long before he is nibbling at my ear and making his way down my body.

He kisses my neck from behind and massages my breasts. He turns me around, finds my lips, and kisses them softly. As our mouths move together and our tongues interlock, I feel the beat of his heart and the quickening of his pulse. His soul becomes radiant and envelops me in its brightness.

He pulls his lips from mine but does not remove them from my body. He uses them to travel from my neck to place my breast in his mouth. As he sucks, he trails his hands against my spine and then gives the other breast the same treatment. He stops only to bite each nipple gently and then continues down to my essence. His moist tongue explores every corner of my being.

When he finishes, I get down on my knees and use my tongue to travel across his length. I lick and caress it with my tongue, treating it as the world's best and longest lollipop. My fangs extend, and I gently pierce the vein there. He moans in pleasure and pulls my wet hair. I detach my teeth and lick the puncture wound so it heals.

Unable to contain ourselves, we exit the shower. He picks me up and walks me over to the bed, tightening his grip on my buxomness and pulling me close to his chest, then he throws me down onto the bed.

"You don't know how long I have waited for this moment," he whispers into my ear.

"I did not know we would ever have this moment again," I whisper back.

We pick up where we left off on the night he asked me to share a bed with him. I am instantly transported to 1591.

After a night of shenanigans, I get Dmitri past my father's guards and into my bedroom. The wind rustles the curtains, and the room becomes draftier than usual. We are laughing, and I must shush him. Father cannot know he is here. We kiss each other passionately as I guide him onto the bed. I lay on top of him and pull off his white linen shirt. His body is that of a man who knows what it is like to labor. I trace my hands over his body and let him undo my gown. He pulls me into his embrace and murmurs sweet nothings into my ear. I smile and bite my lip before sliding on top of him.

We move our bodies to the rhythm of the music in the distance. With every breath we take, we are closer to becoming one. I arch my back and look at the top of my four-poster bed, taking in everything about the night. The softness of the linen sheets and the down comforter. The smoothness of his skin against mine as our bodies move in tandem. How, even though the room is dark, I can make out every crevice and inch of his sculpted body. How the breeze of the room cools my damp, sweaty body. Everything about the moment is perfect.

He gently tugs me off him. "My turn." His whisper drifts off into the night as though spoken by a spirit. He positions himself on top of me and kisses every inch of my body. I muffle a cry of pleasure as he nips and bites the insides of my arms, my sides, the backs of knees, and my calves. When his tongue slides from the back of my neck to the middle of my spine, I must use a pillow to cover my mouth, for I have never known such ecstasy. His hands are those of a person who has embraced the service of Venus and labored leather for many years.

He pushes my legs into the shape of a butterfly and kisses every inch of my treasury before inserting his finger and moving in a circular motion. He inserts a second finger and then a third. Just when I think

I can no longer take it, he eases his pike into me and thrusts until our muffled screams are no more.

His dedication to hitting every one of my pleasure points tells me that he also remembers 1591. The way his hands caress my core as we bite each other.

He is much stronger now than he was then. Some of the more acrobatic positions come naturally to him, so we not only reenact the past, but we also try new things. The way he bends and contorts my body is a testament to how sex has changed in the present day. Much of what we do were not even dreamed of then. And that is a good thing.

At first, we make gentle love to each other. But it is too sweet, and soon, we are—for lack of better words—fucking out our frustrations. The rhythm of our bodies becomes a torrent of sadness, loss, and irritation from being apart for the past four-hundred-plus years. We bite and scratch and roughhouse until we are too tired.

When we are finished, we cuddle and discuss everything from the big bang theory to the weather to our insecurities and doubts. We kiss and laugh and apologize and sleep. And when we wake again, we make love until our bodies are sore and there is nothing to do but sit and admire the beauty of each other's skin and the brightness that is our souls.

Finally, I tell him my plans for finding Mother, and he agrees to help. He brushes my thick curls behind my ear and whispers, "I love you," until we drift into blessed unconsciousness.

Chapter Nine

"So," Anton says, "are you ready to hear what the favor is?"

I try not to let my anger take over. Anton's trickery fills me with disgust. But as I was the one who was stupid enough to agree to a Blood Pact without ironing out the details first, I have no one to blame but myself.

Dmitri gives me a solemn look, but he stays silent and waits for me to finish my response.

"Yes," I say, focusing on Anton. "The sooner I can do it, the better."

"You have time," Anton says with a smug look on his face. He paces back and forth before turning to me and grinning. "The favor is," he pauses for dramatic effect, as though he is rubbing it in, "to marry my son and bear his child."

Dmitri and I both gape at him. "You want me to...to what?" Did I hear him correctly?

"You heard me." His mouth widens into an even bigger smile, his white teeth protruding, and his eyes gleam with mischief. "You are to marry my son, Angelo, and produce an heir."

Angelo's background is almost as horrid as my father's. If the two of us were to marry and have a child, well, there is no telling what could happen. I wait for the punchline, but it never comes. Why does he think I am a suitable candidate to marry Angelo? Why has Angelo not found a wife yet? He is older than me—surely, he has had enough time to woo and charm many women.

Anton tells me what to expect upon entering their family. I try to listen, but my head is spinning with the idea that I will be betrothed to a madman. Then, Anton says something even more strange.

"I am so glad a Bathory is joining the family ranks without any fuckery."

"What is that supposed to mean?" I ask, looking for a hint of his true intentions.

Instead of answering my question, he just smiles. "Ida, dear," he calls.

Ida stands next to Anton. "Yes?"

"Could you be a dear and lift this spell?"

"Of course, Ferenc."

"Ferenc?" I mouth to Dmitri. He shrugs and looks back at Ida and Anton.

"Ida," I ask, "who is Ferenc?"

She stops what she is doing and looks at me with pity in her eyes. "Oh, Lizzy Bear," she says in a condescending tone. "This is Ferenc. Of course, almost everyone still alive knows him as Anton." She explains further, "The only people left alive who know him as Ferenc Nádasdy-Bathory would be Vladimir Tepés, Elizabeth Bathory, myself, and a handful of other witches."

I let her words sink in, and everything clicks into place. In the initial research of my mother, I found a lot of media, from parchment and journals to internet videos, that explored her past. She was married to a Ferenc Nádasdy who took her last name, and she had three children with him. But all the reports said he died well before Mother. If what Ida says is true, the man standing before me is either a descendant, or he is *the* Ferenc Nádasdy.

Ida draws symbols around Anton. After everything has been drawn, she chants one word over and over. It sounds like "unmask" in Hungarian. She finally yells the word, and a bright light explodes around Anton.

I shield my eyes and try to look at Dmitri, but I am not given the chance. Anton—Ferenc—grabs my face and tells me to look at him as a great power emanates from his body.

The darkness of his soul is terrifying. The man before me no longer looks like a teenager trying to play the part of an unhinged vampire. This man is roughly six feet tall, has dark brown hair, the build of a quarterback, and a menacing smile. Starkly different from the person before me a few moments ago.

His beige skin is still vibrant, as are his piercing green eyes. But his clothes have changed too. He wears a simple ensemble of dark jeans and a short-sleeved black workout shirt. His tattoos are more visible this time. The crests on his arm are far more intricate. In addition to the Dhampir and family crest he usually sports, he has crests that represent all beings, including humans. The intricate pattern causes them to mingle and intertwine to form two shapes. On his left arm is the shape of a dragon, and on his right arm is the shape of a unicorn.

Ferenc stretches and sighs. "Ah, thanks, Ida. I needed that. It's good to be back in my skin."

"I'm sure it is," she says.

"You can go now. I am going to have a chat with the young Elizabeth without any interruptions. Do you understand?"

Ida nods. "Yes, Ferenc." She gives him a long kiss on the mouth and winks at him. Then she takes Dmitri by the hand to lead him out. When she passes by me, she whispers, "This is what you get for surviving."

I gape at her, but she just skips away, with Dmitri in tow, like a child who just received a treat.

Ferenc gestures for me to sit on the front pew. I do as he says because I am afraid if I do not, his darkened soul will devour me instead of the other way around.

He clears his throat. "I know you don't understand," he says with seemingly kind eyes, "but you will." He kneels and brushes a strand of hair from my cheek. "You look just like her," he says, staring into my eyes.

I fear he is about to kiss me, but instead, he stands back up and brushes his long, dark brown hair behind his ears, then ties it with a hair tie. "You're wondering why I want you to marry my son, right?"

I try to decipher whether this is a two-way conversation and nod my head to placate him.

"I thought so. Well," he crosses his arm, sits down next to me, and spins me so that I am facing him, "I'll give you the short version of the story."

He boils the story down to mere bullet points, but the gist is that my mother lied to him for years about their marriage, children, and torture parties she held. He faked his death and went to get revenge on my father, only to realize he was too weak. So, he spent several hundred years working with witches and other supernatural beings to become as powerful as possible. But then I showed up. "And instead of going with my plan to kill your father, I decided to fuck his shit up. Because what better revenge is there than to have the spitting image of the woman he loves to marry the spitting image of me?" He takes a deep breath and looks at me. "And you were so easy to fool too. I guess, unlike your mother, you're an imbecile."

It takes every ounce of my willpower to avoid sneering at him and punching him in the face or kicking him in the groin. Instead, I bite my tongue and ask, "And how is this revenge?"

He chuckles. "Oh, you really don't know your father at all, do you? What if I told you that his only reason for treating you how he did was to protect you from me?"

I frown. "What are you talking about?"

He claps with giddiness. "Your father knew I was alive, he just didn't know where. He's been trying to pin me down, but my witches are able to keep abreast of him."

I take a moment to think about that. "So, all those years he was not around..." I let the thought trail off because Ferenc is smiling and nodding.

"Ding, ding, ding, we have a winner."

I cannot bring myself to do or say anything. I just sit in stunned silence. I have spent all these years resenting my father for not spending time with me, all these years looking for a mother to fill the void, and this motherfucker was playing mind games?

I roll my shoulders back and take deep breaths. The anger rumbles inside me. The tantrum rises. Though tantrum is too minuscule of a word to describe the storm brewing. And this time, there is nothing to stop it.

She is coming, and I welcome her.

Ferenc has stopped laughing. Now, he studies me intently. "Was it something I said?" he asks. His face has turned serious, as though he welcomes the monster that will be unleashed in mere moments.

I grit my teeth. "If I were you"—my eyes narrow—"I would leave."

For some reason, he finds this even more amusing. I shake my head. I gave him a fair warning. If he does not want to leave, then what happens next is out of my control.

My alter ego takes over. My dark brown curls turn white with golden streaks, the color that marks a Fae. My eyes burn. They are no longer the color of a Dhampir's eyes—amber with black flecks—but the grey of a sluagh with the red flecks of a Bathory. My fangs and nails extend and become sharper than a nanotip.

My mind is replaced by that of Liz, my alter ego.

Chapter Ten

When Liz takes over, I am a prisoner in my own body. I can see, hear, and feel everything she does, but I cannot speak or control her actions. I am certain she feels the same way for the 90 percent of the time I am in control. Liz is the reason my father and I now have a difficult time getting along. He knew what was happening, knew about her, before I did. And since that training exercise with Andrei, he has been more overprotective than any parent has the right to be.

But to know that Ferenc was the one responsible for some of Father's behavior, that is unforgivable.

Liz tears Ferenc from limb to limb. She literally rips him to shreds as his blood and flesh are scattered and spewed across the cathedral. Ferenc's followers try to stop her at first, but she is a force to be reckoned with. She takes them down, poking out their eyes and ripping off their heads.

Someone starts a fire, but this just gives her more ammo. She finds a pipe and turns it into a hot iron rod. She pokes and prods until everyone's flesh is burnt to a crisp. She shoves the pipes up the genitalia of the females and uses a knife to cut off the genitalia of the men.

I cringe from my front-row seat. Was my body always capable of this much violence?

Once everyone has been slaughtered or run off, Liz relaxes. The shift between our two personalities begins as her consciousness recedes and mine takes over. But then, the room shifts at a rare moment where our two conscious minds can communicate.

"What is going on?" I ask her.

"I'm not sure," she says, "but we can't switch right now."

I give her a small mental nudge. "You do not think you have done enough damage?"

She rolls her—my—eyes. "No, I have not done enough damage," she mimics my accent. "If you would woman up, you wouldn't need me."

"I do not need you!"

"Yes, you do. Just like your mother did, and her mother before her."

This gives me pause. "What do you mean?"

"If I've got to tell you—"

A loud noise causes us to look up. Anton stands before us.

"How is he still..." I begin.

"...alive?" Liz finishes.

Neither of us has a clue.

"You're not ready for this, kid," Liz says.

"Ready for what?" I ask. This is the first time we have ever communicated like this, and she is giving me nothing but snark. I wonder if this is what it was like for Dmitri.

"This," she says.

And then it is upon me. A surge of power like none I have ever felt before. My mind and Liz's meld together, and I see the truth of who I am. Of what I am.

Liz was right. I was not ready.

WHEN OUR MIND MELD is over and Liz has slunk back into her corner of my mind, I take a moment to assess the damage. Like any place that harbors my tantrums, the cathedral is trashed. But this time, I understand where the fire, brimstone, and ash are from. I am part Fae. I thought it meant I had the unpleasant task of collecting the souls of miserable and terrible people, especially since those are the ones that taste the best, and to damn others to walk the Earth as Sluagh or fairy hosts—which I cannot do yet because I am not a full Sluagh. But it is more than that. Since the souls I consume cannot be used, they are turned into raw, unfiltered power. That is why Liz takes over when I become angry. Otherwise, my body would be consumed by its own inferno.

I take in the charred paintings and crumbled pews. Effluvium and the taste of burned flesh linger in the air, giving me a headache.

I am glad Liz is the mental representation of myself that can handle the power of the souls. For lack of a better comparison, she is my subconscious, and that is why we can never communicate simultaneously. It is also why I can usually block out events such as this.

But now that I know she exists, I do not want to hide from it. I kick at the rubble with my combat boot and make my way over to Anton.

"I will not be marrying Angelo, and I will tell both my mother and my father where to find you," I sneer at him.

He smiles wryly and croaks, "You will do what I want."

"Blood Pacts do not apply if you are dead," I say.

"But they do if you are the one to kill me," he counters.

I had forgotten about that. He is correct, though. Blood Pacts can only be broken in two ways: a death of one of the pact members—but it cannot be committed by a pact member—or if the parties involved in the pact break the deal themselves. Neither of these apply to this situation. "I am stuck no matter what." I sigh in defeat.

Anton smirks, "You are."

Liz coming out served no purpose. If Anton's death does nothing but reinforce the pact, then my anger boiling over was pointless.

Except it is then I remember the last thing Liz told me before disappearing into my subconscious again.

I can use the part of me that is Fae, the part of me that is a fairy host, to locate Mother. I must focus the energy within me to work as a tracking beacon. If I can find Elizabeth, she may know of a way to break the Blood Pact I have with Anton. I smile. "It is not over yet," I tell him.

"Perhaps. But, for now, I have won." He stands. His body, which was blown to smithereens, has reattached itself.

"What are you?" I ask. I am too tired to play his games or expend any energy on any emotions besides lethargy.

"I am nothing but a powerful human," he says.

Dmitri is a superpowered human as well. I am curious to know how that happened, but Anton and I are not friends. So, I let it go.

"Don't worry," Anton says. "I will forgive you. This time." He moves swiftly and grabs me by the throat.

Liz tries to come out, but she cannot. I try to fight him off, but I am depleted of all energy.

He holds me up with one hand and presses my back against the wall. "If you ever pull some shit like this again, I will fuck your shit up worse than your parents. Marrying Angelo and bearing his child will be the least of your problems. Do you understand me?" A fire burns within his eyes. He is as serious as they come. He drops me from his grip.

As I gasp for air, he says, "I do hope we will see you at the reunion. It's next month." He straightens what is left of his clothing and walks off.

I slump on the ground, lay my head back, and sleep.

SOMEONE IS CARRYING me, but the only sensation I have is pain and soreness. The gentle bobbing movement from the body below me lulls me to sleep again.

The next time I come to, I am in our hotel room. I sit up and yawn and reach my hand to the other side of the bed. Dmitri is soundly sleeping next to me. I get out of the bed, trying my best not to wake him, and reach for my blood supply. It is empty.

The bed creaks. "You used it all," Dmitri says as he stifles a yawn.

"Of course I did," I say. "Let me guess. You want to talk about what happened?"

"Well, duh," he says. "Ida took me outside, and shortly after that, the entire place went up in flames." He motions an explosion with his hands and looks at me pointedly. "Do you want to tell me what that was about?"

His eyebrows are furrowed, and his eyes are filled with concern. Since we have established that lying does neither of us any good, I opt to go with the truth. "Liz surfaced," I say. His expression tells me that I need to give him more context. So, I recount the events. Several expressions flit across his face, and I find it slightly amusing. There was a time when I thought I was the only person who needed to know about my condition, outside of Andrei and Father, of course, but I know better now.

"So, what, each Sluagh has their own version of a Liz?"

I contemplate the question. "It seems that way. Though, I think the manifestation only exists for those who are born Sluagh. A made fairy host would not have a reason to worry about such a thing. Since, you know, they are damned to walk the Earth for all eternity."

"But what's the difference between the two?"

This is difficult to answer. Growing up, I was the only one of my kind in a mix of supernatural beings. If others existed, then I was none the wiser. So, I tell him what I have learned from books. "Sluagh that are born must consume souls at least once a month. They can have more than that if they want, but once a month is the minimum." I pause, but he seems to follow. "Born Sluagh appear human and pretty much live like humans except for that. When a born Sluagh dies, however, they become more of an entity than a person. They can still procreate for whatever reason, especially since they have to have the ability to seduce men..."

This time he looks wary. I think about telling him that I have never seduced him in that way, but I am not sure he would believe me. The night we shared a kiss was no exception. He would probably argue he wanted to do more than just sleep that night because I seduced him, but I had told him we should just go to sleep because I did not want him to think that it was a trick or mind game.

I roll my eyes and continue. "As an entity, the fairy host can eat the souls of those deemed to be wicked in the world, be they human, werewolf, vampire, Fae, or otherwise. Those souls they eat become fairy hosts as well. Made Sluagh, like made vampires, cannot procreate, and only have the characteristics of the Sluagh as an entity." By the way he scrunches his brow, I am not certain that he understands, but then it seems to click. "Put simply, I am certain that only those born as a fairy host have to worry about having a 'Liz' in their head. And even then, that could just be a part of the Bathory history."

He makes a face but does not respond. I take that to mean that he understands what I am alluding to. A lot of crazy runs in the Bathory family, as evidenced by my mother, aunts, uncles, cousins, and other family members. Liz could very well be a manifestation of the Bathory's mental issues—which I must assume are a byproduct of our genetics or a witch's spell. Most likely, it is a combination of both. Why else would everyone from both sides of my family be torturers and murderers? But I will not know until I find Mother and ask her.

I turn to Dmitri. "By the way, I have a way to locate Mother."

"That's great," he says. "What do you need me to do?"

I smile. "I will tell you on one condition."

"You really love making deals, huh?" he asks.

I shrug. "Maybe. Are you opposed to it?"

"What's the condition?"

"Make love to me."

He smiles and picks me up. "That is something I can do." We spend the rest of the day in bed with our hands and our hearts in sync. The thread linking our souls together is clear, and I know this was meant to be. I rest my head against him and take in his scent of Green Apple Jolly Rancher and Kool-Aid. I have grown used to the scent, which differs from his preferred snack in the 1600s: deer jerky.

I am at ease and protected in his arms. The idea that Father got him out while I was destroying the castle would be unbelievable, except he got what he wanted. In exchange for healing him and making sure the powerful energy I stored in his body would not kill him, Dmitri had to promise he would never reveal who he was. That if we ever met again, he was to act as though I were a stranger. The only way for this pact to be broken was if I fell in love with him again and had my heart broken by him again.

I shake my head at the absurdity. The supernatural community is much smaller than Father realizes. The chances I would never run into Dmitri again was unlikely. Still, maybe he was banking on the idea that I would not fall for the same man twice.

I nuzzle Dmitri's chest with my head and hug him tighter. "I do not care what happens or what Anton says," I whisper, "I will be with you for as long as I live."

Dmitri sits up and looks at me. "But, what about—"

"Shh," I say. "I will handle that. Somehow, I will find a way out of that Blood Pact. There is always a loophole." I feel the fire in my eyes and the heat rising from my skin. I will not let Anton steal my newfound happiness. And he will pay for what he has done.

The Aftermath

I follow Liz's instructions exactly. It has been almost a month since our encounter with Anton. We tried to find Mother the day after Anton left, but she must have been avoiding him. And since Liz had to teach me how to utilize my abilities, we did not have a chance to search for her before today. Dmitri gathers the materials and lays them around me. I focus all my thoughts on my goal to locate my mother, Elizabeth Bathory. I sit in silence and try to control my breathing. In and out. In and out. Once I am calm, I sink into my mind and look for the ball of white energy that blazes inside of me. I stare at its awe-inspiring greatness before pulling it and placing it into a shape that makes sense in my mind. It becomes a rosary like the one around my neck. The energy folds within itself and enters the ruby, causing a bright red glow to be cast against the darkness of my mind.

I open my eyes, and the energy of the souls I have collected are before me. They drift above the rune Dmitri has carved into the floor. The souls, which once belonged to those who would cause harm to others, are now like little children who have been coaxed to behave. They are no longer monsters but gems in search of a purpose. I pay my respects and beseech them to locate my target. It takes several hours of concentration and of Dmitri wiping my forehead with cool, wet towels, but eventually, I find her. She is staying in the luxurious Hellion apartments here in Atlanta, the premier apartments for those who are either supernatural or know about supernatural beings.

I kiss Dmitri, gather my things, and go there immediately.

I AM NERVOUS WHEN I get to the apartment. It is in the most expensive part of town, and from the brochures, I assume it will be large inside. I take a deep breath and tell myself that it is now or never. My palms are sweaty as I ready myself. Every fiber of my being is conscious of the surrounding space. My eyes pick up the tiniest specks of dust floating in the air. My nose picks up the scent of sex, booze, chocolate, and nature throughout the entire floor. On the opposite side of the hall, a bed groans, and a dog whines. The souls and emotions of every person in the vicinity rush through me like a chord being struck by a finger. My senses are on overload, and I am at a loss as to what to do. So, I do the only thing I can. I knock on the door.

At first, there is no sound on the other side. I listen intently for the faintest hint that someone might be home. But there's nothing. I try again. A few seconds later, a light pitter-patter reaches my ears. Whoever it is, they are trying to be as quiet as possible because they know a supernatural is listening. The sound stops short of the door. I take another deep breath, and the door opens.

I gasp in relief. It is her. My mother, Elizabeth Bathory, is standing before me.

"Can I help you?" she asks in a honeyed voice.

My head is down, so she must not have noticed the resemblance yet. I try to respond, but it is as if my vocal cords and mouth have forgotten how to work in tandem.

And her falsely sweet voice is of no help.

She snaps her fingers. "Hello? Can I help you?"

I swallow and finally get the nerve to speak. "Hey. Hi. I mean, hello," I stutter, trying to get the words out. What type of greeting do you give the woman who abandoned you as a child? How do you even start a conversation with her? All this time, I was focused on how I would find her. I did not consider the aftereffects—the heart of the matter. I raise my head so she can see me in my entirety. "Do you know who I am?"

Her eyes crinkle and open in recognition. "You can't be," she begins before moving in closer to peer within my eyes. "Elizabeth?" she asks.

"Yes!" I say. "Can I...come in?" I am freaking out on the inside, but I do not want to let her know that.

She hesitates for a moment, then she steps back and gestures for me to follow her inside.

Part 2: The Blood Queen
Chapter Eleven

I am astounded to see my mother. Father always said that I resembled her, but I could never see it. She is a replica of the woman in the picture. Light brown skin, dark brown curls, an hourglass figure, grey eyes with red flecks, and bloodred lips. A replica of me, but with slight differences. It is a shame the only thing I inherited from her is her appearance.

I inhale deeply and feel the mother-daughter connection between us. The souls of families have a color and smell to them. Had I been paying attention, I would have noticed ours sooner. I could have met her sooner. A combination of Viola tricolor, poppy, and white water-lily scents waft from her body while faint hints of apples and honey permeate the apartment. Mother's exploits are well known throughout the world, so I am surprised by how nature-like the room smells—how nature-like she smells.

I cannot believe Liz's advice worked. At least she was good for something before disappearing. I hope I never have to see her again. According to her, if I can handle the power within myself, I will maintain full autonomy of my body, even when I utilize the full extent of my Fae abilities.

I wait for Mother to finish making her tea. She seems to be the type to bide her time and plan. That is a skill worth learning from her. But there are other things I need to speak to her about before we can get to that.

"So," I say, a little nervous, "about the letter I sent you..." I reach into my book bag and pull out the letter I have carried with me for over four hundred years. It is not as pristine as it once was. The envelope is browned, and the edges are tattered. There are pen marks all over it from being transferred from bag to bag, and a peculiar scent wafts from it. The letter itself is also browned, but it is in far better condition than the envelope, with fewer stains and a less pungent smell. I show her the lipstick mark. "Why did you send it back?"

She looks at me and smirks. I cannot tell if it is sad or calculating. "Because I did not want you to find me." She sips tea from what she said is her favorite cup. "It would have been exhausting to handle you, Vladimir, my husband, and my other children at that time."

Her tone of voice indicates she has some regrets, but the answer still shocks me. After doing extensive research on her, I thought that may be the case. But it still hurts to hear it. I mean, who wants to find their mother and learn that not only are they the bane of her existence, but also someone is actively seeking revenge against her through you. Talk about drawing the short stick.

"Oh, don't make that face, darling," she says. "I know. I know. There were plenty of times where I could have contacted you over the years, but"—she shrugs—"I knew you would be fine with your father and Andrei. The only thing I didn't expect to happen was that you would be stupid enough to get engaged to Angelo when Dmitri was right in front of your eyes."

I glower at her. Perhaps I have more of her disposition than I initially thought. "Andrei," I say, "yes, he has always been there for me. Father, on the other hand..." I let the sentence linger in the air. Clearly, she does not know.

"What is this about your father?"

"We do not get along as well as we once did."

"That is a shame," she says.

"It is," I reply curtly. I try to think of something else to talk about, but anything I could say would just backfire on me. "As for that other thing..."

"What about it?" she asks, raising a perfectly arched eyebrow.

To think I could end up like her makes me shiver in disgust. "You are going to help me with it."

This gives her pause. This is the first time since meeting her that I have seen a stunned expression on her face.

"And why would I do that?" she asks. "You may be my daughter, but you and your decisions are not my responsibility." She takes another sip of her tea and sits the sturdy cup on a coaster. Her actions make it seem as though the discussion is over, but it has only begun.

"Because if you do not," I grin at her, "I will tell Father where you have been hiding all this time." I am not sure this is truly a threat until she narrows her eyes at me, which have turned a dark shade of grey. I follow up with, "We may not be on the best of terms, but he is just a phone call away, and I am almost positive he would love to know why you never responded to any of his letters after 1573."

She takes a deep breath. "Well, when you put it like that," she sighs, "I guess I have no choice. I can't have your father chasing after me." She gives a wry smile, as though remembering a long-lost secret from their past. "I was only a girl when we met. About thirteen."

I am tempted to do the math but decide it is better not to know their age difference.

She studies my face and chuckles. "Don't worry, it was legal then. Thirteen was a bit old for marriage. Especially when most girls married their betrothed around age ten or eleven."

Was that okay with her? It is not a question she is likely to answer—she has made it clear we will not be bonding. This is purely a chance for me to see how she lives and whether it will fit the lifestyle or tribrid I want to become. Or, at least, that seems to be her company line. When she first said she would speak to me and answer any questions, I did not know what to expect. The warning that Moira Morian gave me rings in my ear: *What you seek may not be what you actually want.* I ignore it. I do want this. Few people can profess that they were able to track down the woman that abandoned them and get her to spend time with them. The fact that I did is no small feat.

She stands, grabs her coat, and heads to the door. Once there, she turns toward me and asks, "So, are you coming or what?"

I take a deep breath and consider my options. I could stay here and think about my next move, or I could spend time with my annoyingly snarky mother, who I just met. My mother is a serial killer. My mother abandoned me before I was even born. My mother, although indirectly, is the reason I ended up turning the love of my life into a supernatural being. Going with her could be dangerous, and I could end up dead. Even with these things in mind, it does not take long for me to decide. I nod, stand, and gather my things. I survey the room once more before closing the door. My journey with Elizabeth Bathory begins now.

ELIZABETH BATHORY IS a renowned name. I know this because everywhere we go, someone greets her. They stare at her hair. Her eyes. Her lips. Her breasts. Her hips. Her legs. They undress her with their eyes, leaving no spot unwatched, and if they could, there would be no place untouched. By proxy, that means they stare at me as well. And while my mother struts her body and admires the attention, I do not feel the same way. Their souls tell me their thoughts, and the women are just as bad as the men. Those that ignore my mother and me have a difficult time doing so when we pass by. Whether it's on purpose or by accident, they catch a whiff of our scents, and then they too are staring. It may be Fae glamour, it may just be our presence, but whichever it is, the humans stand no chance against us Bathory women.

I know I am attractive, but there have never been so many people clamoring for my attention at once. One would think I was a famous American by how they act, tripping and falling over each other to open the doors for us or speak to us. The amount of magic it takes to garner this response would be draining, but perhaps it is not magic. Perhaps it just is.

I follow my mother as she flits from store to store, picking up this and that and chatting with people who seem to be utter strangers. They ooh and aah at her, and she takes it all in, basking in her glory. For someone supposed to be in hiding, she is garrulous. It takes everything in me not to question how she has made it this far.

The shop we are in now is obviously owned by witches. The smell of lavender and sage permeates the room. Bags of coneflower, rosemary, valerian, goldenseal, and other herbs, some medicinal, some not, decorate the walls. The stands contain everything from scrying pendants to books to altar kits. I can also see ritual swords, knives, and cauldrons. For human shoppers, the store holds everyday items, like travel gear and cleaning supplies. A part of me suspects these items could also be used as totems, but I try not to make assumptions. One aisle holds forbidden magical items. Voodoo dolls, pins and needles, bugs and creatures that creep and crawl are all held in sealed jars. Andrei and Father were always overprotective of me and did not want me to spend time with witches because they were afraid I would be cursed, which is ridiculous.

I grab one of the sealed jars and hold it in my hand as we head to the checkout line.

Mother flirts with the clerk, who can't be more than sixteen human years, and manages to receive all her items at a discounted price. He is vaguely familiar, but I can't place our meeting. He looks from Mother to me and scrunches his face as though he is also experiencing a sense of déjà vu. I ignore his stares and slide the jar over to him.

"Cash or card?" he asks.

"Card." I insert the chip into the reader. He bends his head down to type something on the POS system, and then I remember where I've seen him before. "Did you happen to be at a convention a few months ago?" I ask him.

"Yes," he answers with no preamble.

Two light puncture marks are on his neck. I sniff the air, and just as when the PI took me to the convention, I can smell apple pie on steroids.

"Why?" he asks.

"Oh, no reason. You just..." I pause. "Never mind. Thanks for this." I hold up my bag and leave. I am almost certain this teenage boy was the one I gave my blood to, but even if he is, it makes no sense to dwell on it now.

"What was that about?" Mother asks me.

"Nothing of importance. But I do have a question for you." My voice is nonchalant, but I am curious.

"Proceed," she replies.

"How did you manage to scam the boy," I ask her.

Instead of answering, she winks and tells me to observe closely at the next store. So, I do.

In the grocery store, she piles the basket high with all sorts of items, some that even seem pointless for someone of her caliber. After all, why would a Sluagh who has access to a twenty-four-seven cleaning service need so many cleaning supplies? It makes no sense, but I let it go. After all, it's none of my business.

When we reach the register, she grabs the cashier's hand, an older woman with long, white hair, and caresses her. The woman's face, which was a sour frown only moments ago, now lights up with excitement. Elizabeth tells her what she wants, and the cashier happily obliges. From the perspective of a human, they could be sharing a joke. But this time, I see the trick to it. When Mother caressed the woman's arm, the spot she touched became a lighter shade than the rest of her body. Mind control, perhaps? When we leave, I ask her about it.

"Mind control?" She scoffs. "As if. It's one of our Fae abilities."

"What do you mean?"

She sighs and shakes her head. "Has your father taught you nothing?"

"I wouldn't say nothing..."

"You are Sluagh, are you not?" she asks with disdain.

She is questioning me. Who I am. What I am.

"Yes, of-of course," I stutter, barely able to answer. I am Sluagh, but no one has ever taught me what that meant. The only thing Father and Andrei told me was that I needed to eat souls for nourishment. If I have any other Fae abilities, well, they are unknown.

"Then why don't you know anything about your heritage?" She rolls her eyes and proceeds to our waiting vehicle.

"Perhaps because you were not around to teach me." I scowl at her.

"Ah, so she does have a bit of a bite," Mother replies.

Mother. Now that I have met her, it seems odd to call her that. The word means many things. Caregiver. Affectionate being. None of these describe Elizabeth Bathory. Other than being the person who gave birth to me, we do not share a connection.

She continues, "Didn't your father introduce you to other Sluagh? Why would it have been my duty to teach you?" The driver opens the back doors for us, and we slide into the limousine. We place our bags on the floor and wait for him to get settled. "Your father knew the stakes of caring for you. He should have done a better job. Or, at the very least, made Andrei do it." She snaps her fingers, and the driver pulls into the lane.

"But neither of them is Sluagh, and besides that..."

She raises a hand at me. "What? All the Sluagh are dead or hiding? Is that what they told you?"

It would be nice to finish my thoughts or sentences without her interrupting me, but it will never happen. "Is that not what happened?"

She doesn't respond, just raises an eyebrow and smirks at me. Since we left her apartment a few days ago, Mother has done nothing but look down on Father, Andrei, and me. Any semblance of bonding I have tried to get in has been met with disdain. How is it that I am spending all this time with her, and yet I still know next to nothing about her?

I take a deep breath. *Be patient,* I think. *Give it time.* Elizabeth has already mentioned she wanted nothing to do with us. She is helping me for purely selfish reasons. I should remember that if I do not want to be disappointed.

"So, why Sandy Springs?" I ask. When she told me to follow her, she wasn't clear about why we were headed to yet another part of Atlanta. We've been staying at a Marriott in Sandy Springs, and there still hasn't been any headway on how to break the Blood Pact with Anton.

"If I know my ex-husband—"

"Which one?" I ask. "The one who loved you, or the one who murdered you?"

"Very funny." She scowls. "Anton, obviously."

I shrug and mutter, "I still don't understand why he chose the name Anton of all things."

"Because it means priceless. As far as names go, it is one that evokes power and wealth." She scoffs. "Anyway, if I know him, and assuming there is a way to break a Blood Pact, he would have left it with a trusted supernatural."

"And who or what would that be?"

"You'll see when we get there. Now shut up and enjoy the scenery."

I start to protest, but then her eyes flash—it is too quick for me to keep up with the color—and I keep my mouth shut. The ride through Sandy Springs is uneventful. The highway turns into a city, and the city eventually turns into an intricate lay of suburban areas. We pass all of that and head toward forests and trees.

"Where are we?" I ask. The area reminds me of home.

"Geographically, we're near the John Ripley Forbes Big Trees Forest," the driver answers. "Physically, we are nowhere."

"What does that mean?" I ask him.

"So many damn questions." Mother rolls her eyes. "You're like a five-year-old. Ignorant of the world but too talkative to just take things in."

I ignore her and listen to the driver. "The John Ripley Forest spans thirty acres. The person you're going to see does not live in the forest, nor do they live next to it. They live around it."

"Around it?"

"In another plane of existence."

My mouth drops. "Please don't tell me that we're here to see..." I trail off because I already know what's coming. The limousine shifts and rises. A gate opens, and we drive through the portal as though this is normal. I close my eyes and brace myself for the large *thump* that accompanies the car's drop.

"We're here." Mother unbuckles her seat belt and waits for our driver to open our doors. "Elizabeth, are you coming?" she asks.

I take a deep breath. Of all the Fae in the world, of all the beings in the world, why did we have to come here? I groan. "Yes," I straighten my clothes, "I am coming." I step out of the vehicle and make my way to the entrance of the home in front of us. As usual, its big, pearly white gates are gaudy. Trumpets blare, and floating beings play and laugh in the clouds around us.

"We're in Heaven now," Mother avows.

"More like hell," I whisper. The gates open, and we walk up the steps to the front door. We are only there for a few seconds when the door is pushed all the way open and a woman appears in front of us. Her short pink hair with golden streaks is cut in a pixie style, and a tall, silver crown has been placed haphazardly on top of it. Her pointy ears, wide eyes, and light brown complexion are both stunning and becoming of her. She is dressed in a long-sleeved white shirt, golden skirt, and white sandals that crisscross at the ankles. She is also adorned with silver jewelry. A pendant in the shape of a circle hangs from her neck, while a gaggle of silver bangles and rings adorn her wrists and hands. She also has a series of piercings on her ears and a nose ring.

"Liza!" she shouts before she hugs my mother. "And tiny Lizzy!" she yells. I try to hide my grimace behind a smile. "Hi, Latina." I take a long pause before continuing, "Long time, no see."

Chapter Twelve

L atina of the Fairies, also known as Queen of the Realms, is the
bane of my existence. She was put on this earth specifically to
annoy the ever-living shit out of me, and I mean that in the nicest
way possible.

Every supernatural meets the Queen of the Realms at least once
in their life, typically when they are first born. It is more of a title
than anything and is bestowed upon the most powerful supernatural
being every five hundred years. There is also a King of the Realms,
but no one knows who he is because the last Coronation for the King
of the Realms was kept a secret. Not that it matters since the title
is passed between the same powerful families. Latina has been the
Queen at least five times, including when I was born and now.

"Lizzy, we have so much to catch up on." She intrudes on my
thoughts, as fairies often do, so I put them aside.

"I am certain you already know everything, Latina." Her guards,
who have just made themselves noticeable, give me a hard stare. "I
mean, Queen Latina, why would you want to speak to a supernatural
as low on the totem pole as myself when you could spend your
time doing more important things, like," I search around the area for
something—anything—to use, "tending to the gardens." The guard's
faces relax now that I have said the correct thing.

What bothers me about Latina is not her overall character, it is
who she becomes when she has the title of Queen. Her powers are
magnified, and she thinks she has the right to control everything and
everyone who crosses her path. And, technically, she does, but she

doesn't have to be so damn cocky about it. Her uptightness and need for power irritate me.

"Lizzy, I know you do not care about my garden. You and your mother are here to discuss the Blood Pact you created with Anton, correct?"

I force myself to avoid rolling my eyes. "Yes, Your Majesty," my voice is clear, "that is correct."

"And you're both hoping I will have an answer," she opines.

"Yes, Your Majesty," Mother answers.

Latina claps her hands together. "Excellent. I love a challenge. And, of course, I would love to help my subjects."

I brace myself for what comes next. The powerful ones never do anything for free. If people like me, or in this case, Mother, did not come sniffing for favors, perhaps we would not have to do their bidding. Wishful thinking, I know, but it is the only way I can sleep at night.

"Your Eminence," Mother courtesies, "thank you for your generosity. I suspect you require nothing of us in return?"

Latina laughs, and it is not a real laugh. She is biding her time. "Nothing in return? Liza, dear, you know better than that."

"Do I?" Mother asks. I want to yell at her to stop challenging the Queen of the Realms, but she will not listen. "I could easily have your crown if I wanted it, Latina. Or did you forget about—"

"ENOUGH!" Latina yells. Her face is red, her nostrils are flaring, and the power of the fairies hums around us. "Elizabeth Bathory, you have come into my home, asking for my services, and this, THIS, is how you go about it? How insolent can you be?"

Mother opens and then closes her mouth as though she wants to say something, but she holds it back.

Latina straightens her skirt. "Now," she says in a deadly soft voice, "do you want my assistance or not?"

This conversation no longer has anything to do with me, so I do not answer.

"We do," Mother says, "but not like this." She curtsies and grabs my hand, dragging me to the door without giving me a chance to protest.

"What was the point of that?" I ask her once we are outside.

"You'll see," she says as we walk toward the car.

I stop walking. "No. I am so fucking tired of this. Why are we doing all this? It makes no sense." I tap my fingers on my leg and shift my weight from one side to the other.

Mother takes a deep breath. "Must I explain everything?" she asks.

Why is she the frustrated one? I roll my eyes. "You know what," I say, "forget it. Asking you for help with this was a mistake. Just take me back to the PI. He and I will work it out."

"Just when you're about to get what you want?" she asks.

Before I can answer, the doors to the castle open, and a flurry of feet surround us. Latina has followed us to the car and, unlike any other time I have seen her, she is flustered and out of breath.

"Wait!" she calls out. "You're just going to leave like that?"

"Well, if you're going to be a drama queen, then what's the point of staying?" Mother smirks, and then an odd thing happens.

Latina laughs. The guffaw is unsettling.

"You're right, as always, Elizabeth, but you know I have to put on a show. You always seem to ruin it for me."

"That's my job, sister."

"Wait, sister?" I ask.

"Sister," Latina replies.

"As in..."

"Your aunt," she says.

"But..." I cannot speak. I have no words.

"It seems like the next Queen of the Realms is speechless," Latina continues. "Really, Liza, you should have kept her and taught her *things*."

"You know why I couldn't."

"Yes, well, it's a shame. But, it's never too late."

"So, is that what you want?"

"Yes. If you want the Blood Pact broken..."

They continue to talk around me as though I am not there, but I comprehend the gist of the conversation. The Bathory and Tepés lines are royalty among the supernatural community. Latina wants to teach me what it means to be Fae so that I can become the next Queen of the Realms, but Mother is against it. Eventually, we follow "Auntie Latina"—the name does not roll off the tongue—into the palace.

They discuss the topic for hours upon hours, and by the time they ask me to weigh in, I am not sure what I want. I already have a lot on my plate, and I make a mental list of what I need versus what I want. I need to learn about my Fae side, I need to learn about Mother and my bloodlines, and I need to know how to break the Blood Pact with Anton. But the only thing I want right now is to discern who or what I am so that I can be with Dmitri. I want to leave the rest of this behind me. I want to have an actual conversation with my father. I do not know the best course of action.

As their stares become unwavering, and as they look at me expectantly, I smile. I will do what they want. I will become the next Queen of the Realms.

"...On one condition." I try not to fidget with my clothes.

"And what is that?" they ask, almost in unison.

I point at Mother. "She has to come too. I want to know everything about this side of my lineage. I can't do that without her here."

"That's not the deal," Mother snarls at me.

"That's not true," Latina says.

"It's part of the deal now," I tell Mother. To Latina, I arch an eyebrow. "Do you know how to teach a Sluagh to control their abilities?"

"I guess not." Latina's voice was low, barely above a whisper, but I heard the comment.

I stare at Mother. She scowls at me, but I ignore her and wait for Aunt Latina's reply. She has the final say.

"It's a fair request," Latina replies, "and we'll all get what we want."

"How do I know you'll find an answer to my dilemma?" I ask her.

"I am the Queen of the Realms, darling." She doesn't hesitate. "If there is an answer, I will find it. If not, well..."

She lets the sentence hang.

I ponder my choices. If there is no answer and Anton comes after me, then I will be forced to do something I am against. But, if there is... I do not like the sound of it, but the choice is simple. "Fine," I say, "Tell me what I need to do to become the next Queen of the Realms."

I HAVE NEVER DESPISED my mother as much as I do right now. Before I knew who, and what, she was, I would daydream about an older, soft-spoken twin who loved me to the moon and back. A mother whose side I would never want to leave. A mother who would do anything to be reunited with her beautiful, charming daughter. But as she jabs her heel into the side of my stomach and curses like a sailor, I want nothing more than to rip her to shreds. I try to conjure up Liz's power, but she is being a pain today. I grunt as I fling Mother off me with my vampiric strength instead.

Then something buzzes.

Above Latina's throne are buzzing numbers and lights that read 100:0. As in, Mother has won one hundred rounds of this insane fight, and I have won none.

"Oh, come on!" I scream, throwing my hands up and wiping the sweat from my face. "What was it this time?" I try to catch my breath. I am tired of getting my arse kicked.

"You know the rules, darling," Mother says smugly. "If you use anything but the gifts of the Sluagh, you're disqualified, and I automatically win."

"This is stupid," I mumble. "What is the point of these exercises? For me to lose so that you can feel good about yourself?"

"On the contrary," she replies. "Your losses do nothing for my self-esteem. It only makes me pity you."

My nose twitches and I ache to make a move on her, but she'll just pin me down like she did the last time. Instead, I cross my arms and look at the buzzer intensely. I have to be smarter about how I approach her.

"Well," she says, "at least you're slightly better than I was at two hundred years old."

"That is a little over a two-hundred-year difference."

"I know. Take the compliment or leave it." Her eyes dance with amusement.

I am about to respond, but then I notice something else. "Your eyes," I begin, "they are...different somehow."

"Oh, Latina," she says condescendingly, "look, she does have some intelligence."

I wonder what Father ever saw in a woman like this, but I bite my tongue and roll my eyes. "So, what did you do to them?" I ask.

Normally her eyes are in the same wide, oval shape as mine. Today, they resemble cats' eyes.

"Glad you asked," Latina says, getting up from her throne. She prances over to us and stands next to Mother. For the first time, I look at her as well. Like, really look at her. The resemblance between the three of us is uncanny. It is not in our appearances necessarily. It is something about our essence. I tap into my Fae powers more until I see it clearly. The three of us, our souls are endowed with silver specks of dust.

"Do you see it?" Latina asks.

I nod. I do see it. I have so many questions, but they stop me before I can ask.

Instead, Latina speaks. "You know about your vampire lineage, correct?" she asks.

"Of course," I say. "Father used to love to talk about his time as the King of Wallachia."

"And what did he tell you of us?"

"Clearly not much," Mother chimes in. "She didn't even know we were related."

I ignore her and answer Latina's question. "Just that Mother was engaged to marry Ferenc while she and Father courted. She had me in secret and had a wet nurse watch over me. Then, for some reason unbeknownst to him or anyone else," I glance at her, "she sent me with the wet nurse to Wallachia to be raised by Father. Essentially, I'm a secret love child."

"Is that all?"

"For the most part." I think on it for a moment. "He was...in a dark place for a while. Could not bear the idea of me even asking about her. Hence the four-hundred-some-odd-year journey." I grin, but I know it does not reach my eyes.

"Well then..." Mother sounds disappointed.

Perhaps she had hoped she would be the star of Father's dreams, not the cause of his nightmares. I shift at the thought. To think this woman caused so much pain. Father's, Ferenc's, mine, and countless others. She is a walking, talking pit of despair that drags everyone down with her. Maybe that is why she is so cavalier with me.

Latina—Aunt Latina, I mentally correct myself—snaps her fingers at me.

"Yes?" I ask.

"I said, are you ready to learn some of your history? It was a part of our deal."

I nod, and Aunt Latina waves her hand in the air. Three large, comfortable chairs and a three-legged table with golden spirals appear in front of us. "Sit," she orders, and we do. She claps, and the servants bring out tiny sandwiches and cakes for us to eat. They also place cups of steaming hot tea in front of us. "Now," she continues, "if nothing else, you need to know this."

I sit up straight and listen. She explains my lineage—our lineage—from the very beginning. We come from a cursed family. Our human ancestors held a grudge against the witches. In retaliation, the witches cursed us with everlasting lives. Instead of knowing peace in the afterlife, we were cursed to roam the Earth after death, sucking the souls of the damned. However, they neglected to take away our ability to procreate with other species. So, even though we were technically dead, our bodies still functioned normally. One day, a fairy and one of our Sluagh ancestors fell in love. Their child, my great-grandmother, inherited the abilities of both Sluagh and fairy. When she was of age, she fell in love with a human. This made it possible for her children to come out as either fully fairy, fully Sluagh, fully human, or a mix. Since this was the first time this occurred, no one knew what to expect.

Anichka Bathory, Shandra Bathory, and István Bathory were born as humans. Klára Bathory—now known as Aunt Latina—was born as a fairy. Mother was born as half human and half Sluagh, which is why her death did not kill her, and Aunt Zsofia was born a tribrid. They were triplets.

"And where is Aunt Zsofia now?" I ask. If anyone has a clue as to what it's like to be a mixed-race Fae, it would be her. She is the one I should be talking to.

"Who knows?" Latina says.

"Who cares?" Mother snarls.

Instead of dredging up what seems like a family feud, I focus on the information I have been given. "So...you were always a soul-sucker?" I ask Mother.

"Bingo," she says. "Again, you're so intelligent."

"And because of our lineage, I am..."

"An Arcane," Aunt Latina says, her eyes lighting up in excitement.

"An Arcane?" I ask.

"It's the equivalent of a multicultural human." Mother nibbles on a sandwich.

"There are few in the world. We thought your Aunt Zsofia would be one, but..." Aunt Latina trails off.

"That's neither here nor there. You being an Arcane makes you the perfect person to lead the Realms." Mother pops the rest of the sandwich into her mouth. "Provided, of course, you learn how to fight properly. No one will accept a weak queen."

"Prove your worth," Aunt Latina continues, "and you will go unchallenged."

"Keeping the title in the family name," Mother finishes.

I gape at them. They want me to hold up a family legacy I just learned about. Were they out of their minds? It was one thing to sit here and pretend it was going to happen. It was a completely different thing for it *to* happen. "And how long do I have before this becomes a thing?" I ask.

"Not long," they say in unison.

"Because there is one person who might challenge you," Aunt Latina says mysteriously.

"And that is?"

"Nothing you need to worry your head about, darling. Now, let's get back to training."

AFTER HOURS OF GRUELING practice, I finally won a match. "Suck it!" I yell in my mother's face as she holds her bleeding stomach. She smells of dead flowers, and her blood is a mahogany so dark it almost looks black. I can see bits of her organs, but she stands like it's nothing. She twists her head and cracks her knuckles as though preparing for a fight. But instead of the *snap* or *pop* I expect, she only stretches, and—for the first time—a genuine smile spreads across her face.

"Well done," she says. "You finally got me." The scoreboard above the throne now reads 200:1. It is not much, but it is progress. "Now, when you can do it two hundred times in a row, you'll be as good as me."

She limps to a bench Aunt Latina had put out earlier. Her body has begun to heal, another trait of the Sluagh, but she still sits as though she is feeble. "So," I say, "in all of that talk, we never did get to why your eyes look different today."

"Was that on your mind this whole time?"

She is being snobby, and I disregard her comment.

"No. Of course not—"

She glares at me.

"Yes, sort of."

"No wonder you're such a sorry sight in battle. You don't know how to focus."

I shrug and arch my left brow to let her know I do not care what she thinks.

"Fine. If you must know, it's one of our abilities."

"Ours as in the family? And just the eyes, or..."

"Ours as in Sluagh. And no. Not just the eyes. Sluagh have several abilities. We can sense the souls of all living things and other Sluagh." She lifts a finger up to count.

"But not of things that have gone from this earth or that others have reanimated."

"Correct. We can suck the souls of the damned and use them as power or release them after they've completed a task for us."

"Like how I found you using Liz's power."

"Exactly. We can communicate with our subconscious." She ticks off two more items using her fingers.

"Which is what Liz is..."

"Are you going to let me finish?" she asks tiredly. For the first time, I wonder if she is tired. Tired of running. Tired of her life. Tired of me.

"Yes," I say. "Sorry."

"Right. We can also bend others to our will, restore lives—for a hefty price, and change our physical appearance, be it race, ethnicity, gender, features, or otherwise." She recounts her fingers as if double-checking she has not left anything out.

"Do we have other abilities?"

"Not that I've discovered." She wipes her forehead with the back of her hand. But she is not sweating; she is glistening. In the dim light of the throne room turned training room, I can almost see the young girl she used to be. Someone who may have been able to love. "But I also haven't tried. None of us have." Her tone is sharp, dragging me out of my thoughts of a young Elizabeth Bathory running around a courtyard.

"So, the extent of our abilities..."

"Is unknown. Now, do you plan to pester me all night?"

"Yes."

"Too bad. I'm busy. Go call Dmitri. Let him know you're fine. I can sense he's worried about you."

"From here?"

She side-eyes me.

"Fine, I am going." I start to walk away, but then I turn around. "You know, this is the most mother-daughter-like conversation we have ever had."

"And it will probably be our last."

"Why is that?"

"Don't push it, Elizabeth."

"I could say the same to *you*, Elizabeth."

She rolls her eyes. "I guess Latina and I should start calling you by your ridiculous nickname so that we can differentiate between ourselves."

"You could, but somehow I do not think it would suit you."

"You're right. You should just stick to calling me Mother."

I turn around and walk away without responding. I do not want her to see the pleased look on my face. After centuries of unreturned letters and what feels like months of banter, we are finally getting along.

Chapter Thirteen

We are NOT getting along. After my call with Dmitri, who was worried about me, Mother dragged me out of my bed and poured a gallon of steaming hot water on me. My skin is still burning and blistering.

"What was that for?"

"Good morning to you too," she says with a foxlike smile. Today, instead of an ocher brown, her skin color is a deep and dark black. "Your first task is to heal yourself."

"I can do that in my sleep," I say. But in my head, I am screaming at the immense pain of being burned alive.

"Using your Fae abilities."

"You mean my Sluagh abilities or my fairy abilities?"

"Either or. They're both Fae, and don't rely on your father and Andrei's silly techniques."

"At least they were there," I mutter. I try to conjure up *that* part of me. The part of me that appeared when Anton lied to me. The part of me that wanted to rip him to shreds after he tricked me. The part of me that longed to tear his spine from his back and feast on his insides. The part of me that craves destruction. The part of me that is my mother. I take a deep breath and open my eyes.

"Excellent," Mother says as she saunters out. "Be sure to look in the mirror before coming out. I would hate for you to have a conniption."

Unsure of what she means, I walk to the small room adjacent to the apartment-sized room Aunt Latina has been allowing me to sleep in. The room, which is right next to the bathroom, is about seven-by-seven all around. It is in the shape of an octagon and has mirrored walls with storage space behind them. One door even leads to a slightly smaller powder room. I tried not to ask too many questions about the setup of my temporary home as it would probably make my head hurt.

When I look in the mirror, I am stupefied by the person I see. She looks like me. She moves with me and does what I do, but this cannot be me. I twirl around in my sweatpants and tank top. The image in the mirror copies me. The longer I gaze at her, the more entranced I become. Has this person been hiding within me the entire time? Is this how I imagine myself? It must be. What other explanation is there?

I use the mirrors to take in my new features. My copper, dark brown skin with warm orange-red undertones is now similar to that of a western coneflower: dark umber with cool, jewel undertones. My once long, tightly coiled dark brown hair is now a white-grey color with loose curls. It frames my face perfectly, and the strands bounce back no matter how taut I pull them. And, my once amber eyes with black flecks, they are now grey with red flecks—exactly like Mother's. There are subtle changes as well. My lips are fuller, almost as full as Mother's. And my ears, which were small, are now bigger. My nose stayed the same, but my once clear skin now has dark brown freckles. As I inspect my body, I grin. I look amazing. The pain from the burns and blisters is an afterthought now that I have seen myself. No, the pain from that was gone the moment I changed into the person staring back at me in the mirror. Dmitri would flip if he saw me like this.

Which makes me wonder, how do I change back? I try to replicate what I was feeling earlier, but nothing happens. I try for a solid ten minutes, but it is no use. In the end, I take a shower and ponder if I should bother styling my hair.

WHEN I FINALLY MAKE it to Mother and Aunt Latina, they gawk at me, but I am not ashamed. I chose to wear colors and clothing that reflected my mood: a black-and-red Lolita style. It looks off in this castle of pastels, but I do not care. Their faces are priceless.

"Do you dig the new style?" I ask with my head cocked to the side. Their eyes are fixed on the bow that sits atop my head. "Oh, this old thing? It was in the closet," I say. I skip the rest of the way to the large, gold-encrusted table and take a seat. I place my booted feet on top of the cushion of one of the chairs. They still do not say anything. "What, is this not fitting for the new Queen of the Realms?" I jest.

"Actually," Mother begins, "it seems to suit you perfectly. Do you plan to stay like that?"

I knead my fingers together and consider it. "Well, it is not like I know how to change back. You kind of forced this on me." I roll my eyes. "Thanks for that, by the way," I mutter.

Mother is still waiting for an actual answer to her question.

"I guess I like it enough that I am not worried about it right now." I pop a piece of biscuit in my mouth and try not to frown at its dryness.

"Well," Latina says, "if you're finished with this act, remove your feet from my chair cushions."

"Who says it is an act?" I ask, and I mean it. Something inside me has been set loose. I rotate my shoulders and crack my neck. It feels as though I have been unchained from something. I sneak a peek at my reflection in the teaspoon by my mug. My eyes flash with an emotion I cannot describe. Anger seems too flimsy of a word, and rage does not encompass it either. I try to smile, but instead of my straight pearly whites, one fang is protruding in the corner. And my ears, have they become pointy between the trek from my room to the table? Are all my abilities making their way into my physical features now that I know I am an Arcane? If so, why? Why now? When I finally snap out of the trance, I hear Mother speak.

"Yes, Latina," she chimes, "stop being tighter than a pig's pussy. Relax."

I almost spit out the tea I am drinking. I have never heard that phrase before. I am shocked, not because Mother said it, but because of the matter-of-fact expression that follows it. I choke back my laughter and remove my feet. "So, what new skill am I learning today?"

"Nothing." Mother sips her tea and smiles slyly.

"Come again?"

"You've learned everything you need for now." Mother places a hand on my shoulder. "You're ready."

"I have? I am? For what?" I slant my eyes and lean my head to the right.

Confusion must be plain on my face because Aunt Latina, who is still seething about Mother's comment, says, "You have."

"As for your second and third questions," Mother gets up and brushes crumbs off her tight black dress, "we'll show you."

I stand and follow them to the entrance to the castle. Today, there are no guards or fairy servants bustling around. It is so silent that if I spoke, my voice would echo against the empty, cavernous rooms. For the first time in three weeks, I take in Aunt Latina's home.

Save for a few portraits of her and a few other people I do not recognize, the place is devoid of any personal mementos. Each room is painted a different color. She has the normal rooms one would expect to find in a home—bedrooms, a kitchen, a washroom, an indoor pool, an entertainment room, a library, etc.—as well as some that are not as common: the throne room, a dungeon, a full-court gym, the servant quarters, and several others that are locked or bolted shut with chains. With all the space, one would expect she would entertain guests often. But no guests have come to stay since we have been here. And the few that have come to visit have only come for the help and wisdom of the Queen of the Realms.

Her life seems lonely, devoid of people and things alike. It makes me wonder if this is part of the Bathory curse. Aunt Latina seems to be unmarried. Mother left the only man she has ever loved for a jealous, backstabbing man that she wanted to divorce, and the gods only know what happened to Aunt Zsofia and the rest of their siblings. If the Bathory family is cursed to be alone and suffer forever, what does that mean for Dmitri and me? If we cannot break the Blood Pact... If I must marry Angelo...

I shudder at the idea of marrying someone I know nothing about. Someone who knows nothing about me. It is an outdated notion. And, as someone who grew up in a time where arranged marriages and marrying for profit was popular, I can say that the twentieth-century approach of marrying for love is much more appealing. Not that Dmitri and I plan to get married, but if we did, it would be our decision together, not some madman's decision, who is out to get revenge on my mother for something that happened centuries ago.

I think back to Anton's words. *What better revenge is there than to have the spitting image of the woman he loves to marry the spitting image of me?*

A rush of annoyance and vexation enters my body. Why am I in this feud? What do I have to do with any of it? Mother did not want me as a child, and Father was so bent on locking me up—supposedly to keep me safe—that he never let me out of the house. How does this Blood Pact, this marriage, count as an act of revenge against him? He is not even aware this is happening. He is traipsing around the country in one of his *moods*.

I take deep breaths and slow down my heart rate. None of this will do me any good. I just need to trust that Aunt Latina and Mother can help me find a way out of this mess, that they can help me fix my colossal fuckup.

They lead me outside to the garden. Just like Mother's apartment, the scent of nature wafts up my nose. I take another deep breath and instantly feel at ease. I want to stop and inquire about our destination once more, but they keep up a steady pace, and I fear any distraction will be unwelcome. For twenty minutes, we walk in silence. The farther we go into the garden, the less garden-like it becomes. Colorful flowers soon turn into dry, brittle weeds, and the trees that were lush with greenery now crack and fall under the lightest pressure. The sky turns from its bright blue to a smoky black. Finally, we reach what I assume is our destination.

Before me is a well with an immeasurable depth. At the bottom is a bright, glowing, red light. I look between Mother and Aunt Latina, but both their faces are solemn. If I did not know any better, I would think someone had just died. I wait a few minutes to see if either of them will speak, but neither say a word. I walk around the well and take in the outside of it. The moon is out now, and its light casts a white glow on the well. I touch the names inscribed in red rubies. All the names are feminine. Analia, Taryn, Klára, Zsofia, Elizabeth. I pause at the last one. The names aren't just feminine, they belong to women from the Bathory line.

"What does it mean?" I did not realize I had spoken aloud, but Aunt Latina grants my inquiry with an answer.

"This is the Bathory Well," she says. She rubs her hand against her God-given name and then continues, "It's been in the family for centuries." She waves her hand, and wind sweeps the fallen remains of trees and foliage out of the way so that we can sit on one of the stone benches surrounding the well. "I tried to find a different way, but in the end, this was the only solution to solving your Blood Pact."

My eyes widen. "You have...found a solution?" I ask. "Does that mean I do not have to become the Queen of the Realms?"

Mother shakes her head. This time, a sad smile plays across her face. I've seen a lot of emotions, felt a lot of emotions, from her. But this one, this one is new. "Quite the opposite, actually."

"Then..." I take a deep breath. I already knew this would be their answer. I have no idea why I thought I might be able to take my quarry and make a run for it.

"The ruby you were eyeing in the well," Aunt Latina begins, "can only be taken out by a Bathory woman."

"What is it?" I ask.

"It's called a Blood Stone," Mother replies.

Why am I not surprised? Our family knows nothing but blood. Based on our history, it would be more shocking if the stone had a normal name, like the rose stone, or something even more generic, like the red stone. "And what does this *Blood Stone* do?"

"It does the bidding of a Bathory woman, so long as she feeds it her blood." Aunt Latina grimaces.

"But only a Queen of the Realms can retrieve it." Mother paces back and forth. Her hands shake, and she is sweating profusely. It is frightening to see her this way.

"You have to pass your Coronation in order to get it."

"And when is the Coronation?" I have a bad feeling in my gut.

"Tonight," they say in unison.

I cross my arms. "And you did not think to tell me this because...?"

"We weren't sure you were ready until this morning," Mother says.

Aunt Latina scoffs. "You weren't sure. You insisted she needed to call upon her Fae abilities when her other abilities were already sharpened."

"If she can't shift into this," Mother waves her hand at my current state, "then she has no business getting into the ring."

I listen to them bicker and try to get a grasp of what they are talking about. Eventually, they stop talking around me and explain it. To become the next Queen of the Realms, I must pass the Initiation and the Emblazon. Then, I can have my Coronation. The Initiation into the Fae world is something I was supposed to do on my two-hundredth birthday, but no one told me about it. It comprises of a magical ability test, but they do not know which one, and a fight. It is the easy part.

The Emblazon is where most Fae fail. The Emblazon is when the candidates for the Queen of the Realms are painted with the first fire of the Fae. The fire burns both your skin and your soul of things it considers unnecessary to your survival. The pain of it can result in anything from mild scarring to death. It is rare for more than one candidate, if any, to be left for the Coronation afterward. That is why the ceremony is not held that often. If someone gets to the Coronation stage, they still have one last test to complete. The individual is given a poisoned crown to wear throughout the night.

"If she survives, then she is named the next Queen of the Realms. A party is thrown, and supernatural beings from all over offer up small parts of their abilities for her to use as her own. It's collected in the previously poisoned crown, and the witches perform a ritual to ensure the transfer." Mother places a hand on her hip and glances at the cave that lies ahead of the path we were just walking on.

"However," Aunt Latina finishes, "should the individual die, the current Queen of the Realms maintains her power until the next ceremony or until she is challenged."

"What happens if you pass the Initiation but fail the Emblazon, or if you do the Initiation just to chicken out before the Emblazon?" I ask.

Mother rolls her eyes before answering in a long, drawn-out voice. "As long as you pass the Initiation, you can participate in the Emblazon at any time. Regardless of if you fail or 'chicken out' as you put it."

"And how many people participate in this asinine ritual?" I ask them.

"Usually two or three," Mother replies. But I can tell from the intensity in her eyes and her shallow breaths that she is hiding something. "Today, it is just you."

"Or so we were told," Aunt Latina says. "I just received word that two others are participating. Some girl and *that* woman."

On that note, I notice a lady with golden hair, fair skin, and a body devoid of curves saunter over to where Mother, Aunt Latina, and I stand. She eyeballs the three of us as though we are gum stuck to the bottom of her shoe. She comes close and takes a deep breath. When she pulls back, she is smiling with a mouth full of sharp teeth. Her eyes widen with recognition, and she twirls around.

"So, you finally brought her here," she says to no one in particular. "Good on you." Her voice is low and smoky, like someone who tells untruths.

"And who are you?" I ask. I cross my arms and look her up and down the same way she did us. "You smell of treachery."

"I've only just met her, and she's already spouting such venom," the woman says. "Dearest sisters, did you not want to wait until she heard my side?"

It takes a moment for it to click. The unsettling hostility in the air. The heaviness. The hard side-eye the three women are giving each other. I use my Fae ability to search for the woman's soul. There, hidden behind a vile green color, is a light purple hue with silvery specks of dust. "Do not tell me..."

"Elizabeth, darling," Mother says, "meet the third candidate for the Queen of the Realms. *That* woman, as your Aunt Latina put it. Also known as your Aunt Zsofia."

Chapter Fourteen

"The one that you two just refused to talk about?" I ask in disbelief.

They do not say a word. The three of them just shift in the uncomfortable silence. I wait. And wait. And wait some more, but there is no sound. The wind does not even dare blow. When the stillness of the area becomes irascible, I break it.

"What happened between the three of you?"

More silence. They stare at the ground like children who have just been scolded. Fine, if they will not talk, then I will just leave them. I begin walking toward the cave, unsure of what to expect, but all three women stop me in my tracks. Mother uses her ability to control desire. Aunt Latina conjures up a stone wall. But Aunt Zsofia, she is the scariest. She combines her shapeshifting abilities, courtesy of the Sluagh in her, with her elemental abilities, courtesy of the fairy in her, to create a human-esque child that pushes me backward into the circle of women. I gape at the three of them. The last of the Bathory women. I do not know if I can live up to that.

"Lizzy," Aunt Zsofia says, "we need to have a chat."

"Not this again," Mother says. "There's a reason no one knows who you are, Zsofia. We've done our best to wipe you and the others from the family tree."

"Not to mention," Aunt Latina begins, "you are an abomination." She glares at Aunt Zsofia. "It's been centuries. Yet no one, and I mean no one, wants to hear what you have to say."

"We'll see about that," Aunt Zsofia says. "Lizzy." Her hand reaches out to me.

How does she know my nickname?

"Or should I say Liz?"

How does she know the name of my subconscious?

"Which one is it today?" she asks softly.

I turn. A half smile plays across my lips as I reply, "Liz. How did you know?"

"Because I was like you."

I stretch my limbs out and throw the black headband off my head. I shed the dress from the Lolita outfit and stand in my black crop top, leather pants, and calf-high combat boots. My fangs pierce my lips, and I can taste the blood in my mouth. "And what does that mean?" I ask.

"The subconscious," she taps at her head. "If you can't control it, it appears around the time of the ceremony."

"How do you know," I ask.

"Good ol' Sof told me when it happened to me."

"You communicate with your other half?" Mother gapes at me as though she's never done this herself.

"All the time," Zsofia says.

"This is why we blacklisted you. You try these *unnatural* things." She says the word unnatural as if it's a disease. As though it is something to be eradicated.

"It's not unnatural. The two of you would be more powerful if you fed into your dark sides."

Latina doesn't do that. Even with the title Queen of the Realms, I've never actually seen or heard of her harming someone. Mother, on the other hand.

"I let out the dark side all the time. It doesn't mean I have to communicate with her."

"Ha!" Zsofia's hard laugh rings out in the forest. "Bathing in the blood of your servants and forcing them to commit heinous acts can barely be called letting out the dark side. If you had full control of it, you wouldn't have turned."

Now Mother lours at her.

"Would you like to speak to Lizzy?" I ask. To be honest, I'm not even sure when the switch occurred. I was on the inside looking out, as usual, but the talk of the ceremony and the swirling feelings of anger and rage took over. It must have been the trigger.

"What do you mean," Mother asks me.

"She's not Lizzy," Aunt Zsofia says to Mother and Aunt Latina, "she's Liz." She turns to me. "No," she says. "I'm sure Lizzy can hear me just fine from where she's at."

That, at least, was true. We share a body, but our minds are free to observe the other's world whenever we want. We retain the knowledge the other has gained as well. She should be able to recall this conversation. "What do you want?" I ask in a voice tinged with sarcasm.

"To talk." Aunt Zsofia pulls back her blond hair.

"You're already doing that, and," I pretend to play with my watch, "you're running out of time. The ceremony will begin soon."

"Exactly. Sit it out." Her sweet smile now disappears. Her golden, red-flecked eyes burn like a thousand suns. It feels as though I will die.

"Why? So that you can claim the throne?"

"Yes."

"I'm the Arcane. You should sit out," my confident voice echoes into the land surrounding us. Had I been Lizzy, it would have faltered. But I know our power. As the Arcane, we can take down nations.

"Being the Arcane is why you should not participate. You can challenge me for the position later." She regards her sisters. "It's my turn to reign."

Mother holds back a laugh, and Latina's expression resembles someone who just ate a sour lemon.

"Why not challenge me, sister?" Latina asks.

"Because you'd lose."

"That's what you said last time," Mother speaks, "and she still kicked your ass."

"Because I was holding back."

Three loud gongs ring from the cavern, interrupting their jibes. "I guess that means it's time," I say. "Can I go now?"

The three of them remove the barriers to the cave, and we all walk toward it. I lead the group. Aunt Zsofia is behind me while Mother and Latina pull up the rear. When I enter the cave, the first thing that catches my eye is the stalactites at the top. The moonlight filters through them, allowing the crystal reflections to dance on the wall. In the center of the cave is a statue of the first Queen of the Realms.

Only two other people are here, a girl who looks like she's in her teens and an older man.

"Why is there a man here?" I whisper.

"A male must conduct all three parts of the ceremony. Part of the rules."

"Ah." I nod as though this makes perfect sense.

He stands in front of the statue of the Queen of the Realms and places an old, torn book on a podium. After a few seconds and a wave of his hand, the book transforms into a glistening blue book adorned with dark blue calligraphy and swirls.

He clears his throat. "Welcome," he begins, "to the Initiation."

The sound of glass cracking startles us. Stalactites are strewn across the ground. The old man whispers a spell—ah, he is a witch—and the fallen stalactites turn into a battlefield of ice.

"Today," he booms like Gandalf from *Lord of the Rings*, "we have two who wish to participate in the Initiation. All who accept, say I."

I expect the voices of Mother and my aunts to chime in, but not the sound of the crowd murmuring. I can't see the other people here. I consider the surrounding space, but there's no sign of corporeal bodies.

This time, his voice is soft. "Will the two women please step into the ring." The girl, with her wild hair and small frame, and I do as he says. "The magical ability test for this ceremony is simple." He opens the book to a page in the middle. "You will speak this incantation." He spins it so that we can read it. "If an ability manifests itself, then you pass. If not, the elements will turn against you."

The other girl's eyes widen, her ears and cheeks turn red, and she traces a pattern on her hand. She's nervous. Good. The old man's desired effect has taken place, which means this test isn't just about magical ability but about mental state as well. The fight isn't just about stamina but critical thinking too. The old man is sharp. I'll have to watch out for him.

After a large gulp, the girl asks, "What do you mean the elements will turn against us?"

"Hard to say, child," he responds. "It could mean drowning in the water from the stalactites or being blown away in a tornado..."

"You can't be serious," the girl chirps in her birdlike voice.

"I don't joke about magic."

She stays silent after that.

"Now, who wants to go first?"

The girl is shaking now. The taste of her fear is sharp on my tongue, and it takes every cell in my body to concentrate instead of thinking about devouring her soul. Her soul—I breathe deeply—smells of sun and lazy days at the beach. I want to eat it now. *Concentrate.*

I will myself to step forward. "I'll go first," I say with confidence.

"Very well. Go ahead. Read."

The words, which are written in symbols, are unfamiliar, but they make their way to my lips. At first, nothing happens, and I think maybe I was too hasty in my need to show up a young girl. But then, I feel it. The warmth of fire, the calm of water, the breeze of air, the coolness of earth, and the everlasting tug of spirit. The five elements spring to life within me. If I didn't know any better, I would think this was witch magic, but then a hint of darkness clouds around each element, and I know I am in Fae territory. The fire burns hot, the water thrashes me in its waves, the air transforms the water into a tsunami, the earth traps me within, and I can feel my spirit leave my body.

"It is an illusion," Lizzy says. "Would you like to switch? It is my body, after all."

I roll my eyes. "I know what this is," I tell her, "and you can't have the reins until this ceremony is over. You'll screw it up for both of us."

She laughs, mocking me. "You are doing a fine job of that yourself. A few outward appearances and you think you are me."

She's annoying. "I know I'm not you because I don't care about the Blood Pact. I just care that I have my freedom."

She says nothing, and all is quiet in my head.

The storm is no longer raging and, when I open my eyes, a crowd of people is before me. Cheers, hoops, and hollers ring out through the crowd. Every kind of supernatural is here. Vampires, witches, fairies, imps, everything except other Sluagh. A stinging sensation prickles up and down my arms. White ink has been inscribed into my arm. One second it's there, and the next it's gone. Invisible ink.

Next to me, the girl is also glowing with white ink. Hers also seeps into her skin like it never existed. She must have overcome her lingering doubts.

"An excellent show," the old man says. He pats us on our shoulders. "Shall we begin the next phase?"

The girl swallows. I grin.

"As you can tell," he says as he strokes his grey beard, "the ice below is thin." The former stalactites have reformed beneath our feet to resemble an ice-skating rink. "You will now fight each other until one of you dies," he pauses to let the fear sink into the small girl, "or until one of you cries for mercy." He smiles and lets out a stark laugh, "We're not barbarians, after all." The crowd chuckles at his joke, but the look in his eyes tells me that it's not a laughing matter. This is kill or be killed. He continues speaking. "You may commence when that stalactite," he points to the one stalactite that doesn't hang over us, "falls."

FIVE SECONDS. THAT'S all it takes for the stalactite to crash and for me to move out of the girl's way. She's small, which means she's fast. Faster than me. But I don't let that stop me. The old man didn't go over any rules, which means anything goes.

I sidestep punch after punch and kick after kick. If we keep moving on this thin ice, it's bound to crack, and one, or both, of us will fall through. I block another of her advances. If she keeps up this speed... I calculate how long it will take the ice to crack. The answer does not work in my favor. I have two options.

I hit her in the back, but she doesn't stumble.

I can either let her keep coming at me, wait for the ice to break and then let her fall through, or—

She gets me in the gut this time. For someone who was timid, she sure knows how to fight.

Or I can let the ice crack, pretend to drown, let her think she's defeated me, and just when she's about to claim victory, pull her down with me.

I survey the ice. The cracks are building up. I don't have much time to decide. But there is a third option.

If she catches onto the first two plans, there will only be one way left to attack.

Ten seconds left. What am I going to do?

Nine seconds lefts. Where is the densest crack?

Eight seconds left. Come on, come on.

Seven seconds left. This is what I've been training for!

Six seconds. I can do this. Just a bit more.

Five. It's going to be freezing down there.

Four. Okay. It's go time.

Three. Get into position and...

Two. Hold my breath.

One.

LIZ RELINQUISHES CONTROL, and I wonder if it is because she could not handle the pressure of the water or because she thought I would be the better choice. Either way, I am glad. It is bad enough she is in my head, even worse that she had the audacity to come out. And in this outfit. Ugh.

I gaze at the crystal blue water. One could travel all over the world and never find anything like it. The water only appears in the Fae realms. Or so I have read. The water is deeper than I—we—thought it would be. It pulls me in and holds me. It is as thick as mud.

The girl is still on the top of the ice. She peers into the water, looking for me, I suppose. It would be easy to follow one of Liz's first two plans, but that is not how we will win. Instead of aiming for an obvious ambush, I swim to the top of the water.

The girl is different too. Gone is the scared individual from the beginning of this Initiation. She had Liz fooled. But the pointed ears, gnarled fingers, and sharp nails gave her away. This girl is a werewolf. She was purposely scratching the ice the whole time. She must have thought it would break sooner than this.

"Good trick," I say, feigning tiredness. "I was not expecting this." Even though I was.

She does not let her guard down. Her entire body is locked on me. Her eyes track my movements, and her ears twitch at the slightest hint of change in our surroundings. Her earlier jumpiness was a façade to hide her true nature. Liz should have seen that.

"So, little doggy, what are you waiting for?"

She snarls at me. Just as I thought, she cannot control the transformation yet. She is in-between, which means I can bide my time.

"It is cold down here. That was a dirty trick, you know."

More snarls. She's about ready now.

"You are not much of a conversationalist." I make a slight movement, as though I am going to get out of the water.

She moves closer to force me to stay in the water.

I put one hand behind my back and use the other to pretend I am going to attack her leg.

Her body reacts to my bluff.

When she jumps back, I fling a piece of stalactite in her face. I jump into the air and use my newly given magical abilities to create stepping-stones out of ice. I make a fist out of the earth and use it to punch in her face. She is not dead, but it is a clean K.O.

"We've gotta thank Dmitri for introducing us to those Japanese animations," Liz mutters.

She is correct. It is the only reason this course of action came into my mind.

I harden the floor beneath us and walk over to the girl. I lean my head to the side and smile so that my fangs protrude. "Would you like to admit defeat?" I ask.

The old man only said that the battle would go on until one of us died or admitted defeat. He did not say we wouldn't pass if we did the former. The latter, however, is probably what got people killed in this asinine ceremony.

Now that the girl is back to normal, her body ripples and shakes like a dog's. The water sprays everywhere.

I wait for her answer.

She mumbles.

"I cannot hear you," I say. "Speak a little louder."

"I," she gasps, "I will not yield!"

"So be it then," my words are low. I summon the spirits and create a sword made of ice.

She stands up and wobbles toward me. There is determination in her eyes. But it is not enough to beat me. I bare my fangs and lunge at her.

One.

Two.

Three.

I cut her into pieces. Even then, I cannot stop. I continue to mince her body until all that is left is her head.

When I lift it for all to see, I am covered in her blood. It drips down my face, into my bosom, down my arms, everywhere. I lick my fingers. The blood of a wolf should be poisonous, but I taste victory. It is then I see it. The piece of her that tries to escape. Her soul. I grab it from the air before it can disappear and eat it. The girl's thoughts and memories flood into me, including her resolve to win. I bow my head in honor and then lift her head higher for all to see.

"She is eligible for the Emblazon," the old man yells.

The crowd cheers. Chants of "Blood Countess" ring through the air.

I snarl. Mother's nickname should not be mine. I am not a monster like her. But this ceremony serves a special purpose. It is not about mind games. It is about death and destruction. The dark side of the Fae. The dark side of the supernatural community. The dark side of those who seek to claim power. It is about the darkness within me.

Chapter Fifteen

The Emblazon is what will set us apart. What I do not know is if I need Liz's help to pass it. Letting her loose is always problematic—she has no regard for her surroundings, whether they be buildings or people.

"But you need me!" she screams.

I push her aside.

The old man readies the arena again. When he chants, the fallen stalactites and the sea of ice water are replaced by brown stone and three black thrones made of onyx.

Aunt Zsofia and I give each other knowing looks as we observe the metal chains mixed with silver and iron and coated in mistletoe, mountain ash, juniper, verbena, and other deadly herbs.

The Emblazon will be a painful event. We may not make it out alive.

The old man speaks. "The Emblazon," he says solemnly but loud, "can result in death." He licks his thin, chapped lips. "If you are not ready, then I suggest you leave now."

He stares pointedly at me. I do not move. Instead, I stand taller, straighter, prepared for what I know comes next.

He clears his throat. "Will the candidates please step forward?"

Aunt Zsofia and I walk up the stone pathway toward the thrones. The crowd hushes. This is what they have been waiting for. "Once I paint your bodies with the fire of the first Fae," he whispers so that only we can hear, "it will be your job to complete the ritual. I cannot stop—no matter how much you scream." He stares at me, but I do not break my gaze. "Do you understand?"

We nod.

"The Emblazon shall commence!" he yells, and the crowd echoes him.

Three elven women lead us down the stone steps and take us to a dressing curtain behind the thrones. They strip us naked and then bathe us with sponges. Then, they rub us down with oils and spray perfume on us. Who knew that one must be beautified before death? The elves slip sheer lace dresses over our arms. The ties in the front are loose. As the lace does nothing to hide our bodies, we are practically naked. With nothing to block our view of each other, it's easy to survey our opponent's natural state. A draft causes our hairs to stand on end and our nipples to harden. Before I can ask Aunt Zsofia the meaning of this, we are led out of the area by the elves.

They lead us back the way we came, wasting no time. Each throne has a plush, red cushion with purple trimmings. The elves lead us to our respective seats. They fasten the chains around our wrists, waists, and ankles. Then, they place something on our heads. There is a prick and sharp pain. I peer at Aunt Zsofia to see what was done.

On her head is an onyx crown with a jeweled pendant in the middle. The pendant fills with a dark red liquid. I sniff the air to find out what it might be. Blood.

But I do not have time to think about that because the restraints have become a new kind of hell. My body screams in agony as my blood reacts to the mix of metals and herbs. The juniper, verbena, and poppy make my skin sizzle and pop, while the iron, boxwood, and blackberry cause an itchy, red rash to spread like chicken pox.

I grit my teeth and watch Aunt Zsofia. She too is trying, and failing, to ignore the pain.

The elves spread ash over our bodies and around our feet. One of them leaves for a moment and comes back with firewood. The three of them build pyres at our feet.

They are going to burn us.

Since I was a child, I was warned of the dangers that fire posed to vampires. I was born with the powers of the Sluagh and the vulnerabilities of humans, and no one was sure what would happen if I were burned at a stake. Would it be a quick consumption of my body like that of a vampire, or slow and painful like when it happened to humans? Or would I be impervious to it since I was part Sluagh? There was no way to tell, and no one dared test it. The one time I had tried, Father caught me and had the witches of the household place a watching spell on me. I could roam the house, but not without him knowing every move I made. It was annoying more than anything.

Today, I will find out what happens when flames lick my body.

The elves leave the throne area, and the old man takes his time to approach us. He removes a paint brush from the bottom of his staff and dips it into a black powder. The symbols he draws are intricate and remind me of the ones from the map that Anton gave me and the etchings I found within Moira's home. He starts at the top of our heads, outlining the crown and moving on to our cheeks and chins. Then, he opens the loose ties of our lace coverings. Anger flashes in my eyes, but he moves about in a clinical manner. He gets no joy from the task. He paints the symbols onto our shoulders, arms, chests, stomachs, legs, and ankles. When he's completed the painting, he drifts down the steps and over to the statue of the first Queen of the Realms.

We are left naked and waiting for all to see.

The old man understands this is a ceremony, but others do not share the sentiment. Some of the crowd, male and female, leer at us. A wink over here, a long gaze there, a lick of the lips, and even some lewd gestures in the dark where they think we cannot see them. It disgusts me. I wish to destroy them. But if I do that, Liz will take over, and this is not the time for that to happen.

The old man speaks another chant and the folds of the statue's dress open. Inside is a thick, green, healthy bush. Around the bush is the most beautiful flame I have ever seen in an ombré of colors and hues. The bottom of the flame is the deepest, darkest black. The flames rising are violet, indigo, blue, yellow, orange, red, and then white. As the bush burns, the shades and hues of the fire change. It is so enthralling that I cannot take my eyes away, and I almost forget about the pain I am in.

The old man places his staff into the flame. Flickers of light burn the staff as he ambles toward us. He says what seems to be a short prayer and then walks to each pyre. He lights them from the bottom, then takes the paint brush and places the tip to the staff. He uses the brush to stroke the flames across the spots the powder occupied.

When he finishes, he rushes down the stone steps and holds up a hand. "Burn!" he commands.

The fire rushes up the pyres. I inhale sharply. My eyes widen and pulse. My body shakes uncontrollably, and black liquid spews from my mouth. I should black out from the pain, but the opposite happens. I am alert. Wide awake. Calm, even.

It takes a moment before the screams resonate in my ear. Are they coming from me? I look from left to right. Aunt Zsofia shakes her head violently. The flame is consuming her legs. The more she screams, the faster it travels. I peer at my own flame. It's like a snake. It slivers up my leg, curls around it, and then travels back down. Unlike the fire around Aunt Zsofia, mine takes its time. The flames on my arm seep into my body. The snaking flame follows suit. My body hums. The power is exhilarating. I focus on the crowd around us. They are awestruck, and it takes a few moments to wrap my head around the comments. Their whispers drift into my ears, even with Aunt Zsofia's screams piercing through the noise.

"This has never happened."

"Could she be an Arcane?"

"But we haven't had one of those in millenniums."

"Is it even possible? That this girl...?"

"She's the daughter of *those* two. Anything is possible."

"How many abilities do you think she might hold? How many species can she transform into?"

"Who cares. It's the other one who should be worried. She's..."

The chatter goes on and grows louder.

What does it mean to be an Arcane? I want to know. I close my eyes and take a deep breath.

"Cease," I whisper just above the sound of the wind.

My fire snakes the rest of my body, finding a place to sink into, and then sputters out. I stand, breaking my chains with ease, the anguish they produced no longer phasing me, and stretch. The crowd hushes.

I look around.

Aunt Zsofia is panting, but her flames have been quenched. I lift my hand to ask a question and notice the symbols etched into them are imbued with the colors of the flame. My body twinkles from head to toe. The colors and sparkles spread across the stalactite-filled ceiling. The entire cavern glimmers.

I turn to face Aunt Zsofia, expecting her to give me the stink eye. Instead, she is on one knee with her head bowed and her right fist clamped over her chest, her panting labored. When I face the crowd, they too are on one knee with their heads bowed and their right fists clamped against their chests. Even the elderly man salutes me and bows in reverence.

I wipe my palms against my clothing, forgetting the dress is barely closed. My skin is not drenched in sweat. Instead, it is clammy and cold. The ink and colors do not run off. Whatever effect has taken place is here to stay.

The room is still silent. Unsure of whether it is the correct protocol, I descend the spiral, stone steps so that I am in front of the old man. "Rise," I say. My voice is cool and collected, the opposite of the panic going on within me. The old man rises.

"What is the meaning of this?" I ask him, gesturing to the room around me.

"What do you mean, Queen?"

"Queen?" I say. "I have not yet been named the Queen of the Realms. There is one test left."

"Correct, but..." he trails off, his head still lowered.

"Raise your head so that I can look you in the eyes," I say.

He does not hesitate.

"Now, explain. I know nothing of...this."

Realization crops into his eyes, but he quickly hides it. "Of course, My Queen." He hesitates. "But may I ask you a question?"

"Yes," I say, "if you must."

He takes a deep breath. "You know nothing of the selection for the Queen of the Realms?"

"If I did, I would not be asking you," I say, harsher than I meant to.

"Ah..." He pauses. Then, "There is a legend..."

"Not a legend," I interrupt.

He clears his throat and continues, "...that says one day a woman born with three of the supernatural races, known as the Arcane, will claim the throne of the Queen of the Realms. She will come bearing the symbols and colors of the first Fae fire but have the strength of the night creatures. Upon her crowning, blood will rain, but peace will persevere, and she will be known as the Arcane, the Blood Queen of the Realms, and so many more."

"And you all think this is me?" I ask. Even Mother and Aunt Latina are bowing.

"It must be. You are the only one here born of three races."

"But Aunt Zsofia—"

"Has tried and failed each time. It is not her. Besides, she's not born of three supernatural races."

"But she is."

"No, she is not. Where you are vampire, human, and Fae, she is only human and Fae. That is a clear difference." Before I can ask more questions, he continues speaking, "My Queen, may we celebrate you now?"

"Wh-what?"

"Latina of the Fairies no longer reigns!" he yells. "All hail Elizabeth Mina Bathory-Tepés, the Blood Countess, the Arcane, our Blood Queen of the Realms!"

A loud cheer spreads throughout the cavern as he lifts the crown from my head and places a drop of something indecipherable in the compartment with my blood. The poison. This is the last test.

"Nothing to fear, Queen," he says. "I am certain. *You* are the Arcane."

I side-eye him and sigh.

"All hail the Blood Countess!" the people chant.

THE CELEBRATION IS about as loud as I expect.

Liz has gone silent. Perhaps she is under the impression there is no need for her to be present for the festivities.

I sing, laugh, and dance with my people.

When someone hands me my ringing cell phone, which also shows several missed calls, I answer it. "Hello?"

"Hi." Dmitri's voice reminds me of home.

"I assume you heard," I say.

"That you're the most powerful being in the world now? Nah."

"Yes," I say, smiling coyly. "Why else would you be calling?"

"To ask you why you let the entire community see you naked."

"How would you know that?"

"Because it's what happens in this ceremony, and—"

Someone taps my shoulder.

I turn around and smile warmly. "Dmitri!" I give him a tight hug and a long, deep kiss. I do not care that everyone is watching. "I thought—"

"That we would keep our distance because of Angelo?"

"Well, that is what we agreed upon."

He shrugs, and I love him for it. His blasé attitude to my mistake gives me hope that everything will be okay.

I show him my fangs.

"Shall we?" he asks.

I nod.

Soon we are together in the forest. Everyone and everything else melts away. I am safe, warm, and secure in his arms. When we tire of the celebration, we make our way into a secluded part of the cavern. I use my newly awakened abilities to build a wall between us and the rest of the world. We take time kissing each other. Slowly, our clothes come off, and we meld into one.

THE NEXT MORNING, I awake to a flurry of activity. Dmitri left a message on my phone that he had to slip out before anyone could see him. It is good to know he is being cautious of Anton's men, especially since they have a knack for breaking the two of us up whenever we try to spend a moment together. They must not like the idea of Angelo's betrothed being with another man.

I ignore the unpleasant thoughts and watch as one of the two thrones disappear from the cavern, leaving mine and mine alone. The grotto is transformed into a receiving ground. Before I have time to process anything, the old man is next to me.

"It's time for your Coronation."

Once again, I am pushed behind the changing board. This time, there is a tub. The sponge bath, oils, and perfumes take much longer than last time. At some time in the night, I must have slightly changed my appearance. My ears are now shaped like an elf's or fairy's. This gives the elven girls an idea. They braid my thick, curly, white-grey hair. When they finish, the two braids hang past my shoulders. They slick down my edges and sprinkle me with golden dust.

The etchings on my skin the night before disappeared, apart from the ones on my wrists and ankles. According to Aunt Latina, they are the marks that notify the community I am the Queen of the Realms. I watched hers fade away as mine grew stronger.

When I step from behind the changing board, I am wearing the crown from last night and, to my dismay, a loose-fitting, sheer, black shift—I refused to wear white. At least I am not naked under it. Instead, I wear a red crop top, tight black jeans with rips at the knees, and red-and-black combat boots.

"Well," Aunt Latina says, "I will have to get used to this. I have never seen a queen wear so much black."

"And yet," Mother replies, "it suits the crown."

I look in the gilded mirror on the back of the board. The crown is now black and metallic and adorned with purple and red jewels. The center has been drained of my blood and the poison. It does suit me, even with the braids.

For the next two hours, I listen to readings of supernatural texts to give me the official title of Queen of the Realms. Afterward, just as Mother and Aunt Latina predicted, supernatural beings come to me. They prick their fingers with a knife and let the blood pour into a bowl. The bowl is magically linked to my crown and allows me to suck in their power. The more blood they give, the more powerful I become. Many give me ten times more than what is necessary. I humbly accept it. The procedures do not bother me as much as I thought they would. Then, the next person in line speaks.

"Hello, Queen of the Realms," Anton says.

Chapter Sixteen

Speaking the devil's name always brings him to you, which explains why Anton is standing in front of me with a tall, white, muscular man. His deep brown eyes are thoughtful, and his dark hair is as long as his father's. This must be Angelo.

As if reading my thoughts, Anton speaks, "Oh, how rude of me," he gloats, "this is Angelo. Your *betrothed*," he says as if I do not know.

"I have achieved the power I need to break this pact," I tell him, thinking of the Blood Stone in the well.

"Even if that were true," he begins, "you have not done it. Which means something is holding you back."

"No," I say, "I simply have not had the time since I have been pleasing my subjects."

He looks around and scoffs. "You mean our subjects."

"Excuse me?" I glare at him as though he is a bug. "I am sorry. I thought you said *our* subjects."

"I did," he says. "Or"—he laughs—"this is rich. You don't know, do you?"

"What do I not know?" I ask through gritted teeth.

"Your mother and aunt didn't tell you?" Now his laughter becomes belches. When he calms down, he speaks, "The Queen of the Realms and the King of the Realms work closely together."

"Your point?"

He paces in front of my throne. "The ceremonies are held at the same time for this reason."

"You are boring me," I say, but dread pools in the pit of my stomach. I pray he does not say what I think he will.

"The King of the Realms was announced today as well."

"Are you telling me that *you* are the King of the Realms?" I suck in a breath and wait.

"Me? Hell no. I would never participate in something like that. But my son here..." He pushes Angelo forward.

This is a million times worse. If Angelo is the King of the Realms, we will spend a lot of time together.

"Don't look so disappointed," Anton says. "Angelo is nothing like me. He will make a wonderful King of the Realms. And," he comes closer to my throne than anyone else, "an excellent husband."

He steps back, picks up the knife, and stabs his hand. He drops an excessive amount of blood into the bowl. After wiping it off with a handkerchief, he says, "I offer my blood to the Queen of the Realms, since she's going to need it." As he walks away with Angelo in tow, he says, "May the Queen reign for as long as she lives."

As they disappear into the distance, Angelo stares back with sad eyes.

But that cannot be. Raised by a man like that, he must be after power as well. I grit my teeth and keep my composure. I refuse to give in to Anton's bait right now. I have better things to do with my time.

"Next," the old man yells.

WHEN EVERYTHING IS over, I follow Mother, Aunt Latina, and Aunt Zsofia to Aunt Latina's home. On the way, Aunt Latina describes the duties of the Queen of the Realms. When we reach the well, I stop her.

"You said I could use the Blood Stone to break my pact with Anton, correct?" I place my hands across my chest.

"Yes," she says, "but is that really what you want to do first?" she asks.

"It is the only reason I agreed to any of this," I say. "My goal was to find Mother. To do that, I had to form this Blood Pact."

"There were smarter ways to find me," Mother says.

I glare at her and continue, "Now, my goal is to get rid of the pact. It really is that simple."

"You're being hasty child," Aunt Zsofia says.

"And who asked you? You tried to stop me from claiming what is mine."

"Because you don't want it," she chuckles. "You preoccupy yourself with these foolish notions and let your mother and that dimwit over there convince you that you need them to do this when all you really need to do is control your subconscious."

"Not this again," Mother says.

"Stop it." My voice goes cold. "I have no interest in what any of you have to say unless it deals with telling me how to use the Blood Stone to break this pact. So, either help me or disappear." I meet each of their eyes, and they cease their complaints. "The fact that I have to stop the bickering of women older than me." I roll my eyes. "The situation is ridiculous."

"She's right," Aunt Zsofia says. "Let's put it behind us for now. I would like to help my niece."

Mother purses her lips. "Of course you would." But she says nothing more.

Aunt Latina pulls a long, red crystal from a crevice in the well. She polishes it with her dress and then hands it to me. I know what I am supposed to do. I take one end and prick my finger with it. The item absorbs some of my blood, reminding me of the needles humans use when they donate blood. The tubes take and take until the bags are filled up. This crystal works the same. The energy it zaps from me would have been overwhelming if I had not just received the gifts of the supernatural community. This is why one had to be a Queen of the Realms to complete this process. When the crystal stops sucking my blood, I take it out. The wound heals instantly.

I approach the well and search for a place to sign my name. One of the stones glows, and it is just long enough to fit my entire name. Mother and the aunts watch me intently. I banish all negative thoughts from my mind and sign my name. The stone flashes a bright red, and the well transforms into a stone stairway. I make my way to the bottom. The Blood Stone shines even brighter than it did the day before. I am entranced by it for the second time. I reach to pick it up, but Aunt Latina stops me.

"What?" I ask.

"If you take the stone..." She looks down.

Mother finishes the sentence, "You will have to sacrifice the thing that is most important to you."

"And how do I know what is most important to me?"

"The stone knows," Aunt Zsofia says. "That's why this is a terrible idea." She sneers. "Liza, this is your daughter. Why would you—"

"None of your business, Zsofia. If Elizabeth wants to do this, then we must let her. Besides, didn't you say my reckless behavior would teach me a lesson. Maybe it will do the same for her."

Aunt Zsofia shakes her head. "I won't stand by and watch this. Lizzy," her face is soft and her eyes are kind, "come find me when you want to hear my story. You'll know how to get to me."

"Will it include the reason you took part in the Emblazon?"

"Depends," she says.

"On?"

"You." She leaves as swiftly as she came.

Was she trying to warn me of something? If her name was on the well, then she must have wanted something too. Regardless, I must do this. It is the only way. I gather up my courage and pick up the stone. "Now what?"

"Tell it what you want," Mother says.

"Repeat it three times," Aunt Latina whispers.

I do as they tell me.

I want to break the Blood Pact with Anton. I picture his face as I say it. *I want to break the Blood Pact with Anton.* I hold the image in my mind's eye. *I want to break the Blood Pact with Anton!* The last one is a scream. And then, the stone responds.

"You Bathory women," the deep voice says. "You always use blood magic to solve your issues. When will you learn?"

"Blood magic?"

"Oh, you're new. You have yet to make the mistake." The voice is taunting me. It thinks I do not know what I want.

"Mistake?"

"Of asking for too much."

The voice of the Blood Stone and I are in the inner recesses of my mind. "So, this is a task you can complete?" Its presence surveys my mind, checking every nook, cranny, and crevice. Is it searching for my secrets?

"I can complete any task. I am a magical object tied to the blood of my master."

I consider this for a moment. "They said I have to sacrifice the thing most important to me. Are you going to tell me what it is?" If I know what it is, then I can determine if this is the only way for me to break the pact. Though I do not have many choices. To be honest, I have no other choices.

"No."

"But—"

"If I told you, you would reconsider. You need to decide to do that without knowing the cost."

I ponder his words. Can he tell I am desperate? If so, I need to be wary. "But you can break the Blood Pact?"

"Yes."

The Blood Stone seems too old to have a master. I wonder if it's satisfied granting the wishes of others. "Are you..."

"There is no time to waste. Do you want this pact broken or not?"

"Yes." If I say no now, it will think I am a coward, and as the Queen of the Realms, I cannot have that.

"Is that your final answer?"

"Yes." Does he think I will go back on my word?

"I will ask one last time. After this, what is done cannot be reversed, and you will have to wait ten years to use me again. Are you sure?"

The third time, the voice is intense. If I did not know better, I would think it too was trying to warn me against this.

A smart person would listen.

A smart person would use the Blood Stone for something more dire.

"Don't be smart," Liz says from somewhere in the back of my mind.

For once, I agree with her. Playing it smart means I have to find another effective means of ending the Blood Pact. Or I get stuck marrying Angelo.

Vampires mate for life. Sluagh and humans are fluid. If I marry Angelo and bear his child, I will never be allowed to marry again unless he dies. Sex might be permissible, but it depends on their faction. And Anton knows I cannot kill Angelo if I have a child with him. Growing up with one parent gone and the other one barely there... I would never do that to my own child.

I cannot afford to be smart right now. My future, and the future of my unborn children, depend on it.

"Yes," I say. "I am sure."

"Then the price that you pay is your consciousness."

"My consciousness?"

"Specifically, the consciousness known as Lizzy. Lizzy will disappear for the duration of time it would have taken you to complete the Blood Pact." The voice has humor now. It is laughing at me. Mocking me.

"And how long is that?"

"Where would the fun be in telling you that? Besides, you accepted the conditions. You have the rest of today, and then Liz becomes the dominant personality."

I close my eyes and bite my lip. That is why she did not stop me.

"You bitch!" I scream at her.

She laughs, almost cackling.

I groan as the realization that I have royally fucked up for the second time hits. Every time I try to fix something, I end up making it worse.

"As for that other matter," the Stone continues.

"What other matter?"

"Come forth, Liz."

"Yes, Blood Stone?" Liz's presence in my mind has grown stronger.

"Since you also made a request..."

I mentally glare at her.

"You owe me something as well."

"Go ahead," she says nonchalantly. "Tell me my price."

The voice of the Blood Stone laughs deeply. "Your sacrifice, Liz, is your love for Dmitri."

"What?!" For someone who got what she wants, she sounds angry. "But he was the whole reason for breaking the Blood Pact."

"That is not all."

"What else could there be?" we ask in unison. For once our minds are working in sync.

"Sacrifice is not the only thing required for these wishes. I am also allowed to add conditions."

"You've got to be kidding me!" Liz yells. She paces in our inner mind. The black space around her lights up with emotion. Red hot anger and passion so bright it scares me.

"What is it?" I ask.

"I cannot break a Blood Pact directly."

We pause for a moment. "He can't—" Liz begins.

The Blood Stone gives off an air of malice, so she holds her tongue.

"I can release you from the conditions surrounding a Blood Pact."

"What does that mean for us?" I ask.

"The only way to break a Blood Pact..."

"Is the death of one of the pact members, but it cannot be committed by a pact member, or for the parties to break it themselves..." I finish.

"Correct." Somehow the Blood Stone nods without having a corporeal form.

Liz tries to cut in. "So, how do we—"

"As I said earlier, I can release you from the conditions surrounding it. For instance, I can change who your pact is attached to, the member who must die, who can commit it. I can also control what they must be killed with, when they must be killed, where the death must happen. Put simply, I can change any of the means needed for breaking it. Six options. Two rolls of the dice."

"Do we get a choice in what factors we want changed?" I ask.

It laughs mockingly. "For a price."

"NO!" Lizzy and I scream in unison.

"Learned your lesson, eh?"

We stay silent. There's the faint rustle of what sounds like two dice rolling in the back of my mind. Finally, he speaks again. "The condition is this: for as long as her love for Dmitri is gone," it mentally nudges Liz, "and your subconscious is locked away," it nudges me, "your souls and the body they inhabit will seek out Angelo."

"Why?" I'm bewildered.

"The roll of the dice. Six sides of a dice. Two rolls. Each side has a specific meaning. Your dice rolled three, so Anton is no longer the holder of your pact."

"Who is?" Liz asks before I can mutter a word.

"Angelo."

Before I can voice my next concern, it continues, "Your second roll was a five."

"What does that mean?"

"Angelo is the one you must kill."

I breathe a sigh of relief.

"You have a year from today."

Before I can get a word in, Liz interjects, "How are we supposed to accomplish that?"

"That is up to you. But if you fail..."

His response seems ominous. "If we fail..."

"You will have something larger than a Blood Pact to deal with."

Liz and I gulp. What could be worse than the fresh hell we've been putting ourselves through? "Will we know the Blood Pact has been destroyed when it happens?" The question will haunt me if I do not ask.

"Yes," its voice is a whisper.

Liz and I get ready to ask more questions, but it disappears. Liz and her frown follow in suit. When I open my eyes, I am alone at the bottom of the well. The Blood Stone no longer glows red. Now, it is just a lump of coal. I toss it to the ground, run up the steps, and make my way back to the forest. When I look behind, the well of names is all that remains.

MOTHER IS THE ONLY one left to walk with me. When I ask her where Aunt Latina went, she just tells me "home."

The air is heavy with silence as we walk back to the castle. There have not been many quiet moments between us, and neither of us knows how to deal with it. For the first time, I really look at her. She is beautiful, but there is something more to it. Her eyes do not shine with mischief. They are dull, lifeless. She does not smile like a fox, nor does she look defiant. She has a deep-set frown and worry lines. Her movements are not as fast as lightning or deliberate. They are sloppy and slow.

I brush my arm against hers, and her memories flood my mind as I walk.

A night in a garden with Father while she was young. Laughs and simpers. The realization they were both night creatures living in a world of humans. Her parents' betrayal when they informed her that she was to marry Ferenc. A young Ferenc doing what he could to please her, but it never being enough because he was not Father. The torture parties she and Ferenc held together as their only true bonding. Him leaving her for his military duties. Her affairs. The letters written to Father but never sent. Her use of the Blood Stone. Screams, torture, and the madness within the castles as she forced the female staff members to participate in orgies, then slit their throats to bathe in their blood and sleep with their corpses. The day the townspeople and government burst down her door. Being locked up in a tower by her family. More screams, torture, and madness—hers, this time. Her death. Her rebirth.

By the time I have lived it all, we have arrived at Aunt Latina's castle. When I look at it, it is obvious that it is a direct replica of their family home. I wonder if it is a coincidence or if there are more things I do not know. I reach out to ask Mother a question, but she pushes me away and walks to her room. Her face is stern. She looks back at me once but then hangs her head and turns away.

There will be plenty of time to ponder that reaction. For now, I go into my room and lie down, because tomorrow, I will no longer be me.

Chapter Seventeen

When I awake, I vaguely hear Lizzy yelling in the back of my mind. She's in the space I've occupied since her conception. As if I would listen to her after that bullshit she pulled at the Coronation. I was able to take over, and I will stay in control. I've played nice long enough—it's my turn to live.

My reflection is different, in a good way. The pointed ears are a nice touch. They make me look like a fairy or some shit. And, although I wasn't a fan of those elves braiding my hair, I have to say they did a decent job. I should hire them as staff in the castle, which, per the rules, is now mine. The question is whether I should kick out Latina and Mother. I've already gotten rid of Zsofia, who is nothing but strife, so why not the rest?

I check my phone. There are a ton of messages from Dmitri, but I don't want to answer them. I can't be with him, and Lizzy is now a part of my subconscious. It doesn't matter.

I send Dmitri a text message in all caps. IT'S OVER. WE'RE DONE.

Those four words mean I don't have to worry about him. This cruel message is something he should be anticipating. I just found him, but I'm not attached. There is no affection or love for him, just a huge, empty hole. I can get it back. Somehow, someday, I can. But for now, the commands of the Blood Stone ring in my ear. They are clear. They give me a sense of purpose.

A plan forms in my mind, and I know it will work so long as Dmitri understands there is nothing between us. It's simple. To break the pact only requires two things. I must marry Angelo and then kill him. The only question is, where and how do I start?

WHEN I RETURN TO THE castle, I call Mother and Latina. They're not as reverent as the rest of the community, but I assume it's because they're older and have held the position I am in now. "How do I move the castle?"

"Straight to it," Mother says, "impressive. Pay up, Latina."

Latina reaches into a bag and hands Mother some crystals. "How did you know?"

"She's my child. I may not have raised her, but we do share some traits."

I pretend to vomit. Lizzy wanted to find this woman, not me. I could have lived forever not knowing who Elizabeth Bathory was or what she did. Lizzy's obsession made us weak, which is why we're in this predicament. Her stupidity will be the ruin of us.

"The answer?"

"Just tell it where you want it to go."

"Fine," I grumble. It seems they are not in a talking mood. "To Midtown then. I'm tired of Sandy Springs, and I don't want to travel in a car if I can just transport."

"Wise child," Latina says.

She's been watching me for the past two days. Her and Mother. It doesn't unsettle me, but it is annoying as hell. "Yes," I say, "I am Liz now, and that's not changing." I might as well confirm their suspicions.

"And Lizzy?" Mother asks.

"Is where I've been, Liza."

"You don't get to call me that."

"I'm one of the subconscious minds that takes over the body of a Bathory when they exhibit Sluagh abilities. I can call you whatever the fuck I want."

"Everyone except Zsofia."

"Well, there's always one who gets away." Lizzy stumbles around the back of my mind. *Great,* I think. *She knows too.* "That's why you ostracize her, right, Liza? Or should I say Mother?"

"You're no one's child," Latina replies.

"Wrong. I am technically your child. I may have been cooked up by some witches, but I do have a living, breathing soul. And I've finally gotten what I want." I pause. "Besides, Your Queen just spoke to you. Show some respect or shut up and leave before I make you." I am delighted. I have never told off a Bathory in this manner. It's liberating.

Their eyes fulgurate, but they walk away. They can't afford to piss off the most powerful person in the supernatural world right now, whether she's related to them or not. Centuries upon centuries of causing madness in Lizzy's subconscious has taken its toll on me.

I underestimated the witch factions that conjured me, but I'm wiser now and tired of playing their games. The Blood Stone gave me what I want. I can retrieve the rest on my own.

MIDTOWN IS THE HEART of Atlanta, and coincidentally, it's not too far from Anton's less than humble abode. Getting what I want starts with one simple task: agreeing to meet with Angelo. Which is why I'm here in the dead of night. I burst into the church and walk down the aisle. The vampires and witches part for me like the Red Sea. I wonder if I should expect this treatment all the time.

"I'm here," I bark in the large cathedral. At first, there is no answer, but then Anton appears. This time, he doesn't hide under the ruse of being an angsty teenage boy. He looks the way he did at the Coronation. I tap my foot. "Can we get this over with?"

"There she is," Anton's voice is filled with vigor. "Our new Queen of the Realms has some cojones."

"Oh, you and I both know that a honeypot is better."

"Oh," he laughs, "the vulgarity. And I thought you were a poised person."

"Then you don't know me."

"Or I have you confused."

"Perhaps. Are we done with the banter?" My eyebrows twitch. I would love to slit the throat of this man-child, but then he'd catch on to my plans. "I'm here to see Angelo."

Anton's eyes enlarge, and his mouth quivers. "You're here to meet with your betrothed. I wonder why." He paces in an erratic and annoying way. He shouts at one of the vampires, "Go get Angelo. Now." He turns and walks toward me. "Why now?"

"Because you forced me to. Any other stupid questions?"

One side of his mouth turns upward, and a wicked gleam appears in his eye. "No. None." He's quiet for a moment. "I like this new you. What happened?"

I roll my eyes and don't answer.

"Something's different about you." He circles me, but I stay silent. "All right, don't tell me. It's more fun if I figure it out on my own."

Still, no words leave my mouth. I refuse to tell him anything that doesn't have to do with this Blood Pact.

"Well, I'm going to work on some things. If you have nothing more to say to me..."

"I don't," is my only response.

"Then I'll let you wait for Angelo alone." At that, he disappears.

"*Tch.*" The sound escapes my mouth before I can stop it. His presence always leaves me feeling—well, something. I don't have the words for it.

The deep, dark blackness of his soul has multiplied tenfold. I can tell without fighting him, this man's dominance was achieved through hatred and sacrifice. He hasn't realized I'm plotting to break this Blood Pact, which means I have the upper hand. So long as I play this right, I could end up getting rid of this entire situation.

My thoughts are interrupted by the man that accompanied Anton to my Coronation. Looking at him in a well-lit room, there are a few differences from the other night. He's tall, 6′8″ to my 5′7″, I'd wager, but he doesn't look white. He has a sand-colored, almond complexion. Light enough to be considered white but dark enough to indicate one of his parents is mixed. His body isn't big like a rugby or football player but his arm and leg muscles bulge like that of a swimmer. His eyes are deep brown with a hint of silver around the pupil. While his dark hair is long, like his father's, it is an ebony black with streaks of dark beige. For him to be the spawn of Satan, he's handsome and thoughtful. Appearance-wise, I can almost imagine this pairing being a success. If it wasn't for his conniving, murdering father.

"Hello." His voice is a deep, raspy baritone but somehow still soft-natured. It soothes me.

"Hi." My response is curt. What are we going to discuss? This isn't like when Dmitri would court Lizzy and me by purposefully leaving flowers and trinkets in our favorite spots. And it wasn't going to be like modern times, where Lizzy and I would date a human or supernatural we met just for fun. Conversation is not necessarily needed in those cases because you already know the goal of the other person. This is uncharted territory.

I try to appraise his features more, but because we supernatural beings have a disposition to heal quickly, there's no telling what field of work he is into. His outfit of jeans and a t-shirt suggest a laid-back profession. And he comes from Anton, which means he's rich. Clearly age doubles whatever he would receive from his father. I can't make heads or tails of him.

I could ask.

"So, are you just gonna gawp at me all day, or…?" He leaves the rest of the question for me to answer.

His elevated vocabulary means he's intelligent, and the remark indicates humor. I sigh. "No, I'm just trying to figure out your father's game."

"His game?" He saunters over and inspects me. "What game would that be?"

"For starters, what purpose would he have for playing matchmaker? He explained it had something to do with revenge on my parents, but that doesn't make sense."

He turns his head slightly, tilts up his chin, and trains his alluring eyes on me. "Is life supposed to make sense?"

He sounds philosophical. A teacher, perhaps? College profession. "Well, what's your theory? You're his son. You should have an idea."

He circles around me. It's a strange behavior, but I ignore him and wait for his answer. He stops. "I never know what my father is thinking. He tells me to jump…"

"And you say how high?"

"No."

"No?"

"I mean, I tell him no."

"Then why are you here?" I cross my arms over my chest, willing him to take the bait. The Blood Pact is in effect, so theoretically, he has every right to try to do more with me than talk. Too bad for him,

I'm not letting that happen anytime soon. I must cultivate this false relationship first.

His eyes follow my motions, and he makes sure I know they are lingering where they shouldn't be. He doesn't come any closer, though. He keeps his distance and leans against one of the pews. He shrugs. "Curiosity, mostly. I wanted..."

I wait, but he doesn't finish. "You wanted what?" I give an imperceptible shake of my head.

"To see if it was possible."

"To see if what was possible?" This game of Q&A has me intrigued. I want to keep playing, but he disappoints me.

"Ah, who cares?" He straightens and heads toward the door. "Are you coming?"

"Coming?" Who does he think I am.

"With me. We're supposed to be getting married, and you're going to have my child." It's a statement, not a question.

I purse my lips, one side of my mouth twitching. I clench and unclench my fists. "To make such a comment, you must be a confident man."

He holds up his hands in surrender. "I didn't mean it like that. I just figured," he pauses before continuing, "well, if you entered a Blood Pact without knowing he would choose this as the condition...don't you think we should make the best of it?"

I scoff. He thinks he knows what's going on here. I can't wait to burst his bubble. "What would you know of our Blood Pact?"

Do you know I'm planning on breaking it? That you're now the holder of the pact? That it's your blood, your death, that will free me? That you and I are never going to happen?

"I'm in the same boat." He continues walking. "Of course, if you don't want to..." He lets the sentence trail off.

In the same boat? Him? That's fascinating. Of all the things I expected Angelo to be, this was nowhere on the list. His attitude and overall sense of self are the opposite of Anton's. Should I be afraid? Confused? Excited? All three emotions well up in me.

Lizzy tells me not to do it, but I shut her out. She doesn't make the best decisions. This is my body now, and I'm going to see what it has to offer.

WATER SPURTS FROM MY mouth as I try to contain my laughter. Angelo's face is priceless. We've been out for hours, exploring the city. Surprisingly, none of it feels forced, which makes me wonder, did Anton do me a favor? Granted, it's only been a little over a month since we've started spending time together, and I don't think this Angelo is the real one; but, if he's playing a game with me, he's succeeding. He's almost as charming as Dmitri.

There's a pang in my chest. When Angelo asked me to go with him last week, I declined. Not because I didn't want to go, but because Lizzy wouldn't shut up in the back of my mind. Luckily, I know how to stop her incessant chatter. She shut me up by sticking me in my own little box. I'll do the same. Once I was confident she wouldn't ruin the day, I told Angelo I'd be willing to go with him. It was more about feeling him out than anything, but it turns out he's fun to be around. Five days of spending time with him has made me realize that it will be sad when I kill him. He would have made a good friend.

We leave the art gallery with souvenirs that neither of us needs and make our way to his car. Before he opens the door for me, a figure appears in the mirror. "Damn it," I say. "Are you actually here?"

"Of course. You wouldn't return my calls." Dmitri's deep voice reverberates against the core of my body. Lizzy stirs in the recesses of my mind. She didn't lose her love for him. I did. Which makes this awkward.

"I didn't return your calls because there's nothing left for us to discuss. We're over. We're done. That was the conversation."

"So, you don't want to talk about—"

Angelo taps him on the shoulder. "She said she didn't want to talk. That's code for leave."

"And you are?" Dmitri's body puffs up as though he's ready for a fight.

"Angelo. Nice to meet you. Dmitri, was it?"

There was a time I would have loved to see two men brawl over me. But being the dominant personality is exhausting, and I would much rather this end without the peacocking. "It's fine, Angelo. Dmitri was just leaving."

"And why would I do that? If you can't find a way to break the Blood Pact, we can always—"

"It is broken."

Angelo and Dmitri both look at me with dazed expressions.

Damn. I let it slip out without thinking. But now that I've told the lie, there's no choice but to stick with it.

"What do you mean it's broken?" Dmitri asks. "If it's broken then..."

"Because I have no feelings for you."

Dmitri backs away as though I've injured him. "You, wait, you what?"

I glance at Angelo. "One second."

Angelo nods, and I pull Dmitri away, aware that Angelo can probably still hear us. "I used the Blood Stone."

"The one you were telling me about?"

"Yes, but there was a price."

"What kind?"

"Do you know who you're speaking to?"

He looks at my face, my clothes, my body as though seeing them for the first time, and then it clicks that this is the first time. Lizzy never showed him that we could transform ourselves. "You look like...your voice is..." he stutters. "Elizabeth? Help me out. I don't understand."

"We used the Blood Stone, Dmitri. What do you think happens when someone uses something that powerful?"

"So, you're not...?"

"I am...and I'm not. It's complicated."

"Then tell me!" he shouts.

I inhale and then exhale. "She's in here," I point to my head, "and she loves you. But I ca—I don't."

"But you're the same person."

"We're not. And you thinking that we are is why I didn't want to have this conversation." I turn away from him and walk to Angelo's car. "Take care, Dmitri."

As Angelo and I drive away, I try not to think of the pained look on Dmitri's face. I want to care that I just broke his heart, but the only emotion I find is pity.

"So," Angelo asks, "want to explain that?"

"It's nothing." I don't need him prying into this. "Let's go out." From the corner of my eye, I see a flicker of a smile on his face.

"So, we're not going to talk about that guy. He's your..."

"Nothing," I roll down the window and let the wind blow in my face. "He's nothing."

"Didn't seem like nothing." His hand tightens on the wheel.

I groan and reach into my boot pocket for some gum, which is difficult to do when sitting in the passenger side of a car. I grind it with my teeth. Not the usual method, but it makes me feel better. "Does it matter?"

"If you want to go out, then yes."

"Fine." I look out the window and watch a few birds leave the nest and soar into the sky. I give him the abridged version of my and Dmitri's relationship. Well, Dmitri and Lizzy's. I was always a spectator, but it doesn't make my feelings any less valid, and when the pact is officially broken, it's me that he'll be with. I just have to bide my time.

"So, wait." Angelo stops looking at the road to give me the side-eye. "You mean to tell me that he left you because your dad made him sign a pact that couldn't be lifted until you fell in love with him again?"

"Yep."

"And then you just accepted him? No questions asked?"

"Precisely." I nod, wondering if it would be rude to turn on the car stereo now.

"And now you're dumping him?"

"Mm-hmm." I flip through a few stations and settle on one that I like.

"And it has nothing to do with the Blood Pact that my father forced you into?"

"Nope." I look back at the road, away from him so he can't detect the lie.

"But..."

"Can't I just want to try something new without being grilled?" I lean back in my seat.

"Not a chance."

"Whatever."

When he puts it that way, it does seem unbelievable. But I know how to convince him.

"We just met," I say.

"Yeah, but that was going to happen anyway, Queen of the Realms."

"Look who's talking, King."

His smile disappears. "That was my father's idea." His hands tighten on the wheel again. "Not mine."

"So, you're not thrilled about being the most eligible bachelor in the supernatural world?"

"I mean, it has its perks. But this was for you."

"For me?" I try to meet his gaze, but he seems focused on the road now.

"So that our future marriage would make sense. If anyone asked."

Anton was planning this far ahead... Too bad I found a way out of it. "And it will."

"You're not actually going to marry me, though, are you? If the Blood Pact is broken, then you have no reason to. Especially if you're just 'trying something new,' as you put it."

"Perhaps," I say, rolling my window back up. "Or maybe," I lean in close to him as he parks the car near a nondescript building, "maybe I think this could work," I whisper in his ear.

He turns his head to push me back, but I kiss him.

I wait to see how he reacts. If it's disgust, then there'll be a hitch in my plan. But if he likes it, then the plan will work. He searches my face with his eyes, and I don't back down. This is step one.

In case he still isn't sure, I move in closer. He does too. We kiss until our hands are tangled in each other's hair. He pulls me closer and some primal instinct takes over. Before I know it, he's on top of me, and his fangs are in my neck. Even as Lizzy shrinks away in my mind, I welcome it. I've felt the effects of this before, but it's always been secondhand. If Lizzy did what she wanted, then I should be able to do the same. The seats of his car lean back, and his hands roam my body. I like it, but if I let this continue, there will be no point in the wedding night. And I have big plans for that.

"That's...enough." I gasp. My future preparations aside, this is too much for me right now.

"I thought you wanted to?" He looks disappointed, but he quickly untangles his body from mine.

"I do, but remember, I'm trying something new."

"What does that have to do with anything?"

"I'll show you."

Chapter Eighteen

I spin some truth into the lie I tell Angelo. Ever since the stay at Father's, I've kept a journal. When I came up with my plan to kill Angelo, I pre-wrote entries for an occasion such as this. The journal's leather cover depicts the scene of Lucifer falling from the sky. It's a little on the nose, but I think it works.

"So, your mother forced you into the Queen of the Realms thing too?"

"Essentially. She is not what I expected."

"I bet."

"Our parents are dicks."

"You could say that again." He takes a sip of beer. "So, is that all you meant by trying something new? Listening to a parent that was never there for you?"

"That's part of it."

"And the other part?"

"I've been with a few men over time, but there's only one I've ever cared about."

"That guy from earlier?"

"Yep."

"If you still care about him, then why..."

"I don't. You could say that it was a long-term relationship gone awry."

"How long?"

"None of your concern. But the point is, I want to try a few different flavors before committing. Do you know what I mean?"

"Yeah, but why stop me?"

"So many questions."

"Are you opposed to answering them?"

"Not really."

"Then?"

"You seem to be an interesting flavor. I want to save you for last."

"Which is why we're here?"

"Which is why we're here."

He looks at me skeptically.

"What? I've never been to one." A place like this was never on my radar, but if I'm going to sell the lie, then I have to start somewhere.

"Well, then you're in for a treat."

"Oh, I'm banking on it."

MUSIC POUNDS IN MY ear. The lights flicker and rotate in the club, and I feel like the Queen I am. I lick fresh blood from my teeth. Drinking a human's blood and feasting on their soul simultaneously has never given me as much pleasure as right now. Lizzy would never do something like this, but that's all right. I'm in control now. And who knew a place like this existed? A place where the Fae, vampires, werewolves, and humans in the know can gather and just...be.

All kinds of species fornicate around me, and it gives me a thrill. The ass in this building is unrivaled, and be they human, Fae, vampire, or other, I like it. Since Lizzy never went to the fun places in town, this is the first time I'm experiencing this. It's even more worthwhile since I can get the men here to do my bidding. I have a better range when it comes to our abilities, so I'm able to use them more effectively. Free booze, drugs, and magical items that enhance libido flow freely around the room.

But when I'm asked what I'm into, the words tangle in my mouth.

"The Queen of the Realms doesn't have a type?" one woman in my newly found entourage says.

"Of course I have a type, sweetie," I say, eyeing her up and down. "I'm just not sure I can find it here."

"What about foreplay, sex, positions?" a man asks.

He looks like a snack. Both figuratively and literally.

"Now," I wink at him, "I can't tell you that. It would be unbecoming of me as your ruler."

He's piqued my interest, but I can't let him know that.

"Your mother used to come here all the time," an older man says. He looks like he's fifty, but his soul tells me he's in his hundreds.

"Is that so?" I'm more interested in this development.

"Yes," says someone else, "they don't call her the Blood Countess for nothing." They laugh.

The man speaks again, "This is one of the places that she, well...I shouldn't have to tell you."

I try not to choke on my drink. When I muster up my confidence, unexpected words tumble out. "I can do it better."

"What are you saying?" the first woman appraises me.

"I'm saying that when it comes to me or my mother, I'm more than a countess. I'm the Queen." It's not a complete lie. Liz did participate in one, but it was lackluster compared to the ones I've seen and heard described in books, movies, and television. "I'd be happy to show you," I taunt them. I wonder if they'll take the bait.

"Well, Our Queen of the Realms has spoken," someone says. He must be the owner or manager of the place, because his next words are, "Clear the VIP room in the back. Let's show Our Queen some hospitality."

Everyone clears out of the area I'm in and uses their abilities to create a large open space. A curtain is brought in to obscure the vision of those who do not belong in the VIP section, mostly low-tiered creatures or those deemed too ugly to be in my presence—the VIP group's words, not mine.

"Now," the man says, "come."

I smile. I had picked out the most eligible males and females for this exchange. They follow me behind the curtain.

If not for the neon jewelry that everyone wears, it would be dark behind the curtain. Humans jacked up on aphrodisiacs and spells lie on plush blankets and pillows. They beckon us to come toward them.

I look for Angelo, and it doesn't take me long to find him already half-naked. His body is attractive. When he notices me looking at him, he smiles, walks over, and pulls me toward him and the human woman next to him. Her pale white skin is easy to see in the pseudo-darkness of the room. Her blond hair is just long enough to cover her breasts.

Angelo pushes the two of us together. He commands me with his eyes. I smile mischievously and cock one eyebrow in his direction. I know what he wants, but he will have to wait.

I take in the other guests. They've already made short work on the dietary properties of the humans. Now, they've begun the fun part. I turn back to Angelo and mimic what I see. I push back the woman's hair and expose her neck. I let my hand travel the length of it and then bite into the vein. Her lifeblood pours into me, but the taste is magnified. I drink and drink until I feel a hand on my shoulder.

"Did you plan on saving some for me?" Angelo asks.

"Apologies," I say. "I thought this is what you wanted."

"A small part of it, yes."

"And the rest?"

He gestures around the room.

"Okay."

When he bites the other side of her neck, the blood trickles onto his chest. I lick the droplet, and the smell of expensive cologne intrudes my senses. The aphrodisiac. It's gotten into me. The moment our eyes lock, I am his. We kiss and caress each other, and when the human woman stares at us in a haze, we include her as well. Body parts tangle together. Another couple joins us, and then more humans, and before I know it, my senses go out of control.

Thoughts, memories, feelings, everything that makes up sentient beings flow through me, and I gladly take it all in.

THE FIRST HAZE I AWAKE from, everyone is covered in blood. I search around for clues as to what happened, but there are none. Then I see a replay in the depths of my mind. It must be one Lizzy is holding on to because I don't remember anything from it.

The humans gather around my body, which hums like electricity. I nibble and bite and stab and gash and claw at them until they bleed into baths of water. Angelo and I sink into the blood as we feed on the humans. The other Fae watch in amusement, but then I bring them in too. Before the end of the playback, we are all doused in blood.

When the fuzziness disappears, we are still covered in the blood of the humans, and the woman I was drinking from has now run dry, the taste of her long evaporated. Everyone is caught up in their own visualizations, and they don't even notice when I call upon water to rinse the blood away.

Once everyone is clean, I smile. They turn to me, and the vibe from before the blood bath returns.

To say this experiment was pure ecstasy would not do the moment justice. I lay on a plush bed, surrounded by naked bodies. Everyone is tired from the hours we just spent participating in undulating fornication. Every pore of my body is filled with the emotions and climaxes of those around me. Erotic, satiation, pillow-biting, basket-making, none of these words describe the velvet-tipping, green gowned, burning shame, sword-swallowing, bar-dashing, pin-cleaving, arrow-breaking, spunking group sex I just had.

Was this what I was missing out on all those years Father attempted to keep me locked away? Is this what people warn of us when they speak of lust and desire? If so, then I wonder if losing out on such pleasure is worth having a stick up their arses. Something as beautiful as a group coming together for an orgasm should not be considered sinful. Though, if Lizzy had something to say about it...

"I do," her voice is faint in the back of my mind. "It is not that I never wanted to try. Just... How could you—we—do this to Dmitri?"

I don't want to dignify her with an answer. I mean, come on. Had I known what we were missing out on, I would not have let Lizzy or myself pine after Dmitri for so long. Our few sex partners were a result of that loss. Now that he's back in our life—or *was* back in our life—it seems pointless to have been so preoccupied with mourning him. Even now, I don't see the point. And with the threats looming over us...

I stop thinking and look at my smartwatch. I groan. It's early morning, and Dmitri has left several messages. I don't want to deal with him. I don't want to think about him. I ignore the messages. When all is said and done, the choices Lizzy made are what they are. Dmitri and I will have to reap the consequences.

"It was a great evening," I say to the mix of men, women, and supernatural beings splayed before me in their naked glory. "But we have to return to reality. To our duties as your king and queen."

They murmur in acknowledgment, which makes me chuckle. Even in a state of drugs and stupor, they still manage to answer me. It's uncanny. As we walk out the door, the owner approaches us.

"Do come back," he says.

I stare at him for a moment. Something seems...familiar. I brush it off and continue walking with Angelo in tow. The last thing I need is cryptic remarks from a stranger.

"So, did you experience something new?" Angelo asks as we walk toward the car.

I laugh. "I did. Thank you."

"Me too."

"Wait, you've never?"

"No."

"Even though you're...?"

"What? Even though I'm...?"

"Nothing. Never mind."

He shrugs, and we keep shuffling until the car is in sight. But then he stops. "What is this, really?"

"What is what?"

He groans in exasperation and then grabs my hand. He leads me down an alley where no one can see us and corners me. My heart races. I am excited, nervous, and scared. And I don't think I've ever felt scared. He leans into me. "What is this? Us?"

"Would you call this an 'us'? I mean, it's barely been a month."

"And yet..."

"And yet?"

He leans in closer and kisses me. Electric sparks flow between us, and I'm wondering how this is even possible. Is it because I've lost all romantic feelings for Dmitri? Is it because there's a large, gaping hole where his love once was?

"You can't tell me that you don't feel this."

"We're Dhampir. Everything is extra." These words must leave my lips. He must die, or who knows what will happen to me. Even if I wanted to feel something for him, I'm not allowed to. Lizzy is still a part of me. Even if I hate her guts, there's nothing I can do about her being in me. And while my love for Dmitri is gone, her love burns for him. And that's enough. That's enough for me to kill Angelo to get what we want. Everything will be fine once he's gone. "There is no spark here, Angelo."

His face sinks. He begins to talk, but I shush him. I didn't forget the plan.

"That doesn't mean one won't form for me," I tell him.

His face brightens. It's just a little, but it happens. I smile and lean in to kiss him. Yes, this is his weakness. Love. He wants it. Needs it. And I'd bet he's never received it from his parents. There's nothing better to break a man than love. It's the most natural feeling given to living beings—and the most toxic.

Chapter Nineteen

The last three months have been a learning experience, but I am finally ready to inform Mother and Latina that the Bathory and Nádasdy homes will be consolidated. Or, at least, the King and the Queen of the Realms castles will be. Apparently, it had been done in the past, but there hasn't been a king and queen who could work that close together in centuries. With nine months left, I've got to move fast. Neither woman was excited about the prospect, and they're not in on my plan, so they left for Mother's apartment. Now, I have a large, empty castle to myself. At least, empty of people Lizzy and I potentially care about. As if summoned, the only person who could get a handle on Lizzy or me calls at that moment.

I try to contain myself. He doesn't know. "Andrei!" I yell.

"You're not Lizzy." He doesn't greet me or begin with any pleasantries.

We sit in awkward silence. How did he know? I squint at one painting and purse my lips. "How is it that you're the only one to figure it out in zero-point-two seconds?"

"Because I was there from the beginning, Liz."

Ah, right. The first time I appeared, Lizzy couldn't control me. I sucked that man's soul out of his body until he was nothing but a shell while *she* soothed him and promised him he'd be okay. The one and only time we'd worked in tandem. "I should have known."

"I'm surprised you'd call me when you know I can suppress you. You're not the dominant."

"I wish everyone would stop saying that. I *am* the dominant. At least, I am now."

I wait as he mulls that over. "You used the Blood Stone, didn't you? Or she did."

"We both did." I lick my lips. "You know?"

"You said you're the dominant. There's only one way for that to occur." His voice is so matter-of-factly that I want to crush his head.

"And you know it exists because..."

"Your father and I looked for a way to get rid of you and keep Lizzy."

"Huh, but you couldn't use it."

"Unfortunately, no. Only the Bathory's can use it. If they had been married..."

"But they weren't."

"No. You said you both used it? You used it to become the dominant. Does that mean that she...?"

"Used it to break the Blood Pact."

"Did it work?"

"Sort of."

"What do you mean sort of?"

My phone beeps from someone else calling me. "Phone's going dead," I say as I view the caller ID. "Talk later?"

"Liz!"

I hang up with Andrei and take the next call.

"Elizabeth Mina Bathory-Tepés!" the voice yells.

"Trying to warn me of something, Father?"

I LISTEN TO HIM RANT and rave for what feels like hours, but it is only a few minutes. I guess three of the largest names in the supernatural community united in one home was too much for him.

In my defense, he's never paid my activities much attention before. The difference this time is that I'm willingly getting involved with the son of his enemy. This is never going to sit well with him, but the castles in the sky have merged.

"Can I go now?"

I must sound like a surly teenager to the great Vladimir Tepés because the disappointment in his voice could crush worlds.

"Yes," he says. "You can go." He hangs up the phone.

"Rude much." I narrow my eyes, scrunch my nose, and frown.

"Who's rude?" Angelo asks me.

I smile. Dating Angelo first was a good idea. He thinks we're together because I want to be here, and he finds me trustworthy enough to not rat me out to his father, which means Anton thinks I've accepted my fate.

Lizzy is still angry with me and has been quiet ever since I decided to break up with Dmitri. As though his heart breaking caused hers to shatter as well. No matter. She'll get over it, just like I had to. It's all for our freedom.

I hug Angelo tight. "My father."

"Your father?" He's shocked. If nothing else, I tell him the truth about our family dynamics. The Tepés-Bathory line must appeal to him if I'm going to convince him to marry me. "You called him?"

I shake my head. "He called me."

"Yikes."

"Yikes indeed."

"Well, do you want to invite him over?"

"So that he can strangle you?" Angelo is strong, but he's not that strong. Besides, the Blood Stone specifically stated that Lizzy and I had to do it. "I don't think so."

"Suit yourself." Angelo says, "I'm headed out. Need anything?"

He's so domesticated. Nothing like his father. "No," I say, "I'm fine."

"Great. Be nice to my mother."

"Your almost stepmother. They aren't married yet."

He shrugs. "Same difference."

I shiver. It is not the same. The difference is huge. Idabelle should not be anyone's mother, especially not mine. The fact that she's Anton's third wife is suspicious. Vampires mate for life, and they are resilient. For his previous wives to die, Angelo's mother included, foul play had to be involved. But I don't know how that fits in with Mother and Anton. And, honestly, I don't know if I want to.

The woman who used to be a close friend acting as my mother-in-law must be some cruel plot to fuck with me.

"Lizzy Bear!" she shrieks.

"It's Liz," I tell her for the thousandth time.

"Lizzy Bear, I just want us to get along."

I ball up my fists. "The best way for us to get along, Idabelle, is for you to disappear from my home."

"Tch, tch, tch," her voice sounds like a cheese grater, "*our* home, Lizzy Bear. You let Angelo move in, and by extension, the rest of us." To the untrained nose, her breath smells like cotton candy. It would be a nice scent, but what I smell is nothing less than betrayal and treachery.

This is her thousandth reminder. "Don't make me regret it."

She didn't warn me about what was to come. She was supposed to be my friend, but she was a spy. All those years of unanswered phone calls and messages because she was shacking up with the enemy. And, when she did call, it was to be Anton's lackey. We could never be family. She is the one wife that Anton should axe, if that's what he's doing.

"She won't," Anton, who is behind Idabelle, wraps his arms around her. "Neither of us will." He gives her a full kiss on the lips, with tongue and everything.

Anton needs to be the next one to die after Idabelle.

"Love what you've done with the place." His grin is foxlike. "It's homey."

I ignore his jibes at our décor. I used my Fae magic to combine the homes into one, but it didn't go as well as I had hoped. Instead of two spaces for everything, all the furniture pieces ended up merged together. If someone entered now, they'd think we were setting up for Halloween. I'm in the middle of explaining this, but there's a knock at the castle gate.

"One minute," I tell them.

I open the door, expecting it to be some Fae waiting for me to kiss their child's forehead and help them with their crop magic. What I find is an irate Andrei, a vexed Mother, and a frightening Father.

"Great. More family."

Chapter Twenty

Anton and Idabelle laugh as the trio make their way in. Father, in all his 5'6" glory, tries to make a beeline for them, but Andrei holds him back.

"It's not the right time," he tells my father.

Father straightens his blue shirt and black tie, and Andrei drops his hand.

Mother dismisses them both.

"I need to talk to you." Father's voice is stern and has more bass in it than a beat. "Now."

I lead him to a room where we won't be disturbed. "So, my protector has finally come to save me. To whom do I owe this great pleasure?" I lean against one of the walls in the room and cross my arms.

"I do not care if you are the Queen of the Realms," he says in his thick Transylvanian accent. "You will not disrespect me."

"It's my house, and I'm not Lizzy."

"I do not care."

"And that right there is the problem."

He steps back, stunned, like I've just tasered him.

"All of this," I motion to the castles, their contents, and the people within it, "is your fault."

"How? How is it my fault? I have done nothing but try to protect you from this madman."

"Who you angered!" I shout. "He did this because you slept with his betrothed wife. Because you faced him and showed him overwhelming power. Because he could never be good enough for

205

Mother when all she did was pine for you." All my rage and anger spill out of me and into my words. I mean for them to pierce him like a knife and to seep into him like venom. It works. "You did this. And now I, I can't..." For the first time in a long time, I cry.

But not onto his shoulder—I won't give him the satisfaction.

His wide shoulders droop. His thin and reddish face softens. His eagle-like nose and swollen nostrils stop flaring. His long eyelashes flutter, his amber eyes with black flecks widen, and his bushy black eyebrows furrow as he strokes his mustache. His stocky, strong, and terrifying frame shrinks, and the only thing left before me is a shell of a man wearing black pants and black loafers with blue trim.

For the first time in my life, in our life, I've reached him. Lizzy would never have been able to do this. I dab at my eyes with a handkerchief. "You have never been here for me, for us. You never wanted me to meet Mother..." Lizzy's words mix with mine, and I have to control the power that buzzes at my fingertips.

"Because I knew that this would hap—"

"No. Because you're a selfish fool who doesn't give a damn about anyone but himself. Anton has already told me why he's doing this. Why he did this. And Lizzy, the sweet personality you've always preferred over me, has slunk into a corner of this mind." There's no need to tell him that I put her there. "There's no one to blame but yourself." I take a deep breath and walk toward the door.

"I just wanted to wait until I got my soul back," he whispers.

"Doesn't matter," I mumble and close the door behind me.

I leave Father to sulk in the room so I can confront Andrei and Mother. When I return to the living room, Mother, Andrei, Anton, and Idabelle are talking about something, and they hush when they see me, but the tension in the room—their souls and body language—tells me that a matter of grave importance has been discussed. Before I can ask anyone what's going on, Anton speaks.

"Elizabeth," he says.

"Liz," I correct.

He nods. "Liz, as the Queen of the Realms, you have the ability to decide certain *things*." He says it slyly, as if we're scheming.

"Yes, your point?" I tap my foot. I knew it would only be a matter of time before he asked me to do something for him apart from the Blood Pact.

"If a supernatural person were to have a grievance with another supernatural being that they could not resolve, you would be forced to step in."

It's not a question, but I answer. "Possibly. It depends on what it is. I refuse to settle trite debates."

"What about age-old feuds?"

"What do you want, Anton?"

Anton is not the one to answer. Instead, Mother does. "You know of our *history*," she says.

I nod. Why can't the old ones just get to the point?

"Liz, he had me murdered for his own selfish reasons."

Anton grumbles, "You were cheating on me. And you still didn't die."

"You wouldn't let me live my life, you were never there, and even when you were, you tried to control me. I—" She stops talking to him and turns to me. "Supernatural law says that you have the power to revoke any union, with the exception of your own."

"And Idabelle and I would like to be officially married." Anton glowers at Mother.

"Pause," I say because the gears in my head are turning, and I don't think that I like where this is going. "What exactly are you asking me?"

"We'd like you to annul our marriage," Mother says.

"Grant us a divorce," Anton pleads.

"Please," Mother begs.

I try to hold back the laughter welling up inside me. All this time and the two of them are still married. "Why?" I ask to give them a hard time. "You could have asked a previous queen to do this," I say, referring to Aunt Latina.

"I tried," Mother says, "but the rules say we must both be present, and he"—she points at Anton—"refused to meet with me."

"I'll admit, I wasn't ready to let her go," he says cunningly. "But I am now."

Knowing Anton, there's more to the story than that. Granting them the divorce would put me in both of their good graces, but anything Anton wants must be denied. "Why not ask your king?"

"Only the Queen can grant this request," Andrei pipes up.

"Oh, and what's your stake in this? I assume there must be one since you seem to be a part of the discussion." I wait for his answer, but Andrei just shrugs.

Then he says, "I am indebted to Elizabeth," there's a telling gleam in his eye as he speaks, "for things I am not allowed to discuss." He takes a deep breath. "Her marriage being annulled would lift some burdens off me."

Andrei has secrets too. His eyes are sad, and a part of me thinks he might have slept with Mother. But I can't see him betraying Father in that way, so whatever his reasons are, they probably have to do with Anton.

"I'll think about it," I say. Just as the words leave my mouth, Angelo walks in, Dmitri storms into the building after him, and Father enters the room.

"Shit," I whisper.

WHY ARE MEN SO ANNOYING? The question plays through my mind a million times a minute. They don't listen. They can't take a hint. They chase after you when you're trying to plan the murder of your future husband and ignore your father. I grimace as they stand before me. "Yes, come right in," I say. "We're not discussing anything important here." Did I mention being a queen sucks too? Because it does.

"Go away. She doesn't want to speak to a toff." Dmitri pushes Angelo away.

"If she wanted to speak to an insolvent, then she could have done better than you." Angelo pushes him back.

"Enough!" I yell. Father and the others watch on as I drag the men across the room. "What the fuck is this?" I ask them.

"I came to give you this," Dmitri says and holds out a paper, "but asshat over here wouldn't let me in."

I take the slip from his hand and put it in my pocket.

"And then he said something ludicrous," Dmitri continues.

"What did you tell him?" I ask Angelo.

His face is set in a hard expression before his eyes soften and he looks at me. He's been doing that a lot lately. "I just told him that we were moving in together."

My jaw drops. No, no, no. Dmitri was *not* supposed to hear about this. It's been months, but I wanted to keep him out of this life until I killed Angelo. If he gets in the way, the months of planning will be for nothing.

The plan was simple: Meet. Joke. Seduce. Date. Move In. Score a Marriage Proposal. Marry. Kill Angelo. We're only at step five. Why does Dmitri have to pop up at the worst time?

"...I'm just saying that I love you, and I want you to dump this guy. If the pact is broken, then you can't be happy about this." Dmitri's voice is loud.

"Shut up," I say, and it comes out low.

"You have to understand—"

"I said *shut up*." I'm louder this time, and he hushes. Everyone becomes silent. "Get out."

"What?" His eyes crinkle.

"You heard me. I said get out."

"Bu—"

I don't give him a chance to continue. I can't save our relationship if he doesn't listen. "I don't want anything to do with you," I say. "Get the fuck out of our house."

His expression shifts from flabbergasted to curt. His eyes narrow, and he looks between Angelo and me. "That's what you want?"

"That's what I want."

"Fine."

"Fine."

"I'll go then." He turns away from me.

The emptiness in my stomach wells up. It's not love, but it's something.

"I'll tell the Morian Coven you said hello," he calls over his shoulder as he walks out.

I say nothing. I watch him go for the third time, probably the last time. I turn toward the others. "Get out," I whisper. The mock clouds above us darken, and the air in the room becomes heavy. Everyone besides Angelo begins to leave. Anton is the only one who smiles.

Once we are alone, Angelo and I sit in the living room. In all the chaos, Angelo must have found a way to rework the home permutation spell because the castles are finally merged into an appropriate home. I sigh as we lean back against the couch. I lay my head on his shoulder. If only this relationship were real. If only I could confide in him, confide in anyone. Someone needs to know the truth. I let these thoughts flutter in my mind. I raise my head to look into his eyes. He looks down at me and kisses my forehead.

"Busy day?" he asks.

"Yes." I relax my body and snuggle into him.

"Want to talk about it?"

"Not particularly."

"Okay."

"Okay."

We sit in silence for a little while, and then, "Will you marry me?"

I am taken aback. He wants to marry me now? Why? Our marriage is part of the plan, but I was expecting it to take more time to convince him it's the right decision. Our relationship is only in its fourth month. For beings with long lives, beings such as ourselves, that's nothing but days. "You're asking me to marry you?"

"Yes."

"Isn't it too early?"

"Not at all."

"Why?"

"Because I think we'll be happy together."

"Do you even know what happiness is?"

"No idea, but I think we will be."

I stop talking. I can't have him thinking that I'll say no. I must tread carefully. "What happens if I say yes?"

"Then we plan for a wedding."

"That's it?"

"That's it."

"No other caveats?"

"None."

"Then yes."

"Yes?"

"Yes." I grasp his hands with mine and look him straight in the eyes. It's now or never. If my plans to kill him are to succeed, then this is the time. Angelo is a lot of things, but like everyone else of our kind, he's sure to have done crooked things, and his death will be just as valuable as anyone else's. I just have to bide my time until that day. "Let's plan a wedding."

Chapter Twenty-One

"Less magic, more work," one fairy screams as they put the finishing touches on the venue. I watch as the others follow her orders. Fairies really do make the best wedding planners. They populate quickly, so there's an overabundance of them, which makes it easy to use them as a labor force. There's a reason Latina used them as her guards when she was queen, and I will keep the trend going.

Except there's no one guarding me today. Instead, they're all working to ensure the King and Queen of the Realms have a wedding that will be written in the history books. While the fairies handle the small details, I focus on the hardest part of planning a wedding: inviting my family.

The first person on my list is Father. He immediately tells me there is a 0 percent chance he will come to the wedding, let alone support it. We argue for what seems to be an eternity until he hangs up the phone. When I try to call him back, it goes to voice mail.

The next person I try is Mother. She too refuses the invitation.

"I thought you were wiser than this," she says in a condescending tone.

"And I thought you would be a great mother. I guess we were both disappointed." I hang up the phone and toss it on the bed, then fall back onto the plush mattress and groan.

Latina already made her feelings clear when Angelo moved in, so there's no need to call her, and Zsofia is long gone. The only other person on the list is Andrei.

"If you do this..." Andrei's voice trails off. Out of everyone Lizzy and I have ever cared for, his approval is the most important. If

Andrei is on my side, then I have nothing to worry about. "If you do this," he starts again, "I don't know that you can come back from it. Dhampir mate for life, save something happening to their significant other."

"Yes, I know that. That's why..."

"I'm not finished."

I pause and wait for him to tell me what's wrong.

"This is a big decision. Most Dhampir wait much longer. I'm not telling you that you can't or shouldn't marry him, but look at the bigger picture."

"The bigger picture is my happiness."

"Yes, but what happens when Lizzy wakes up and takes control again? Huh? What are you going to do?"

"It's a risk I'm willing to take if it will get me what I want. What we—Lizzy and I—need."

"And what's that?"

"I can't tell you."

"Then I can't give you an answer."

"What does that mean?"

"I want to make sure you're doing this with the right person and for the right reasons."

"Do you even trust me?"

"I trusted Lizzy. You..."

I clench my fists. Andrei has never liked me. It's why they hired a witch to extract me from Lizzy's body, but the process would have killed me, and my will to live was too strong for her. Lizzy didn't even know I existed until this whole thing with Anton began. I would have been content living in her shadow if it weren't for that. But now, I want a life of my own. That's my quest, once Andrei is dead and Anton is destroyed. "Fine. Don't answer. Just remember that Dhampir mate for life. Which means a wedding between Lizzy and another happens only once. This will be your only opportunity..."

"To see her on her wedding day." His voice sounds defeated. "I will be there, but you don't have my support."

"That's fine. Care to convince the others?"

"Not particularly."

I groan internally. Fine. I don't need them anyway.

THE WEDDING VENUE IS beautiful. It's a shame that by the end of the night it will be covered with blood instead of flowers. Or, at least, I imagine it will be. Andrei and Anton have invited far too many humans for this to be considered a normal wedding. And with only six months left to kill Angelo, the night will be just as bloody.

I don't know how many people have come in person, as I am still being handled by one of the house-elves. I gaze at my reflection in the mirror. My white hair transforms into burgundy braids. The locks are long and reach the middle of my back. I have the house-elf—Lena, I think her name is—bundle the locks in the front into a crown and let the rest of the hair fall behind me. The bath water is warm and filled with soap and flowers that give off an earthy smell. A smell like my mother's. I sigh and stand to view my profile in full, my naked body on display for all in the room to see.

I trail my hand across my thighs and notice tiny stubbles of hair growth, so I use my abilities to get rid of it. My entire body is silky smooth and blemish-free. If there were ever a day I needed to look perfect, it's today.

I call to Lena's friend and ask her to help lotion and perfume me. She does as I ask. When she's finished, they both help me into my undergarments. The cups used to support my bosom in the dress are awkward. I almost prefer to let them hang free, but I was told it is not proper decorum for a woman of my status. The next thing they put on me is a crinoline. These, I am used to. Then, they help me into my dress.

It's a typical wedding dress, one that's Disney-esque in looks, much like Cinderella's—the 1997 version with Brandy, not the 1950 cartoon. But instead of white or blue or pink, I have an ombré of black and red. The dress is strapless. The top is a corset with many ties and is beaded with onyx stones. It is constricted in all the right places. The bottom flares out, and a small amount of red trim sticks out from under it. And, of course, I do not wear traditional heels. Instead, I have opted for studded, black boots with red shoestrings. They do have heels on them, but they're steel-toed and hold my sharpened knives. If there is any nonsense during the wedding, well, let's just say I won't have any issues protecting myself.

Once I am dressed and the crown for the Queen of the Realms is placed upon my head, I walk out of the large room and head toward the ballroom where the ceremony is to take place. When the doors open, everyone stands and looks at me. Lena takes my hand. She said that she would walk me down the aisle, but she stops and moves away from me. When hardened hands grab mine on either side, I look both ways. Father is on my left, and Andrei is on my right.

"You came?" I whisper. It's not my real wedding, and I'm not one for tears, but the surprise on my face must be evident because they both nod and walk me down the aisle. I want to ask them why, but we are silent. After giving Angelo a death stare, they sit in their respective seats in the front. Mother glares as well, but a part of me knows she's enjoying this. Anton and Idabelle sit in stock silence. Almost everyone else here is either Fae or human, which means anything could happen once the ceremony is over.

As we stand under the archway, both of us with crowns on our heads and staring intently at each other, I think of Dmitri. This is all for him. Under no circumstances may I waver. Once this marriage is complete, I will have six months to kill Angelo.

But I don't plan to let him survive the night.

"Do you take this woman to be your wife under the rules of world laws?"

The rules of world laws...it's our way of saying any marriage law for any species. I'll have to uphold them all during this marriage.

"I do," Angelo says easily. When I gaze into his eyes, I see no deception, nothing fake. Only love. I wonder if that love would be there if he knew my plans.

"And do you, Elizabeth Mina Bathory-Tepés, take this man to be your husband under the rules of world law?"

I give Angelo a small smile and say with clarity in my voice, "I do."

"Then, with the power bestowed upon me by hundreds of years of officiating weddings for all species, I declare you husband and wife. Angelo, you may now kiss the bride."

Angelo is quick to grab me into his embrace. His kiss is gentle but firm. He pushes his tongue into my mouth, and I can feel he wants me. I want more, but he holds back, and then we pull ourselves apart. The kiss was less than a minute, but it was filled with all the emotion and passion of someone who wants to love but hasn't been able to until this moment. Damn. Killing him really will suck.

THE RECEPTION HALL is filled with black and red decorations, from flowers and ribbons to linens and tableware. Everything is perfect. Once Angelo and I are seated, Anton claps his hands. The humans, who were moments ago talking and eating, all halt. They form a line and walk to the front of the dining hall.

"What's going on?" I ask Angelo.

He shrugs. "I'm not sure. Perhaps..."

The humans tilt their heads and stop moving. Their heart rates pulse faster and faster. Then, Anton speaks.

"Hello," he says in a voice that can't be trusted. "I would like to present the main course to the bride and groom." He gestures to the humans. "Bon appétit."

Angelo and I stare in confusion. He can't mean...

"He wants us to drain them," Angelo completes my thought.

"And why would we do that?"

"To show them our power." He gestures to the crowd of vampires, Fae, and the like.

"Is it necessary?" I ask. The scent of their nervous blood is sweet. I want to indulge, but, draining them seems excessive.

"If we don't want challengers to the throne..."

I consider it for a moment. Father's and Mother's eyes gleam with amusement as though this is the norm for them. Andrei rolls his eyes and scrunches his face in disgust as though the idea of a draining is revolting to him. After all, it hasn't been done in centuries. I turn to Angelo. "Let's do it," I say. "Let's show them our power by killing a few. The rest we can reserve as a snack." I grin, and so does he. This feast will be one to remember.

The moment I bite into the neck of the first human, my senses disappear, and the only thing left is the hunt. I tear through her neck and drink my fill. The expression of pleasure on her face mixed with the fear I can taste in her blood is a delicious contradiction. I drink and drink and drink from her until there is nothing left. Andrei follows suit with the woman next to her. Then we share one together, and it's a feeling I've never had with anyone—that *we've* never had with anyone. As the blood of the woman flows into our mouths, we come to a silent agreement.

After our shared meal, we have the rest of the humans sent to our bedroom, which we finished combining yesterday, and address our guests.

"Eat, drink, and be merry," we command them. And they do.

We give the guards instructions to kick everyone out at sunup while we retreat to our bedroom.

I use my magic to command the humans to sit and watch as he peels off my boots, dress, crinoline, and panties. He observes my naked body with pleasure. He strips to nothing as well, and I take in his fine specimen of a body. It's a pity that tonight will be his last to enjoy earthly pleasures such as drinking and copulating.

He pulls me into him, and we make out. Our hands explore each other's bodies. He pushes the braids in my hair behind my ear and nibbles on it. His lips trail from my ear to my neck and down my back. He stops right above my tailbone before stepping away and gesturing to one of the males. He offers the human like a platter.

I smile and accept. I push the man's neck to the side and bite into his carotid artery. The blood is sucked into my teeth, but some of it trails down the side of his neck. Not wanting to rush my meal, I pull my teeth back in and lick the trail of blood. I turn the man so that he faces me.

"Am I beautiful?" I ask.

He nods.

"And what else?"

He hesitates to speak. But then he says, "You're a beautiful monster!"

Before he can shriek, I climb on top of him and say, "Then be sure to savor this last moment of life." Then, I cut open his neck with my nails. Blood sprays in several directions, including down his chest and right above his waistline. I lap up every bit on his body.

For good measure, I suck up the essence of his soul as well, and I feel empowered. An entire human soul, including the memories and experiences, I've never had that before. It's like walking on cloud nine. I gasp in pleasure. Nothing can compete with this.

The other humans watch, expressionless, though their heart rates tell me that they're aware of what's happening. I grab the next male and do the same to him. Each death is more violent than the last, and each one is drained of all their blood and their life essence. By the time I've finished off all the males, I am drenched in blood, and the empty shells of humans are left by my feet. I don't feel bad, though. All of them were scumbags, which makes me wonder if Anton knew this when he picked them, or if it was just pure luck these men were monsters. Either way, my body and soul are satisfied and, when I finally look in the mirror, I recognize my true self.

I turn toward Angelo, and he is smiling.

"You're violent," he says.

"And you," I ask, "do you not want to partake?"

"After you have your fun."

"Why don't you show me now?"

He bares his fangs.

ANGELO AND I, MUCH like our bedsheets, are drenched in blood. I am fascinated by the way it slowly drips through the sheets and onto the floor. I can see why the vampires of old hate using blood bags.

We smile at each other. I kiss him once more, and this begins another round of sex. Just when he's about to enter me, someone knocks on the door. I groan and roll my eyes. Angelo chuckles and answers.

"Come in."

One of the guards opens the door. His face contorts into shock and disgust for a second before he controls it. "The guests are leaving."

"Your point?" I ask.

"They would like parting words from their king and queen."

"Of course," he mumbles. "We don't have time to change."

"Then let's not," I say.

"What?"

"Guard, take these bodies out in carts and present them to our guests."

"What?" he echoes Angelo.

"You'll see," I say. I've finally caught on to Anton's plans for this night. And, for once, I want to play right into his hands. Let him think he's won before I destroy his life.

"Do as she says," he commands the guard.

The guard nods.

"And what about us?" Angelo asks me. "We're going out there naked?"

"I've got a better idea." I don't bother rinsing off. Instead, I go to the closet and pull out a black robe and red heels. I throw Angelo a pair of black jeans and red shoes. "We have to match," I say, "to show our unity and all." It doesn't seem like he gets it, but he goes along with it anyway.

When we reach the throne room, the dead bodies are in carts, and our people are murmuring. I clap to get their attention. All eyes are on Angelo and me as they take in our expressions, the blood on our bodies, and our lack of clothing.

"We were told you all wanted parting words," I say.

They're mesmerized, in awe of how we're still radiant even with dark rivulets of blood dripping down our skin and soaking into our clothes.

"Be merry," I continue, "and know that the Realms are safe with us as your rulers." I look at Angelo. "And don't worry," I make eye contact with each person, "this is not the last time you will see us like this. I promise you that." At this, there are cheers. "I'm not a countess, and I am *not* the Queen of the Realms." I look at Mother and Latina when I say this, "I am the Blood Queen," I look at Father, "and this will be my legacy." I gesture to the dead bodies. "If you have a problem with it, then feel free to challenge me for the crown."

I nudge Angelo.

"The same goes for me," he says in a bored and lackluster voice. "If you wish to challenge your new rulers, know that you will face the same fate as these souls here." He gestures to the dead human bodies.

So, he did understand.

"If you've eaten and drank well..." I begin.

"Then see yourselves out," his voice booms across the room.

The crowd bows and everyone walks out. Our families are the last to go, and by the looks on their faces, Father and Andrei are disgusted. But they don't have a right to be. I'm not Lizzy, and Father's rampages were a hundred times worse than this.

Once everyone's gone, we retreat to our room. The elves and fairies have replaced the sheets and cleaned the floors. Not one speck of blood remains, almost as though nothing occurred here.

Angelo and I shower together. The blood rinses off our bodies and into the shower drain. His eyes are soft, but I can feel them calculating.

"What is it about you that I can't figure out?" I ask.

"What do you mean."

"You're always quiet. Observing. Calculating. Plotting. Why?"

"Am I?"

"It seems that way to me."

"I'm not."

"Only someone who is would claim their innocence right away."

"Perhaps," he grabs my hands, "or perhaps you're overthinking it."

"Mm-hmm..."

He pulls me into an embrace. The water washes over us, around us, and between us. He kisses me. It's deep, as if he's clinging on to something. Instead of pulling away, I pull him closer, and then I bend to my knees and place my mouth around his erogenous zone. With my tongue, I please him, but he stops me. He picks me up with one hand and spreads my legs open with the other one. This time, his tongue pleases me. Circling around, in, and out like no one—not even Dmitri—has done before. When he's finished, he places me down softly.

The hot water slowly turns cold. My nipples become erect, and that is the moment he squeezes, kneads, and sucks on my breasts. He steps out of the shower, picks me up, and walks me to the bed. He bends me over, and before I can protest, he's inside me. Between each thrust, he picks a spot and nips at me or bites me. He uses my hair to pull my head back. Once he's finished, he turns me around and pushes me onto the bed. He pulls a rope out of a bag and binds me to the bed. He runs a feather across my body, then caresses and licks those areas. Someone moans. *Is that my voice?* I think. But it has to be, because there's no one else around.

He hovers over me and asks me with his eyes if this is okay. I nod, and he continues. He pinches and licks and grabs and suckles and plays with my body using his hands and everything in his bag. The only thing he does not use is his quimstake. He teases me with his arsenal until I can barely breathe.

I wiggle and writhe to get out of the ropes, but they don't budge. I sniff the air and realize it's because they're coated with herbs that weaken our kind. The more I move, the tighter they get, and the more excited he becomes. When I can't take any more, he unties me. He pushes himself into me, and it is pure bliss.

We take a small break, but now I'm a mix of emotions that can only be sorted out in one way. "My turn," I tell him.

I push him onto the bed, bite at his neck, and scratch at his back while riding him until he makes a sound I've never heard a man make in my entire existence. I use my hands to stroke him, and when he least expects it, I squeeze his balls and play with the tip.

I kiss his waistline and then use my tongue to travel his length. Left to right, up and down, back and forth, around and around. And when he's at the brink, right before his white gold can spill over, I stop. I lick him from waistline to chest and then kiss him like my life depends on it. When he tries to place his steed into my treasury, I keep him at bay.

I torture him with this come-and-go game until I've teased him long enough. I use my hands to guide his nightstick back into my phoenix nest. As I move back and forth, he massages and sucks on my breasts and nipples. He pulls my head back and rams into me with the force of an Olympic runner.

Before I know how, he's back on top.

As our breaths mingle and we become one, I let out a squeal. As I bite and scratch, my frustration and emotions pour out into the world.

Once we're finished, he brushes my hair back, kisses me on the cheek, and lays next to me. The both of us pant, out of breath from our extracurricular activity.

Instead of breaking the silence in the room, we continue to stare into the depths of each other's eyes. The windows into our souls.

It dawns on me that, somehow, he knows this is his last night alive. Somehow, he has seen my true intention and has made peace with it.

But that's ridiculous, I think. *There's no way. Even if he did know...*
I let the thought trail off.

I stroke his dark hair and lay on top of his chest. Our breathing syncs until we are the only beings on Earth. We stay like that until I fall asleep.

WHEN I WAKE UP, IT'S dark. I remove his hand from my waist and sneak to my drawer. The dagger I've hidden is still there. I sigh in relief. I trace its ornate design of dragons and swords before picking it up and moving back to the bed. I place it under my pillow and wait for sleep to overcome me. When the first rays of light shine, that's when I'll commence the final step of the plan.

Toward the Future

The ceiling of the bedroom depicts a scene I'm unfamiliar with. Instead of pondering its significance, I think about last night. I haven't been a virgin in a long time, but a part of me feels as though I've just lost my virginity. I wonder if it's because being intimate with someone in this way has always been reserved for Dmitri.

Damn it. I *must* stop thinking about him. If this is going to work, if I'm going to fulfill my bargain to the Blood Stone, then this had to be done.

Do I want to be with Angelo?

Unknown.

Do I dream of a life with Dmitri?

Sometimes, but it's lackluster and doesn't hold the excitement and joy it once did. Memories of him, with him, are slowly fading, replaced with thoughts of Angelo. His kindness, his wooing, his love, his touches, his...everything.

I shift under the covers. Angelo is next to me, still naked like I am. He turns in his sleep, and now we're facing each other. I brush back his dark locks and examine his face. It is perfection. I don't say that as his wife or someone entranced by him. It's an objective fact. Every part of him, from head to toe, is symmetrical perfection. It's a good thing too. If he'd been abhorrent to look at, I don't think I would have the strength or the courage to do what I'm about to do.

I close my eyes and pray that it works. I pick up one of the pillows that fell to the floor and use the wind magic from the part of me that is a fairy to float it above his head. Silently, I slam it onto his face and hold it there. I use the moment to seize the dagger from under my pillow and plunge it where his forehead should be. Once the deed is done and blood stains the pillow, I lean back in relief.

But then, the blood from the pillow recedes.

He sits up and removes the pillow.

"Nice try," he says. "But, if you're going to kill me, you're going to have to do better than that."

Part 3: The Blood Bond
Chapter Twenty-Two

It should not be this difficult to kill someone, no matter how much power they have. Yet, my husband still breathes. *Why?* I groan inwardly. Lizzy scoffs in the back of our mind. She won't say, "I told you so," but the thought lingers.

"How did you know I was trying to kill you?" The answer is obvious, but I want to see if he'll indulge me.

"Well, for one, I'm not stupid," he replies. "And, two," he looks me in the eyes, "you don't strike me as the type to say yes to a marriage so quickly. Especially not one that locks you into eternity."

Crap. So I was too hasty. I chastise myself for being deluded into thinking this plan would work.

"This led you to believe that I would attempt to murder you on our wedding night?"

"No. But I'm good at reading people, so..." He shrugs and rolls off the bed. His feet land on the floor with a *thud*. "I'm hungry, you?"

His demeanor is so nonchalant that I'm not sure what to say. I leave the knife on the bed and follow him to the kitchen.

Everyone has left, so it's just the two of us.

"What do you think of downgrading?"

"Excuse me?"

"Downgrading. I mean, do we really need to stay in a place this big? I just think it's a bit overbearing. Especially when we don't have any children, and I doubt anyone will come to bother the Royalty of the Realms."

"I just tried to kill you, and you want to talk about home development?" I'm beginning to wonder if Angelo is terrifyingly and unnaturally smart or if he is unbelievably stupid.

"I don't care."

"Excuse me?"

He looks at me and repeats his words. "I. Don't. Care."

"You. Don't. Care?"

"Nope. To be honest, I haven't had anyone attempt to murder me in a while, and though amateurish, I appreciated your attempt. It was intuitive and ingenious."

"What do you mean no one's tried to murder you in a while?"

He becomes silent.

I wait for a minute.

"Well?"

"Nope. Not doing this today." He walks out of the kitchen with the sandwich I didn't even realize he was preparing.

"Not doing what?"

He walks faster, dodging my questions the same way he dodges the mess of clothing and decorations on the floors.

"Angelo!" I yell.

He stops, turns, and saunters toward me. "If I told you, it would be the end of... Well, whatever it is that we have here. This marriage. I'm not ready for that. You'll have to be patient."

"Okay. And what do I get in return?"

"I promise not to pry into why you want me dead. Unless you want to tell me." He furrows his brows. "Why do you want me dead?"

This is the moment that will make or break our plans. *Just tell him*, Lizzy whispers in my mind. *He might be able to help us.* I give her words some weight before answering. "I could tell you, but I think it's better if I keep it to myself."

"Then we have a deal. But I will tell you one thing."

"What's that?"

"I'm truly immortal. I can't be killed by anything."

If someone else were saying it, like Anton, I'd think he were being smug. But I've gotten to know him pretty well between the time we met and now, and Angelo is anything but. His eyes are sad; the creases on his face have deepened. Could it be that his existence is forced?

I consider this before grabbing his hand and leading both him and his sandwich back to the bedroom. If he considers himself truly immortal, then I'll just have to find more creative ways to kill him. But—just for right now—we'll have sex, fight over his sandwich, and talk about home development.

THE WOMAN OF BLOOD. The Blood Countess. The Blood Queen. These are names I have gathered over the past month. My exploits to kill Angelo have not gone unnoticed, but no one has dared try to stop me. Not even him. Instead, he proposed a road trip. When I asked where to, he just looked at me and smiled. Now, we're in a car with a couple of thralls.

"Why don't you resent me?" I ask him, trying to ignore the way his thralls are looking at me through the rearview mirror.

"Because I know why you're doing it," he says. "Or, at least, I have an idea."

"So, your suggestion is a road trip?" I turn to look at him.

"If I'm going to die, I want to at least complete my bucket list." He smiles at me and squeezes my hand.

"And that includes a road trip?"

"Yes, dear, it does."

I scowl. He always does this. "Is this a ploy to make me love you?"

He shifts in his seat before answering. "How long do you have until impending doom?"

I count on my fingers. "Four months. I've spent the last eight trying to concoct a plan and carry it out. Remember?"

He tilts his head, and his eyes shift as he pretends to recall something. "Oh, yes, I do." He pauses for a moment. Then, "Your attempts to hide it were cute," he says, winking at me.

"As you keep reminding me."

He won't tell me how he's able to stay alive. I've tried everything the past month, from sending a knife into his head, to poison, to beheading, but nothing works. He either finds out beforehand or comes back to life after I've completed the deed.

"And you didn't answer the question." I pick up my drink from the cup holder and take a sip.

"It's not that I didn't answer it." He snatches the cup from me and takes a swig before handing it back. "You just haven't asked the right one yet."

"And what's that, pray tell?"

"Do I look like I give spoilers?"

I groan. This is what I deal with every day. "Just die already."

"I would if you were better at killing me." He chuckles, but then his voice gets serious. "Liz, I love you. You know that, right?"

"If that were true, you'd tell me what I need to know."

"Can't." He stares at the back of the passenger's seat of the car. "I have my reasons too."

"Right," I mumble.

It's always the same conversation. I can't give him the details on why I have to kill him, and he can't tell me why it seems impossible to do. We're at an impasse. And yet, somehow, he still loves me. He laughs with me, cares for me—he is there for everything I need. Did Anton really think this through? I find it hard to believe this is all a part of his plans. If it is, then I can't believe a word Angelo says. No matter how much I want to.

Regardless of how I look at it, the situation is impossible.

"We're here," one of the thralls says.

"How do you know?" I ask.

"We can feel it," they say in unison.

"They're right," Angelo says. "We are here."

"And what's here, exactly?" I ask as the car stops.

Angelo opens the door and steps outside. "Where it all began," he says, grabbing my hand.

"And that would be?" I get out of the car and dust off my jeans.

I follow him and the thralls to what looks like a coastline. In front of me lies a place that I've only seen and heard of in myths. A sea of blood. Humans with bite marks. A land of night creatures that survive from blood. Dhampir, made vampires, Celtic fairies, German Alps, and others skulk around. I know exactly where he's brought me, but I don't know why. I walk out to the sea and touch the thick, burgundy liquid in front of me. I taste the iron, salt, and the fear within it.

The Bloodlands.

We continue past the shore and into the marketplace.

"I'm going over there," I tell Angelo before he can stop me.

He nods and gestures for me to take one of the thralls.

I roll my eyes because arguing is pointless. Especially when I don't plan to let him continue breathing.

When we get to the dwarf's stall, I ask him to show me what he has.

"No, no, no," I say, looking at the trinkets of magical and non-magical items. "None of this will do."

"Well, what are you lookin' for exactly?" he asks.

"Something to kill an unkillable being."

"Why can't he be killed?"

"Couldn't say. But show me what you have anyway."

The dwarf shakes his head. "There ain't nothin' here for that. Not without the why."

That figures, Lizzy says in the back of my head. *Surprise, surprise. You made a deal you knew we would not be able to keep. Classic Liz.*

I rub my temples and ignore her. She's been getting sassy lately, and I don't like it. I never bothered her when she was in control, so why is she hassling me?

Because you bit off more than you could chew, and now we are both going to pay.

I build a mental image to block her out.

"There must be something," I say. "Anything?"

The dwarf shakes his head.

I throw him across the stall and snarl at him. "Seriously? Nothing!" I crack my knuckles and get ready to knock him to the ground again, but the thrall shakes her head. Something about being told that even dwarves, the best supernatural craftsmen in the world, are unable to create a magical item that will kill Angelo really ticks me off.

"As I've told ya before," the dwarf says, standing up and brushing himself off, "it's impossible without knowing *why* he can't be killed. Come back when ya have more information."

I want to protest, but between the gaping strangers and the group of dwarves in the back who look like they're about to swarm me, I give up. "Fine," I huff. "But if you're lying..." I threaten him with my knife.

"I would never lie," he says.

I glare at him. "Sure. Because dwarves, like Fae, never lie." I turn toward my thrall. "Come on. Let's go find Angelo."

This is bullshit. As a child, the Bloodlands was a place I could only dream of. It was to me what baseball is to Americans. Being here as an adult, I take back every word I ever uttered. On the surface, the

Bloodlands seems like a place where all sorts of creatures can mingle. Where anything is possible. But it's really a black market where those same creatures come to sell and exploit each other. Yet they can't make me a simple killing spell. Preposterous. I should have shown him my true form, but Angelo said we should keep a low profile. So, I do.

No one knows that he's the King of the Realms. I changed my appearance, so the dwarf didn't recognize me as queen. But maybe I should have shown him what he's dealing with.

"My Queen." The thrall points me in the direction of Angelo. Her voice is raspy, and I cringe a bit. Even a woman like me, the Blood Queen, is nervous around the likes of thralls. Their purpose is to feed us. In return, we give them just enough of our blood for them to be strong, heal, and have night vision like vampires. Some of them are even able to live as long as us. But the cost is high. Sunken eyes, frail bodies, and raspy voices tell other humans that they're not quite right. Give humans too little of our blood, and they either stay humans or go insane. If we exchange too much blood, they become made vampires. Thralls are the in-between creatures that sustain us and act as servants.

I asked Angelo to leave ours at home, but he pointed out that not everyone can have a magical bag that keeps blood fresh. Apparently, they're rare. I didn't tell him that I knew someone who could provide us with one. Especially because the terms that Dmitri and I left on were not—are not—the best.

"Thank you," I tell her. I tap Angelo on his shoulder. "What are we doing here?"

At first, I think he's ignoring me, but then I see he's looking at something. He puts the trinket down and gives me an earnest look. "We both have things we want, right?"

"Yes." Is this a trick question?

"Well," he continues, "we're here to gain those things."

"Uh-huh." I don't pry further.

We pass by tents and stands that contain everything from jewelry to weapons and hexes. Some areas display fresh human corpses, which the thralls cringe at, while others have slivers of kappa and mermaid skin. Other pieces of creatures, like pounds of werewolf meat, are kept in magical refrigerators. If I didn't know that magic was encasing the area, I would be surprised it smells of roses and daisies as opposed to rancid, rotten meat. If he's brought us this far into the market, he must be looking for something important and rare.

I try to make small talk with Angelo and the thralls as I take in my surroundings. "There are a lot more humans here than I would expect."

"That's because they have to get the fresh meat from somewhere," one, the male thrall replies.

"Explain," I order him.

"Well, when something loses value, what do you do with it?" His voice is guttural. Did they join Angelo together, or did he start his journey as a thrall before her?

"I throw it in the garbage," I say.

"And that's what happens to humans who can't pay their debts," Angelo replies.

The thralls look at him in surprise.

"Don't worry," he gives them a gentle smile, "I'm not going to sell you all."

They sigh in relief.

"Yet." His voice is stern but playful.

I guess the thralls don't hear it, though, because they shiver at his response. In their defense, they have served their purpose. Now that we're in the Bloodlands, we don't need them to feed off anymore. We could send them home.

As Angelo lurks from stall to stall, I walk toward the water and gaze at the sea. Its red waters push and pull, back and forth, in a rhythmic pattern. I think back to what I've been taught.

Geographically, the Bloodlands are located between Hungary and Romania. It's an interesting magical realm. The bloodred water it's known for is a combination of the surrounding seas: the Adriatic, Ionian, Mediterranean, Aegean, and the Black Seas.

The rumor is that it was created as a never-ending blood supply for my parents. When everyone began hunting the Sluagh, the Bloodlands became a black market to sell their parts. Over time, it's become a hub of human and supernatural trade. There are multiple ways to enter; you don't have to be in Hungary or Romania to get in, but if you're not in one of those countries, teleporting capabilities are a must. It's a dangerous place. As a young girl, Father and Andrei forbade me—or, rather, Lizzy—from coming.

"Liz," Angelo calls my name, breaking me from my thoughts of the history class I took so long ago.

"What?" I shout at him.

"Come here."

I roll my eyes and walk toward him, stopping only when I see a familiar boy with two puncture wounds on his neck. "You? How did you get here?"

"You recognize him?" Angelo asks.

"Yes. He's the boy from the convention."

"From the what?"

"The—"

But I don't get to finish my statement because the boy is lashing out for my throat.

Chapter Twenty-Three

Angelo's thralls—I don't know either of their names—jump in front of me and pin the boy down. The thralls pull him to a secluded section behind one of the meat stalls. Angelo and I follow. I take a good look at the boy. The puncture wounds in his neck have festered and look diseased. The boy's eyes are red, and it looks like they are beginning to sink into his face.

"Fuck." I crane his neck to the side and look closer. "Fuck, fuck, fuck. How? When? What?"

"Liz, is this your thrall?" Angelo raises an eyebrow at me. Then he smiles mischievously. "After all that crap you gave me about bringing Edina and Brax?"

"Those are their names?" I look at his thralls. "I've just been calling them 'the thralls' this whole time."

"Yeah," Angelo says, confused. "But we're not talking about that. We're talking about this." He gestures to the boy. "Mind explaining?"

I give him the gist of the situation. How this kid was at the anime convention—Angelo winces at the sound of Dmitri's name—and how I drank too much of the kid's blood and gave him enough of mine to heal him. As I explain, Edina leaves to get a sedative used for catatonic thralls. When she comes back, she administers it to the child. Once he's docile, we move to some picnic tables out of earshot of the other patrons in the market so that we can talk. As they ease him from the ground to his feet, the other shoppers snarl for us to get out of their way.

"But it was clearly too much," Angelo says, examining the kid.

I shake my head in disbelief. "I swear I didn't. I would never."

He looks at me, this time raising both brows.

"Okay, I would. But Lizzy wouldn't. And she was in control during that time." I cross my arms.

Throwing me under the bus? Lizzy asks.

No, I tell her, *I just said that you wouldn't.*

I can feel the mental rolling of her eyes. "Anyway, what do we do?"

"You described his blood as apple pie on steroids?" Angelo paces between the tables.

"Yeah."

"I don't smell it now."

He's right. The boy is wearing ripped jeans and a t-shirt with a band logo I don't recognize. The clothes smell like burnt cedar, leaves, and batteries—not the tantalizing smell I remember. If it wasn't for his face or the way he lashed out at me, I wouldn't even know he's a thrall.

"Well, I've only smelled it one other time," I say.

"Yeah? When?"

"Well, again, it was when Lizzy was in control, but it was when I went shopping with Mother. A boy bumped into me at the store..." My eyes widen. I snap my fingers to get the boy's attention. "Hey. Hey! Were you at that store too?"

He doesn't respond.

I wave my hand in his face again, but there's still no response.

"Ugh," I groan. "He's useless. When will he be able to talk?"

Brax's guttural voice answers me. "He should be okay after a meal and a good night's rest."

Edina's raspy voice joins Brax's. "You should also give him some of your blood. About this much." She pulls out a vial to show me.

I turn to Angelo. "What is that?"

"It's what vampires new to creating thralls use to ensure they don't give too much blood."

"Wouldn't it be better to turn him into a made vampire? Isn't that less messy?" I ask. I don't want a creepy servant. We already have two; we don't need a third.

"Maybe. But since you created him without his permission—"

"It's up to me to clean up my own mess and figure out what the kid wants to do."

Angelo nods. "Are you sure you're older than me?" he jokes.

"Not funny," I say. "So, what now?"

"We wait."

"We wait." I sigh.

I WAKE UP EARLY IN a tent, with Angelo snoring next to me. Thirty-one combinations of available poisons in the Bloodlands, one for each day of December, and still he lives. Why couldn't my Christmas wish be answered? I sigh. It's okay. It's a new month. I have new plans. My New Year's resolution to kill Angelo WILL happen.

I yawn and look for my jacket. The brisk wind from being in a bubble of magic doesn't make me cold, mostly because I don't get cold, but I have to put up a front for wandering eyes.

Angelo still wants to pretend we're common people. Why we couldn't stay in a real hotel and teleport back to the Bloodlands is beyond me. But whenever I ask, Angelo says something about "ruining the experience." Whatever that's supposed to mean.

I get it. Neither of us wants to deal with challenges to our positions. So, this is for the best.

Our thralls, Edina, Brax, and Arch—the boy Lizzy accidentally turned into a thrall—are sitting by the fire. As Arch almost burns himself from handling the fire, the others laugh. Any sense of joy leaves their faces once they spot me.

"Did you need something to drink?" Edina asks.

"No, I'm fine," I say. "The food, it smells good."

"Would you like some?" This time Brax asks.

"No, thanks."

Brax and Arch share a look, but Edina continues staring at me like she's waiting for me to say something.

"Actually," I sigh, "could you tell me something?"

"What do you want to know?" Edina asks.

"Why did you all sign up to be thralls? I mean, I know what the perks are, but why would you want them?"

"Well, I didn't have a choice," Arch says.

Edina and Brax hit him at the same time.

"Don't talk to your master like that," Edina scolds him.

Brax chuckles. "Why?" he repeats. "That's easy. It's because humans are pieces of shit."

Edina nods. "And we wanted to be better."

"Speak for yourselves," Arch says.

I roll my eyes at him and turn toward the other two. "But are you? Better, I mean?"

"Yes," Brax and Edina say in unison.

The conversation ends there. I huddle next to the fire and, when they offer it a second time, I take a piece of the meat.

I want to talk to them more, but the three of them seem preoccupied. So, I ignore them, opting to play on my phone instead.

I didn't think it would be possible to get service here, but it is. Good thing, too, because Andrei has been sending me updates on Father's whereabouts. I told him I didn't want him in my life, that Lizzy didn't want him in her life, but the truth is that we do, and that won't happen with him running around without a soul.

I pull up the most recent article in a string of news clips Andrei sent me about Father. The title of this one is "50-Year-Old Model Found Dead, Drained of Blood." It says that the story is from Botswana, but Father would never go there. Father is soulless, not stupid. It's more likely that he drained her body somewhere else and had someone dump the body there. I have to fix this on top of my Angelo problem. As I mull over how to do this, I overhear the conversation the thralls are having.

"I swear it's true," Arch says.

"You're telling us there's magic stones out there that can control the world?" Brax says. "I think you're getting the real world confused with comic books."

"No," Arch says. "Is it really that hard to believe? Dude, we're thralls. Undead beings. Witches, the Fae, vampires, all of its real. You're telling me you don't think magic stones can be real too?"

Edina watches the two in amusement before commenting, "Okay, Arch, let's pretend you're telling the truth." She pushes her long, curly hair out of her face and puts it in a ponytail. "What do these stones even do? And where would you find them?"

Arch looks between Edina and Brax conspiratorially before saying, "Well, my *master* has already used one of them." He says master like he's annoyed by it. Which, to be honest, I can't blame him. He was turned against his will. But he's the one who decided he'd rather stay a thrall than be turned. "The Blood Stone is in the Bathory Well. It can only be used once every ten years, so it's no good to anyone right now."

"Plus, it belongs to the Bathory's," Brax says, scratching his auburn hair. "You'd be crazy to steal from that family."

"Ahem." Edina gestures toward me.

I pretend I'm not listening and wait for Arch to continue.

"Anyway," Arch says, lowering his voice—as if I can't hear him from this distance; does he not understand the meaning of super hearing? "There are at least two other stones, if not more. There's the Soul Stone."

"Let me guess," Edina says, "it sucks out people's souls?"

I hadn't noticed before because I typically don't pay attention to the thralls, but her raspy voice has an accent. I can't place from where, but it sounds familiar. I might have to ask her where she's from the next time we're able to chat.

Stop letting your mind wander and listen, Lizzy says.

I am, I snap back.

Sure you are, she says.

I click my teeth. She's annoying, but she's right. I should be listening to Arch instead of letting my mind wander.

"You can kind of say that," Arch tells her. "It lets you place someone's soul inside of it in exchange for your soul."

Brax stands from his seat and stretches. Then, he grabs a thermos of water and drinks from it. "But how does that work? Like, how would that help you?"

Arch shrugs. "No idea. It's just what I heard."

"And the other one?" Edina asks. "What does it do?"

"Ah," Arch says. "The Death Stone."

"Death Stone?" Brax and Edina say in unison.

Arch nods. "You like the sound of that one, don't you?"

"Not particularly." Edina's demeanor changes from uninterested to engaged.

"Just a little curious," Brax says, his eyes shifting from left to right.

Something isn't right about the way the two of them are avoiding Arch's gaze. But even if what Arch is saying is true, what would Edina and Brax need a Death Stone for? They just said they were happy being thralls.

Arch doesn't seem to notice how off the whole thing is. He continues talking, oblivious to the situation. "The Death Stone allows you to kill anyone or anything in exchange for another life."

"Whose life?" Edina asks a little too quickly.

Arch raises his head and looks at the sky like he's thinking about it. He must have come to a decision because he starts talking again. "It has to be a life of equal or greater value."

"And how do you determine that?" Brax this time. He sits back down and leans in close to Arch.

Arch shrugs. "It's subjective. What I think someone's life is worth and what you think someone's life is worth are two different things." He shifts in his seat and takes a sip from his thermos. "But I imagine the Stone Spirit would decide."

Edina raises an eyebrow at him. "Stone Spirit?"

Arch nods. "All the stones have one. Magical spirits, or guides if you prefer to call them that, who tell you the cost of using the stone and what you'll gain."

The three of them sit in silence for a bit. Then, Arch stands and stretches.

"How do you know all this?" Edina asks.

"And how do you know the info is trustworthy?" Brax asks.

Arch looks at them and grins. "A guy at this nightclub showed it to me. He said he'd be selling it here. Apparently, he's a big deal in the supernatural world."

"What's his name?" Brax stands and moves closer to Arch.

Arch crosses his arm. "Can't say."

Edina stands and moves in close too. "Are you sure about that?"

Arch backs up.

I try to figure out if he needs assistance or not, but before I can jump in, Angelo is bursting out of the tent.

"Good morning," he says with a cheerful voice. He's smiling, but it doesn't reach his eyes, which have turned from deep brown to shining silver. "What's going on here?"

With Angelo's height of six feet, eight inches, and his eyes screaming, *Murderer*, it's no surprise the thralls are quiet.

I use the moment to walk back over to the campfire. "Good morning," I say, giving him a hug.

He squeezes me back, and I smile.

"What's that look for?" Angelo asks me.

"What look?"

"You look angry." He gestures to my face. "The lines around your eyes never lie."

"I'm fine." I'm not fine. I don't know if he heard what they were talking about or if he slept through it. All I know is that he interrupted before I could get the information I needed. A Soul Stone and a Death Stone might be the answer to my problem. With them, I could separate Angelo's soul from his body. If I can kill one or the other, the conditions for the Blood Pact would be met.

But he said, Lizzy starts.

I know what he said, and I've got a solution for that too. Now, go away! I lock Lizzy in a mental prison that will take her several days to get out of. Long enough for me to formulate a plan.

If what Arch said is true, I could imprison Angelo's soul within the Soul Stone in exchange for my own. Except it won't be my soul that I give to the stone...it'll be Lizzy's. Then, I can have this body to myself. As for the Death Stone, I can use it to kill Angelo's physical body. I just have to figure out whose life would be equal to his. Although, if the spirits that Arch talked about are present, then things might get complicated. They might be as vindictive as the Blood Stone and choose the sacrifices themselves. If that happens, it might not be worth it.

I close my eyes. It's worth it. If I do this, when I do this, I'll be able to have a life of my own, one free of Lizzy and Angelo. My love for Dmitri will come back. I won't have to share a body anymore. What could possibly go wrong?

"You're sure you're okay?" Angelo asks.

"Peachy," I say. "I just have some business to take care of before we leave."

Arch said that the person who told him about the stones is here, in the Bloodlands. If I can find them, then I'll be set. I could order Arch to tell me the name, but he could lie. We can control our thralls to a certain point, but it doesn't include the mind—unless you're me. I thank the universe I was born an Arcane, immune to the limitations imposed upon normal supernaturals. I'll have to probe Arch to see what he really wants. Only then will we be able to make a trade that benefits us both.

Chapter Twenty-Four

After breakfast, Angelo goes for his morning run. But when Edina, Brax, and Arch get ready to do today's shopping, I pull Arch back.

"You're staying with me for now," I tell him.

"Wh—" he begins.

"Don't argue," Edina says. She turns to me. "We'd like to show him how to address you properly." She eyes Arch. "Will you send him our way when you're finished?"

I smile. Edina is sneaky. She wants the same info I do. "That's fine," I tell her. I turn toward Arch. "You, here, now."

Edina and Brax go ahead, and I wait until they're out of earshot to ask him about the stones.

"I want something in return for the information," he says.

I don't have time to dillydally. "Name it." I wait for his response and pray it's something simple.

"I want to be human again."

I look him squarely in the eye. "That's what you want?"

"Yes."

I'm dumbfounded. Of course, it wouldn't be simple! Of all the idiotic, impossible things this little brat could think to ask for, he chooses his mortality. I guess this shouldn't be a shock to me. When I asked him whether he wanted to stay a thrall or become a vampire, he said he'd rather die than become a blood-sucking creature. That was interesting, considering a quick look through his mind told me that he loved the idea of having powers. What he said and what he thought were contradictory. But who am I to tell someone what they really want?

"I don't know if that's possible," I tell him. I can't recall a moment when a thrall was reverted back to their initial state.

"You're the Queen of the Realms. Find a way."

"You don't even know what that title means," I say.

"I know enough about it to know that it gains you entry into even the most secluded and off-limit places. And that it allows you to have an audience with whomever you desire."

He's right. Being the Queen of Realms does grant me those things. But I can't just do whatever I please. There are rules. "I'm not going to make a promise that I can't keep." Now I'm the one being contradictory. I'm in this entire mess *because* my other half made a promise she couldn't keep. Or didn't want to keep anyway.

Arch doesn't reply.

So, I offer something I know he can't refuse. "Tell me where to find the man with the stones, and I'll give you information on who might be able to help you."

He looks at me skeptically. "But you just said—"

"I said I didn't know if that was possible. Not that there wasn't someone else who might be able to help you."

I try not to sift through his mind, but with the amount of time I have left to figure this out... Well, it's better if I know how to win him over. I try to hold back my glee until he tells me. The last thing I need is for him to realize I've been reading his mind to get what I want.

"Fine," he says. "But we're going to exchange information at the same time. After waking up in that closet, I don't trust you."

"Fair enough."

And that's how I ended up at the River of Blood. When Angelo came back from his run, I told him I was chasing a lead regarding Father. It wasn't a complete lie. If the stones really do exist, then the person who holds them might also know how to find a lost soul and replace it—without the help of a person born of human and Sluagh or human and witch lineage.

The smell of the sea fills my nostrils. I'm tempted to drink from it, to see if it's anything like a normal sea, but I don't. Instead, I make my way to the cabin that Arch mentioned.

Everything about this screams trap. Arch knew I'd been trying to kill Angelo. Even if the vials didn't give me away, Edina and Brax would have. It's a bit too convenient that he had knowledge of something that could help me and knew where I could find the items I needed.

I sigh and pace in front of the cabin.

I check my phone. It's 9:45 a.m.

Regin Niall is fifteen minutes late.

I tap my foot.

The longer I wait, the antsier I become. I'm about to call it quits and come back later when a whooshing sound reaches my ear.

I turn around. Behind me is a man who looks like he stepped out of *GQ Magazine*. "We meet again," he says.

"Again?" I try to place where I've seen him before. Although there's something eerily recognizable about him, I don't think we've met.

He nods. "You may not remember, but you were at my club with a tall gentleman. An Angelo, if I recall correctly."

His accent reminds me of the old ones on the Dhampir Council. But somehow, he sounds more ancient than them. I take a moment to check his soul. It's a brilliantly bright light, filled with millions of colors with only the smallest speck of black. I've never seen a soul like his—even the purest ones have some darkness to them. But this one...

I'm at a loss. He's clearly dangerous, but I need what he has. And then it dawns on me where I know him from. "You're the nightclub owner."

He smiles. "That I am."

"You said we'd meet soon."

"I did. And we have." He scratches his pointed ears and looks at me expectantly.

"You're Regin Niall?" I purse my lips. The nightclub we went to was shady, but I didn't think it was Bloodlands type of shady.

"Yes, that is my name."

His silver eyes pierce mine, and a shiver runs up my spine. His appearance, the way he speaks, and the way he answers questions—short and curt—can only mean one thing. My lips start to form a question, but Regin stops me.

"Let us not bore ourselves with trivialities," he says. "I have something you want, and you have something I want. How about we just skip to making a deal? I haven't got all day."

I'm stunned into silence. He wants to make a deal. Right here, right now. My instincts tell me to run, but there's nothing to run to.

His unassuming appearance disturbs me, but I don't have the luxury to think about it. He's right—at least when it comes to him having something I want.

"I told the boy to get you up to speed. But young ones can be daft, I suppose." He shifts. "I see I will have to tell you what is at stake then." He pulls a black box out of his pocket and presents it to me. "Come closer," he says, "I do not bite."

I give myself a mental shake and walk toward him. He just wants to show me something—there's nothing to be afraid of. When I'm close, he opens the box.

Within are four stones. One is a grey agate stone in the shape of a house. The second is a black lava stone in the shape of a skull. The third is a blue tanzanite stone in the shape of a heart. The last is a purple amethyst stone in the shape of a clock.

"These are the stones," I say, slightly breathless. They are all beautiful and ominous in their own right. I reach out to touch them, but Regin pulls them back.

"Do not touch them," he says. "Unless you plan to use them."

I nod and pull my hand back. "Which ones are the Death and Soul stones?"

"Straight to it," he says. "I like that." He puts on a glove using one hand before continuing. "This one," he says, pointing to the lava stone, "is the Death Stone. And that one," he points to the grey agate, "is the Soul Stone."

"What about the other two?"

He closes the box. "The other two are not for sale at this moment. There is no reason for you to inquire about them." His voice is almost robotic.

"Fine," I say. "I will take the two I came here for. But what do you want in return? Arch didn't tell me."

"What I want is simple." He smiles slyly.

My body tenses. I'm not desperate enough to enter another Blood Pact, but I am willing to do almost anything else.

"I want you and Angelo to come back to my nightclub."

I stare at him, dumbfounded. "You're...nightclub?"

"Yes. Business was wonderful the night you all gorged yourselves on impropriety, lust, and blood. I would like to recreate that."

I'm not stupid. This man is part of the Fae. If I'm not careful with my words before entering an agreement, who knows what will happen. I check to see if Lizzy is listening, but she's still blocked off. Hopefully this memory won't be one of hers.

"When do we have to come to your nightclub? How long do we have to stay? What are the specific conditions of this deal?"

Regin smiles gleefully, and for the first time, I see his sharpened teeth. "It looks like there is an intelligent being in my midst. Most people take the deal without considering the terms. Impressive." He closes the box and puts it back into his pocket.

I'm about to protest. After all, it's not like I said no, but I change my mind when he pulls on his other glove and hands another pair to me.

"The gloves and the two stones are yours if you and Angelo, the King and Queen of the Realms, come to my nightclub twice a month for six months, beginning in April. You can choose the days and the time, but you must stay for a minimum of two hours. Does that sound fair?"

I don't say anything, and I don't make any gestures. I don't even nod to let him know I understand. Instead, I say, "I understand the conditions."

"This deal is only good for the next," he checks his watch, "five minutes. Decide quickly, or I will go on my merry way."

"What happens if I don't complete my side of the bargain?"

"A deal with a Fae is like a Blood Pact. Break it, and you die." His smile is wide this time, but his teeth aren't showing. "You now have three minutes."

I mull the deal over in my head. Is this feasible? "What if Angelo can't come to the club?"

Regin sighs in frustration and clasps his hands together. "Fine. I will amend it. As long as you or Angelo is present, the agreement is satisfied."

"Great. Do we have to be there physically? And if so, define physically."

"You are trying my patience Liz Bathory. Regardless of what form you take, you must be able to perform the duties outlined in the contract."

I think back to that night. The duties outlined in the contract are impropriety, lust, and the drinking of blood. On that night...I smile. This deal is fine. "Last question," I say.

"Speak." This time, his voice is annoyed. "And after this, if you do not agree, I am leaving."

"Does it matter if it's me or the other one?"

"The other one?" Regin raises his eyebrow in question. Then his eyes widen, as if it's just now dawning on him that there is another being inside me. "Last adjustment," he says in a warning tone. "You, Liz Bathory, your alter ego, Lizzy Bathory, or Angelo can complete the terms of this agreement."

I nod. "Wonderful. We have a deal."

"Excellent," he says, pulling out the box.

I put on the gloves that he handed me a moment ago.

Regin pulls out the box and opens it. He takes out the Soul and Death Stones and places them into a pouch. "That will be $4500 in American money," he says.

"But you said..."

"The gloves and the stones. I said nothing about this pouch, which you need to hold the stones. Unless you have a better idea."

"I don't," I say, taking the pouch from him.

"Then I expect payment the next time I see you. Ciao." With that, he disappears. No warning, nothing.

I open the pouch and take out the stones. Their designs are a bit on the nose, but for some reason, that comforts me. Regin didn't give me instructions on how to use the stones, but I assume it's similar to the Blood Stone. If I touch them, I'll be sucked into a world with the Spirit of the Stone. But is it the same spirit? And will Lizzy be able to make a deal with them the same way that I was able to make a deal with the Blood Stone?

There are so many unknowns to this, and I'm not sure if I'm ready to dive into those waters.

Chapter Twenty-Five

It's another three days before we leave the Bloodlands and return home. Angelo must not have found whatever we came here for because the only things we've picked up are a few trinkets and the stones I plan to kill him with.

Now, four days after our return home, we're leaving again. This time to Augusta, Georgia, to meet with the Morian Coven.

I think about the last visit there. Lizzy was in charge then, and she fucked up. But this time, I'm in the driver's seat, and I'll be damned if I ignore the words of a witch. She told us what we sought might not be what we wanted, and she was right. All these years, Lizzy, and even myself, to some extent, were focused on finding Mother. The journey led us to her, but at what cost? And Elizabeth is hardly worth calling "Mother" after all these years of abandonment and neglect.

Finding her was supposed to be the end. It was supposed to be a chance for us, for Lizzy, to get to know her. But it feels like a bust. I don't know if it's because she didn't turn out to be who I thought she was—who Lizzy thought she was—or if it's because I never cared about it either way, but all this effort to find her was wasted.

She hasn't even given us what we need to find and bring back Father's soul. We would've been better off trying to do it ourselves.

The problem isn't that what we—what Lizzy—sought and needed were two different things entirely; it's that neither of us knows what we need to begin with. This time, I'll be sure to make the witch elaborate.

Angelo touches my shoulder and breaks me out of my thoughts.

"What's wrong?" He strokes my face with his free hand.

"Nothing," I say. "I was just thinking."

He takes his eyes off the road for a moment and looks at me skeptically. "Right." There's a brief moment of silence. Then, "So, why are we going to the witches again?"

"I made a promise to Arch. I'm just fulfilling it," I say.

"And you made me drive because?"

I smile. "Arch doesn't know the way there, and you forced me on a three-month camping trip with the shortest notice possible. This is payback."

He laughs. "Noted. Next time I'll just leave you."

"Next time," I murmur. There won't be a next time. This always happens. We'll be talking, and it feels like we're just humans, and I forget that I'm supposed to kill him and end up loving the conversation, loving him. Then he ruins it by saying something like "in the future" or "later on" or "next time," and I'm stuck questioning if I should kill him.

Is that his plan? To make me love him so I won't kill him? How much does he know about why I have to kill him in the first place? It sounded like he believed me when I told him the Blood Pact was broken, but did he really? Or does he suspect the truth?

"Liz!" Angelo's shout breaks me out of my thoughts again.

"Oh, right, what?"

"We're here. Wake up the kid." He pulls into a parking space on the Morian's vast lawn.

"Great," I say. "I told her we were coming ahead of time. She should be expecting us."

Angelo nods.

"And you wake up the kid. I'm going to go say hi."

He's about to protest, but Moira and her granddaughter, Misha, are waving at me.

"Fine," he says, "I'll wake up the boy."

I leave him to deal with the kid and walk to the front door. "Hello, Misha. How are you?"

"Well," she says in her childlike voice, "you're the Queen of the entire magical community, so I guess I'm doing great."

I smile. "Are you telling the truth?"

She nods.

"That's enough, Misha," Moira says. "Go in the house now. The grownups are talking."

Misha sighs, waves at me again, and then goes into the house.

"That façade isn't fooling anyone. You're not even trying to hide your true nature."

"Well, isn't that a way to greet your queen," I say.

Moira gestures to the chairs and tables on the front porch, and we sit.

I watch Angelo and Arch talk by the car before turning to her. "You know why I'm here."

"Yes, you told me why on the phone."

"Then?"

"I only know of one person who completed that spell successfully."

"Let me guess," I say, "Mira?" My skin prickles when I say her name. I still don't know exactly what happened between her and the PI, and I couldn't care less, but the reaction isn't from me. It's from Lizzy. I sift through my mind and see her behind the wall I put up. She's pining for him again, and I wonder for the zillionth time why the stone didn't take her love for him away too.

"Yes," Moira says, pulling me back to our conversation. "But it means that it *can* be done. Where is the boy?"

I point at Arch. "The red-headed one, obviously."

She stares at him for a bit. "Obviously."

I guess Arch said something that Angelo didn't like because Angelo is hitting him fairly hard with the back of his hand.

"He can stay here," she says.

"What?" I ask.

"The boy. He can't go home in that state." She strokes her chin. "Yes, he can stay here, and I will try to find a way to complete the reversal."

"But he needs my blood to stay alive, does he not?"

"That's a misconception that you vampires made to force thralls into your ranks and good graces. Thralls can survive without your blood for up to a year. However, because your blood is addictive, they wind up following you around in hopes of more."

"But Arch hasn't even—"

"What? Asked you for any? If his goal is to become human again, he probably wants to mitigate how much he takes from you." She closes her eyes, which are creased and wrinkled, and shakes her head. "Of course, it doesn't help with the insanity that he's battling."

"Insanity? He seems normal to me." I observe Arch some more. Now he's leaning against the car. I guess he and Angelo are giving Moira and me time to talk.

"Is that how he appeared when you found him in the Bloodlands?"

I shift in my seat and twiddle my thumbs. "Well, not exactly. He was in a frenzied state of mind. We gave him a sedative and some of my blood, and he mellowed right out."

She doesn't say anything. She just sits there and watches them.

I don't know what she's playing at, but if she's implying something...

My thoughts trail off. No. She's just stating facts.

"So, he was going insane, and then you gave him some of your blood. Now he appears to be fine. But, tell me, have you ever given your blood to another human?"

It doesn't take me long to give her an answer. "No. He's the first."

"Hmmm," she ponders.

"What?"

"Well," she says, "a normal vampire's blood—made or otherwise—works the same. But you're an Arcane. No one knows what properties or effects yours might have. Except maybe—"

"What are we talking about?" Arch pops his head over the railing, interrupting our conversation.

I groan. "You," I tell him. "You're staying here."

"Why?" Arch asks vehemently. "You promised—"

"That she would find you someone who could help," Moira replies. "And that's what she did."

Arch looks at her skeptically.

"This is Moira Morian," I tell him. "She's a witch who knows a spell that can reverse the effects."

"Why do I need to stay here then?" he asks. "Can't I just take the potion or whatever it is with me?"

Moira shakes her head no. "It's more complicated than a potion. You can stay here, and I can try to help you, or you can take your chances of becoming a permanent thrall. It's up to you."

Arch looks between the two of us before answering. "I don't care how it's done. Just make me normal again. This she-witch," he points to me, "is impossible. Queen or not, she sucks."

Moira laughs. "I think we're going to get along just fine."

"Great," I say. "Then Arch can go in there and play with Misha while we finish our conversation."

"What about my bags?" Arch seems annoyed.

"You'll grab them before Angelo and I leave," I say. "Unless you have a problem with that?" I raise an eyebrow at him. I shouldn't let him disrespect me, but at this point, I have more important things to worry about.

"Fine," he says. "Who's Misha?"

"Moira's granddaughter," I say.

"She's in her room," Moira tells him. "Ask her to show you around."

He rolls his eyes, but he does as he's told.

I turn back to Moira. "Who?"

"What?" Moira stands from her chair.

I follow suit. "Who might know the properties of my blood?"

"Isn't it obvious?"

I cock my head to the side and stare at her in puzzlement.

She takes a deep breath. "Angelo was born human. His father—Anton, Ferenc, or whatever you wish to call him—found some of your blood and fed it to him as a baby. And now—"

"He's immortal," I say, cutting her off.

Well, fuck.

ANGELO AND I WAVE GOODBYE to Moira and Arch and make our way to the nearest Walmart to load up on snacks. The drive takes about fifteen minutes, but the only thing I can think about is the fact that Angelo might be immortal because of me—because of Lizzy. But if he knows that, why wouldn't he share? And if he doesn't, does this mean that Anton's plan was never about screwing over my parents but about making a more powerful supernatural being that he could control? Was this entire thing just a ploy?

I want to think it's all a conspiracy I've concocted. But when I think about all the moments that led to this. About the hatred Anton has for supernaturals even though he is one, about the way he talked about my parents, how his face beamed with glee when he dropped the news about the pact. It's all too convenient. Fuck, fuck, fuck. How could Lizzy fall for something like this? How could

I let her? Years of being trapped in her mind, years I should've been talking to her about these things, and I just...

"Is that Dmitri?" Angelo is looking at the entrance to Walmart.

A tall man with dark hair and sepia, reddish-brown skin is talking to someone. When he turns around, I see the dark brown eyes with flecks of amber.

"Yes," I say, as the scent of his soul, of familiarity and comfort, enters my nose. "That's him."

"Let's say hi," Angelo says.

"You just want to gloat," I reply.

He grins. "Maybe. Still?"

"Fine," I say. "Let's go."

We get out of the car and walk toward Dmitri. The person he was talking to left, but the meeting still feels awkward. The last time I spoke to him, I essentially told him to get lost. I then preceded to block all his texts and calls. We haven't spoken since the wedding.

"Hi," I say, waving at Dmitri.

He startles, but then his eyes widen in recognition for a split second before narrowing. He doesn't say anything.

"It's nice to see you," I say, pushing a lock of hair behind my ear. Today, I'm in a classic Lizzy look instead of my own: jeans and a t-shirt, sneakers, long black and purple locs with silver hair jewelry, and—of course—the dark skin we were born with.

Dmitri's eyes look sad. "You look just like her," he says, crossing his arms. "To what do I owe this pleasure?"

I open my mouth, but he doesn't let me get a word in.

"The King and Queen of the Realms have blessed me with their presence," Dmitri says sarcastically. "Does that mean there is a god?" He laughs, but it's humorless.

"It's nice to see you again," Angelo says.

Dmitri raises a brow at him. "Sure it is."

The silence drags out for a bit. With it comes a heaviness in the air.

Dmitri caves first. His eyes soften. "How is she?"

And I know he means Lizzy. The version of me that still loves him. The one who didn't cause this part of the Blood Stone condition. I feel nothing for him. But Lizzy...

She stirs in the back of our shared mind. I can feel her in there, gazing out through my eyes. The pining from earlier intensifies. She wants him—in more ways than one.

But I don't.

For the first time, the thought occurs to me. I don't want Dmitri. But have I ever truly wanted him? I loved him, but the way Lizzy is subconsciously reaching out for him, I've never done that. And when I think of who I'd rather be with, love aside, it's Angelo that I want in my life. Angelo that I can't live without. Dmitri can fit into that life, as a friend or a sex partner, but he's not the one for me.

The Spirit of the Blood Stone.

It must have known. But why would it...

"She's around." I don't want to lie to him. "She misses you."

"I miss her too." Dmitri sighs and rubs his head. "Well, I have shopping to do, so..."

"Right," I say. "Right, we wouldn't want to hold you up."

He purses his lips, and I think he's about to say something, but he just turns on his heels and walks inside.

"So, are we still getting snacks or no?" Angelo asks.

"Yeah," I say. "Yeah, we're still getting snacks."

He leads me into the store, and I follow him.

My plans are always changing. First with the pact, then the Blood Stone, and now with Angelo. Is it fair of me to send Lizzy into the Soul Stone just so I can kill the man I love?

The Blood Stone's condition would be met, but what would I have left? *What you seek may not be what you actually want.* I think I know what it means.

Before I can ponder any more, my phone rings.

I answer it without looking to see who it is. "Hello?"

"You need to come back to England. Angelo too. It's a matter for the King and Queen." Something is muffled in the background. Then, "Your father has—" Andrei's voice cuts out.

I frown.

"What is it?" Angelo asks.

"That was Andrei. It looks like we're needed in England."

"Great," he says. "I've been wanting to see your childhood home."

ANDREI SLAPS ANOTHER article on the table in front of me. The title of this one is "Copycat Killer Strikes Again: Another Impaled Body Found!" and has an old black-and-white photo of my father—or, at least, some iteration of him from long ago. It turns out that parents really were invented to make their children's lives miserable.

Underneath that article are several others spanning over the last year, each containing some trace of Father. "I think they got his good side," I joke.

Andrei doesn't laugh. "This is not funny, Elizabeth."

"Liz," I say.

Andrei rolls his eyes. "If he is discovered—"

"Yeah, yeah," I say. "If he's discovered, the entire supernatural community is doomed. Blah, blah, blah. What do you want us to do about it?" I gesture between myself and Angelo.

Angelo sucks the last drop of blood out of his bag. "I think he wants us to handle it."

"No shit," Andrei says, glaring at Angelo.

"Why are you mad at him?" I ask.

"I'm not." Andrei crosses his arms and leans back against a pillar. "Liz," he spits.

Okay, yes, I did take over his precious Lizzy's body, but we're technically the same person, and he would never act this way with her.

"Well," I say, "you could've fooled me."

"We've been here two days, while you've been looking at this for months, and you're the one complaining?" Angelo clasps his hands together. "What are we supposed to do that you haven't already tried?"

"Plus," I say, "you're supposed to go up the chain. Does the Council know about this?"

Andrei throws his hands up in frustration, "We've already been through this! Yes, the Council is the one who told me to call you in. I am not ecstatic about it either."

"Okay, okay," I say. "So, what, this is their way of testing us?"

"And your capabilities," Andrei says. "You are the King and Queen of the Realms now, and it's time you both start acting like it. Honestly, who spends all that time in the Bloodlands without checking in on the real world?" He shakes his head. "If this is the future, I'd hate to see—"

"There," Angelo yells. "Found something."

"What?" I ask. We've been scouring all the recent articles to figure out where exactly Father could be. Ever since the wedding, he's been on a killing spree. I don't know what he's like with a soul, but it has to be better than dealing with him running around the world the way he is right now.

"See this?" Angelo points to a building in the background.

"Yeah," I say, "what about it?"

Angelo spreads all the articles out. "Look at the backgrounds in the others."

I do as he says, and then I see it too. "We're all idiots," I say. I turn to Andrei when I say this part, "But especially the lot of you."

"What does that mean?" Andrei asks.

I tap on the articles. "These pictures are photoshopped. Look."

Andrei peers at where my fingers are resting. Then he looks at the other articles as well. He rubs his eyes and massages his temples. "So, genius, where is he?"

"Where do you think?"

Andrei shrugs, Angelo laughs, and I roll my eyes.

"Andrei," I say, "he's clearly with Mother."

Andrei sits with a loud thump. "And why do you think that?"

This time, Angelo answers for me. "Because of this." He points to the emblem for the Bathory family. "It's the same as the one on Liz's necklace."

Andrei stares in confusion, and then he sees it too. "How did I miss this? How did the Council miss this?"

"Because you're all a bunch of old geezers," I say. "It looks like we can handle 'difficult' tasks." I roll my eyes. "It's late. I'm going to bed." I turn to Angelo. "Coming?"

Angelo looks from me to Andrei and shrugs. "Yes." He turns to Andrei. "We'll talk to them tomorrow." Then, he follows me to our room.

I lay on the bed and groan. "He's so exhausting," I say. "When I was younger, he never wanted to listen to me. He always shut me out."

"Weren't you trapped in Lizzy's mind then?"

"Well, yes," I say, "but not always. Sometimes when she slept, or if she was unconscious, I would come out. You know, just to get an idea of what living was like."

"Is that why you know more about our world than she does?"

I nod. Father and Andrei liked to pretend I was inferior or didn't exist. But I always thought of myself as their second daughter. Not in a *love conquers all* kind of way but in a stepchild kind of way. I was to be seen but not heard. I existed but wasn't to interfere. Still, when I thought things were headed in the wrong direction for Lizzy, I'd step up and talk to them. It took them a while to figure out it wasn't her, but when they did, they never listened to me again. It's why I had so much resentment for her. For my so-called sister with whom I share a body.

I lay my head against Angelo and snuggle close to him, and he kisses my forehead. I smile and give him a peck on the cheek. The next thing I know, he's kissing me hard and pulling off our clothes.

He starts at my collarbone and makes his way across my shoulders, caressing me in all the right places. Then, he massages my body and licks me from my bosom to my naval, only stopping to ask if I want more.

I tell him yes, and he continues by spreading my legs and letting his tongue do all the work.

I grip the headboard and bite down on my lip so that I don't scream, and when I open my eyes, I see the evil gleam in his. He flips me over and places his silent flute into my altar of Venus. As we dance in the temples of ecstasy, we become one with each other and the universe.

Long after his life-forming essence has entered me, I lie awake thinking about what my future might hold.

Chapter Twenty-Six

"I've thought about this long enough," I tell Andrei.

"Eleven days is not long enough to make a decision like this. Besides, have you even considered what Lizzy wants?"

I pretend like I'm consulting with Lizzy. "Uh-huh, yeah, she says it's fine."

Andrei looks at me disbelievingly. "That was not your 'commune with my other half' face," he says.

I scrunch my face at him. "And you're acting like I care. Look, you should be happy. This is what I want."

Andrei scratches his head. "I just... I don't know."

"It's foolproof. I can keep an eye on him," I gesture toward Father, "and you'll have someone capable to run all of this," I gesture toward the business room in general. "You asked me to do this last year, so why don't you want me to do it now?"

"I asked Lizzy to do it," Andrei says.

"We're the same person!" I scream at him.

"You're not," he replies.

"Might I have a word?" Father says.

I roll my eyes. "No one's talking to *you*."

"I, for one, am intrigued," Mother chimes in.

"Well, no one asked you either," I say.

The fake articles were a ruse to get me to reach out to them. Mother used several of her connections in the supernatural and human world to pull it off. I guess they found something to bond over after their mutual disgust in my choice to marry Angelo. They won't tell me exactly what's going on, but there's a lot less distrust and hate between them.

Actually, it's more than that. For a soul-sucker and a soulless person, they seem to be completely absorbed in each other. It makes me want to throw up. Where was this when I—when Lizzy—was younger?

"You should let her do it," Father says, surprising me.

I smile. "Okay, you may speak. This time."

He raises a brow at me but continues. "Even if this one," he gestures toward Mother, "agrees to help—"

"Which I haven't," Mother says.

"When she agrees," Father continues, implying there is no room for debate on this, "I am going to spend my time reacquainting myself with what it is like to have true feelings. And you, Andrei, will need to help me with that. It would be good for my child to know how to run things while we sort this," he gestures to himself, "out."

"But she's not—" Andrei protests.

"But she is," Mother says. "Speaking of which," she pulls a book out of her bag and hands it to me, "this is a gift from us to you. We're... Well, you know."

Here's the thing. Mother doesn't say sorry. As I learned last year, there isn't a remorseful bone in her body, which means there's another reason she's giving this book to me. But I won't question her motives right this instance. Instead, I just take the book from her.

"Thanks," I say, eyeing her.

"You should read it right away. There's a lot of information about the Blood Stone, as well as things you need to know about us Sluagh."

I nod. "I'll get right to it."

"Now," Mother says, "if that's all, your father is supposed to show me around."

Andrei looks at each of us. "But we haven't finished—"

Father holds up a hand. "I am still the master of this house, Andrei," his voice echoes throughout the room. "What I say is final."

I don't know what's gotten into them, any of them, but something has changed. My childhood home is crowded. Andrei is more irritated than usual. Father and Mother are talking instead of running away from each other, and I'm, well, I don't know what I am. The chaos is too much for me, but *all* of this is necessary.

They don't know about Angelo, at least not yet. Me becoming the heir to the Bathory and Tepés fortunes will give me a leg up to deciphering Angelo's, and Anton's, plans.

I want this. I need this. And I'm going to get it because, unlike Lizzy, I know I can do this.

A COUPLE OF HOURS LATER, I'm perusing through the book that Mother gave me. *Stones, Magic, and Powerful Families in the Supernatural Community* is more riveting than I thought it would be.

Mother was right. There is a ton of information about Sluagh in it. For instance, our unique physiology and how our transformation from human to creatures of the night works, or the way our bodies convert souls into energy or damn others.

But there's also information about the powerful supernatural bloodlines. All the witch covens are listed. So are werewolf bloodlines—which I don't know much about—and powerful Fae bloodlines, including the Sluagh bloodlines—like Mother's and Idabelle's; vampiric bloodlines—like Father's and the Council's; fairy bloodlines—like Aunt Latina's parent, and several others.

But the most impressive thing in the book is about the Spirits of the Stones.

The section isn't long. In fact, it seems like the shortest section in the book, but I find myself reading and re-reading the pages over and over again.

Spirits of the Stones

The Spirits of the Stones are not one entity. They are a network of entities that control the five stones of the supernatural world. *See Stones* in index.

The Spirits are some of the oldest Fae in the universe, and it is their job to protect the stones from those who would use them for inappropriate reasons. *See Curses* in index.

The Spirits grant users of the stones wishes and/or abilities based on the unique properties of their particular stone. It is said that once a user has initiated a condition with the Spirit(s) of the Stone(s), they must complete the condition, much like a Blood Pact. *See Pacts, Promises, and Conditions* in index.

However, the key difference between a Blood Pact and a Condition of a stone is that <u>the user of the stone may renege on their deal if they return the wish and/or ability that was granted to them</u>. Few people utilize this unique aspect of the stones because they fear the retribution will be too great or that they will be caught in the fabled "Monkey's Paw." *See Returns, Refunds, and Reneging* in index.

I read the underlined section again. No matter how many times I see it, I have a hard time believing it. But if I play my cards right, there is a way out for Lizzy and me. I go to the book's index and flip to the sections listed in the passage—Stones; Curses; Pacts, Promises, and Conditions; Returns, Refunds, and Reneging. I read the fine print in each and every one.

By the time I finish, I have formulated a plan. All I have to do is make one phone call, and then I can set the pieces in motion. It only has a 34 percent chance of working, but it's better than nothing. And, if all goes well, Lizzy and I will be free of each other. We'll be free to live our own lives.

I pull down the mental block between us to see how she's doing, but she's nowhere to be found. She's either found the darkest corners of our mind, or she got tired of waiting for me to talk to her. Regardless, she doesn't need to know the plan. Not yet. I put the mental barrier back in place and steel my resolve.

Zsofia picks up on the first ring.

"How did you get my number?" She's annoyed.

"Perks of being a queen, I guess," I say.

"Oh," her voice deflates, "it's you. What do you want?"

"It's nice to speak to you too, Aunt Zsofia." It comes out the opposite of how I wanted it to sound, condescending.

"Apologies, *Queen*," and then in a muffled voice, "who stole my title."

"What was that?"

"Nothing. How can I help you, Your Majesty?"

She's still bitter about the contest.

"If you want the position, you can always challenge me for it."

"I could," she says, "but I'd rather win it in a true battle. You know what happens to challengers."

I don't know, but I don't want to acknowledge it and give her the satisfaction that she might be better suited for parts of this. "Anyway," I say, lightening my tone, "I have some questions for you."

"Hurry up and ask then. I'm busy."

She can't see me, but I nod anyway. "Right. I want you to tell me about your other half. Sofia."

"Oh? And why would you want me to tell you that?" A creak in a chair lets me know she's intrigued.

"Just humor me."

"Fine," she says. "But I want something out of this exchange of information."

"Yes," I say, "I expect you would. Name your price."

"Favors are better than prices."

"I've done enough favors for people. Name something else." She doesn't need to know one of those favors was recent.

"Fine. I want you to un-blacklist me from the family tree."

I flip open the book that Mother gave me to our family tree. White Xs indicate living, red Xs indicate permanent death, purple indicates turned into Sluagh, and black indicates blacklisted from the family. "Why?"

"Money, riches, gold, wealth in general. That kind of thing."

"Succession rights?"

"Yes, if you must know."

I tap my fingers against the bed before answering. "I'll do it if, and only if, your information is worth my while."

"I'll take those odds."

"Great. Then let's hear it."

She sighs and gives me a long explanation of how she found out about her other half, Sofia. And how, when she told her family, they mourned because it meant the curse hadn't been lifted. Since her, Mother, and Aunt Latina were triplets, they all found out around the same time. Where previous family members decided to place binding spells on their other halves, only letting them surface in times of danger or great pain—i.e., Mother's entire marriage to Anton—Aunt Zsofia decided to try a different approach.

"Sofia and I became friends," she says, reminiscing. "She completed me. Opposite in every way, yet the same."

"Why are you speaking in the past tense?"

She exhales, "Because she's gone."

"Gone? Like, dead? How?"

"No. Not dead. Just not in my head anymore."

I wait for her to elaborate.

She clicks her teeth. "The stones," she says. "Specifically, the Blood Stone."

"What about it?"

I hear her pacing in her home.

"I asked it to grant me a wish. One hundred years before you did."

I frown. "What did you ask for?"

"I wanted—" She takes a deep breath. Like what she's about to say will be painful for both of us.

"You wanted?"

"I wanted a body of my own. To be separated from Sofia."

I mull this over. "But it clearly didn't work. You said that 'good ol' Sof' told you I was Liz and not Lizzy."

"It's true, she did tell me. But it's not because the wish didn't work. It did."

"Then?"

She's trying to tell me, but I have so many questions.

There's more pacing on her end. "Let me just tell you from the beginning," she says.

So, I let her talk. And the more I listen, the angrier I become.

She asked the Blood Stone to give her and Sofia separate bodies so they could live separate lives but still see each other. The Spirit of the Blood Stone granted her wish. She and Sofia were separated. But the price she had to pay was a love life. But not her love life. Mother's. Aunt Zsofia is the reason Mother stopped contacting Father. She's the reason Mother married Anton. My life is like this because she made a wish.

"I tried to renege on the deal, to have the Spirit of the Blood Stone take it all back, but it was too late."

"And when Father was looking for his soul, you didn't help because?"

"By then I'd been blacklisted. I told everyone that Sofia and I were in contact, but they thought I meant in my head. They never asked if she had a corporeal form."

"And during the ritual?"

"Sofia did tell me that you were Liz. But not because she was in my head. It was because she was there that night. She wanted to go to the event, but she didn't want to participate. I told her to wait for me there. She's like a sister to me, you know?" Her voice has a smile, and it makes me think about Lizzy. "Anyway, she has an ability that not many of us possess. She can see the number of souls in a person's body and can tell which personality is dominant. And because we'd been aware of you all this time—"

"She was able to tell when Lizzy and I switched."

"Exactly."

This conversation didn't go the way I'd expected it to. "I still have questions."

"Go on then, ask them."

"Have you ever used the other stones?"

"Why?"

"Just wondering."

A long silence follows, and I'm about to tell her to forget about it, but she speaks first.

"I have."

My eyes widen in excitement. "Which ones?"

"Just the Soul Stone."

"Why did you choose that one?"

"Energy cannot be destroyed, only changed. A soul has to be housed somewhere at all times."

"But what does that... Father."

She takes another deep breath. "The Soul Stone allows you to place a soul into it in exchange for your soul, is what everyone believes."

"That isn't the condition?"

"Sometimes it is. Other times..." she trails off.

"Other times what?"

"Other times, the Spirits like to collude and plan."

"Meaning?"

"The Spirit of the Blood Stone told me how to get what I wanted. 'Place Sofia's soul into the Soul Stone,' it said. 'After, you find a body that can host her, replace her soul with someone else's.' And when I asked with whose, the Spirit of the Blood Stone told me that your father's would suffice. And when I did as I was told, well, you know the rest."

I do know the rest. This means she was responsible for Father's missing soul too. I don't linger on the thought for too long.

"Is it a mistake to use the stones?"

"I can't answer that," she says. "But I can tell you this. The Spirits of the Stones always have a reason. They are the closest things to gods on this planet. If you obtain a stone and decide to use it, make sure you're willing to pay the cost. And if you decide to renege on a deal, make sure you do it before any irrevocable changes to your life are made. Do you understand?"

"Yes." And I do. She's warning me that my plan might fail. Yet, I still have to go through with it. If nothing else, her story confirms I can make this work. "Thanks," I say. "I'm still angry, but I'll do as you ask."

"You're going to take me off the blacklist?" she asks in surprise.

"That's what we agreed to, is it not?"

"Well, yes, but..."

"I'm not doing this for you." I take a deep breath and push back my anger. I don't have to let my rage define me. "You destroyed my family, and you deserve to stay blacklisted. And I know you have ulterior motives besides succession."

"Then...why?"

"I have my own reasons. You don't need to be privy to them."

"This is true," she says, and I hear the grin in her voice. "Good luck, Liz," she says.

I lay on the bed. The past, the present, and the future, it's all coming together. *Don't worry, Lizzy,* I say. *I've got this covered.*

She doesn't respond.

I GAZE AT ANGELO'S sleeping form and come to a decision. I'm not going to kill him. At this point, it isn't just impossible, it's unfathomable. Since I met him, he's been a perfect complement to me. It was unsettling at first and one of the main reasons I wanted him dead—next to fulfilling the condition that the Spirit of the Blood Stone set up. But it turns out that I've grown to enjoy his company. He can't die. It would destroy me. But the Blood Stone knew this. The roll of that die wasn't coincidental, it was intentional, and it's up to me to figure out why.

Then there's the problem of Anton. If my suspicions are correct, and I get the feeling that they are, he created Angelo specifically to cater to me. It isn't impossible. Vampires and other supernaturals have been playing with genetics for millennia. He said he wanted to get revenge on my parents by having the spitting image of my mother marry the spitting image of him and create a child just because, but that's too shallow of a plan. With the way he tricked Lizzy into doing his bidding, I know Anton is smarter than that.

Lizzy and I didn't consider it then, but it's preposterous when you think about it. Anton's goal must be more sinister than we initially thought.

Moira said that he experimented on Angelo with my blood, making Angelo immortal—or, at least, unkillable. And if Anton was born human, it's not too far of a stretch to say that Angelo is also human. But then why does Angelo drink blood? For appearances? Or because my blood changes the composition of others? Or maybe a deficiency? The only way to find out is to experiment. But I'm not willing to do that right now.

What matters is this: If my blood can turn human people immortal, and if Arcane abilities are few and far between, what would the supernatural community do when an immortal child with Arcane abilities is born? And what would happen if the person who raised that child was vindictive and power-hungry?

Nothing good comes to mind.

Which means my plan can't fail. It must work. To protect the world from Anton and to give Liz and me the lives that we want. But will Liz agree to it when she sees what I've cooked up?

Every time I take down the mental block to discuss it with her, she slinks into another part of our mind. It's like she's losing herself. Which means this is ultimately up to me. It's my decision.

All these years, I took it for granted. I thought being in the driver's seat would be amazing. And it was, for a bit. But these decisions, ones that affect us both... I didn't expect that part to be so difficult. And Lizzy never had to worry about it because Andrei and Father made sure I couldn't tap into her world that often. But now, there are too many questions and not enough answers.

I get up from the bed. It's taken three weeks to set up the chessboard. All the pieces are in place, and all I have to do is make the winning moves that will lead me to checkmate.

I don't plan to just roll over and let the conditions of the Spirit of the Blood Stone kill us. The answers will come before that. After all, I plan on being the Queen, figuratively and literally.

Which is why, before coming home, Angelo and I made a pit stop at the Bathory Well. While he was distracted, I picked up the Blood Stone.

And since the thralls were nowhere to be seen, I can assume I got away with it.

There is one month and roughly nine days until I'm supposed to kill Angelo. It's now or never.

My plan starts tonight.

Chapter Twenty-Seven

Everything is set for the ritual. I check my phone to make sure Angelo will be out for the rest of the night and lock the door to our room. I even went as far as to put up enchantments to ensure he couldn't enter during the ceremony.

I lay the three stones on the altar I made on the dresser and wipe my sweaty palms on my dress. I don't know if the Spirits are above human and supernatural wiles, but, just in case they are, I donned a revealing black gown and satin robe, along with bloodred rosary earrings and a black choker necklace. I transform to look more like me and less like Lizzy: pointed ears, long white-grey hair, and everything else that marks me as Fae.

When I'm ready, I touch all three stones at once. But instead of saying what I want aloud, I show them. And, just like the first time we used the Blood Stone, Lizzy and I are transported into the inner recesses of our mind.

"Blood magic again," says a deep voice. I recognize it. It belongs to the Blood Stone.

"And this time, she's dragged us into it," says a lighter voice.

"Oh, stop it now." This one is meek. "She clearly has a plan."

"Hello again," I say to the Blood Stone. "I'm sorry, I don't know which of you is—"

"Did we ask you to speak?" The lighter voice sounds annoyed.

"Well, no, but—" My lips are zipped shut.

"Grab the other one, Death," the Blood Stone says.

Something slithers past me.

"Found her," says the meek voice. "She doesn't look great. Almost like me."

There's a moment of shakiness from the Blood Stone. "You had one job," it says.

"One job," repeats the lighter voice, which I assume is the Soul Stone.

"You couldn't do it without dragging all three of us into it," the Blood Stone continues. "Let me guess, you found out how to renege on our deal?"

"Yes," I say without hesitating. "I did."

"And you?" The Blood Stone seems to be talking to Lizzy, but she just stares blankly at the space in front of us.

"I've got this," says the Soul Stone.

There's a sensation of being kicked and throttled; it's unpleasant, but it seems to work.

"Gah," Lizzy screams. "What in the..."

"Nice of you to join us," says the Blood Stone. "Liz was just telling us why she called us all here."

"Liz?" Lizzy looks around, and then she spots me. "You," she yells, lunging for me.

I block her and put her in a hold. "Yes," I say.

Lizzy pushes me off her. "You selfish asshole! You blocked me out for—"

"We don't have time for this," the Soul Stone says.

"I do," says the Death Stone. "It's pretty lonely in my stone. Nothing to do, etcetera, etcetera."

A sense of irritation builds up. The Blood Stone is about to bust a gasket.

"Right," I say. "Well, you all know what I called you for. I just need to know what I have to sacrifice to get it."

The three Spirits of the Stones circle around us. Their conversation is whispered, but it seems like they reach a consensus.

"We'll help you," the Death Stone says with glee.

"Because balance has to be restored," says the Soul Stone.

"Not because we like you or anything," the Blood Stone replies.

"What deals are you making now?" Lizzy huffs.

"Don't worry," I say, "you'll like this." I address my question to the stones. "What do I owe you?"

"A soul for a soul," says the Soul Stone. "If you want both, you'll have to deliver two."

"A death for a death," speaks the Death Stone. "If you wish for a body, you must provide a body."

"A deal for a deal," states the Blood Stone. "If you want to renege on our original deal, you must fulfill the original pact."

"Does it matter who or what?" I ask. If the conditions are broad, then this will definitely work. But if they put restrictions on it...

"I'm not picky these days," says the Soul Stone. "Provide whomever you wish."

The other two stones discuss something while I wait.

The Death Stone speaks first. "After some deliberation, I've decided I won't be picky—this time. Here's a list of things you can kill to equal the body you wish. They MUST die if you want a life."

"Have you thought through what it means to renege on our deal?" asks the Blood Stone. "The time limit I placed still applies regardless of which deal you fulfill. Shall you fail—"

"I'll die," I finish for it.

There's a sensation of a nod from the Blood Stone.

"I'm prepared for that. There's just one thing."

"Oh," the sensation of moving happens again, "and what's that?" asks the Blood Stone. "I've been generous so far."

"It's just that... Well, I want to renege on Lizzy's deal too. Just pile her consequences onto mine."

"We have a martyr," says the Death Stone.

"Or a brave person," speaks the Soul Stone.

"She's just in over her head," states the Blood Stone. "But I'll allow it—if, and only if, you succeed in breaking the original Blood Pact." There's a feeling of movement. "Otherwise, your fates are intertwined now. Fail, and you both suffer the consequences. Good luck."

There's a jolt to my body, and I get the feeling that the conditions have been put into place.

I make my way back to the bed, close my eyes, and pull down the mental blocks for good so I can communicate with Lizzy.

What the hell was that? she asks.

Me, correcting our mistakes, I tell her.

It seemed like you were making more. She throws up her hands. *What is all this about bodies, and souls, and deals?*

You would know if you'd been paying attention for the past month or so.

You mean AFTER you made Dmitri walk away again. I hate you.

I'm doing this for you!

You are doing this for yourself. She crosses her arms and walks in another direction.

I would agree with her, but she's wrong. *Do you know what I just did? What I just gave up?*

No, she says, *and I do not care. You are in the driver's seat, remember.*

You really don't know, I ask her.

She ignores me.

I guess you'll find out in about a week then.

I don't hear anything from her for the rest of the night.

I SPEND THE NEXT WEEK writing letters and gathering the items that I need for the plan to succeed.

"We're going to the store again?" Angelo yawns. "We've been like, a million times."

"Yes, well, I still need a few more things." What I don't tell him is that the "few more things" I need are 135 pounds worth of rats, Anton and Idabelle, and a prayer.

"What's this party even for?"

"It's a celebration."

"Of what?"

"That would ruin the surprise."

"So, it's a surprise celebration?"

I stop moving around and stare at him. He's smiling at me and staring at me with those big goofy eyes. I bop him on the head. "Yes."

"Okay, what are we picking up?"

"Rats."

"Rats?"

"Rats."

"Can I get Edina and Brax to do it? I don't really like rats. There was that whole plague, you know."

I laugh and hit him. "No," I say. "It has to be you." In all honesty, I don't trust Edina and Brax. Ever since the ritual, they've been hanging out a little too close for comfort, and I get the feeling they're spying on me. "Hey," I reach out to Angelo.

"Yeah?" He gives me his full attention. As in, full-on stops moving just to make sure he's holding my gaze.

"Edina and Brax," I say, "how did they..."

"Become thralls?"

"Yeah, and why do they hang around us so much?"

He shrugs. "Father told me to bring them with me, so I did."

"That's it?"

"That's it. What, expecting something more nefarious? Thought I tricked them into it?" He smiles and winks at me.

I give him a nervous smile back. "No, just, never mind." If he's telling the truth, then they might be a bigger threat than I thought.

"Whatever."

"Actually," I say. "Do they have a family? Edina and Brax, I mean."

"Nope. Any family they had is long gone. They've been around since I was young."

"I thought thralls died quickly."

He frowns. "Usually, yes. But Father told me that they're a special type of thrall." He shrugs. "Anyway, let's go get your rats."

I run through the mental list the Death Stone gave me again. A death for a death. I can kill someone of my choosing if I provide an equal exchange. The only limitation it gave me was that the weight had to be equal. If Edina has no family, she's a perfect candidate. "Actually," I say, "I don't need the rats. Let's just finish setting up."

Several hours later, the house is decorated in nondescript streamers and balloons and there are party favors on every table. The kitchen is filled with blood, snacks, and drinks. There are party games in the corner, and the room where I will complete two of the three stone conditions has been prepared.

When the guests start trickling in, I pray that I've made the right decision.

I'm immediately rewarded when I spot Edina and Brax making their way toward me.

"May we talk to you about Arch?" Edina asks.

"Is this a conversation we need to have in private?"

"Yes," Brax says, "it is."

If I'm right about Anton's plan, whatever they're up to won't lead to my death. I should use the opportunity to get as much information as I can. "Okay," I say. "But I need an answer to a question before I can tell you about Arch."

Edina and Brax give each other a knowing look.

Edina speaks first. "What is it you'd like to know?"

"When exactly does Anton plan to kill me?" I lead them into the dark room I prepared earlier.

Edina is silent, but Brax, he cracks wide open like a nut hit with a hammer.

"Wh-what do you mean?" he asks.

I raise a brow at him. "So, he does plan to kill me. Before or after I get pregnant?"

"No one said anything about killing you," Edina says, glaring at Brax.

"No one had to. Your response tells me everything I need to know. Now, if you want an answer to your question, you'll answer mine. He's going to kill me. Before or after the child?"

Edina hesitates, and I use the moment to climb into her mind and take a better look at her soul. She's done some nasty things in her past, including murdering her own family. I pull those images to the forefront of her mind. After what feels like an eternity, she breaks. "After," she says. "After his grandson is born."

"Thank you," I say. "Now, what did you want to know about Arch?"

It doesn't matter what I tell them because they won't be leaving this room. At least, not alive.

Brax, whose eyes are large and buggy, asks, "Where is he? You said you were going on a trip, and we never saw him again."

"Oh, that's all?"

Edina looks at me skeptically.

"I'll tell you," I say. "I always keep my word. Just, give me one moment." I walk over to the altar and put on the gloves for handling the stones. I pick up the Death Stone and gesture for them to sit at the table.

They do as I say, and I set the stone in the middle, just like I was told to do. "He's with a witch coven."

"Which one," Edina asks.

"Does it matter?" I look at her pointedly.

"It does," she says.

"Well, I could tell you, but then I'd have to kill you," I say.

Edina and Brax smile.

"Not if we take you down first," Edina says. "We just need enough for this." She holds up a tube for blood.

"And we can get it using this," Brax chimes in, pulling out a familiar container.

My eyes widen in surprise. "It's a sedative," I say.

"And it works like a charm," Edina replies. "Get her, Brax."

I smile like a wolf before entering their minds at the same time. I bring up every vile deed they've done and put it on repeat for them.

I don't know the extent of my powers. Lizzy and I never explored. But I have always been able to bring out the worst part of people and paralyze them with the fear of themselves. That's what I do now as I pluck the sedative from Brax's hand.

I never expected them to make this so easy. I whistle as I inject his body with the weapon he planned to use against me. His body stiffens, and he's knocked under. I lay his body on the floor, and then I work on administering the drug to Edina.

She's a bit stronger than Brax. She has more willpower and is resisting me. But it doesn't matter; once the syringe is in her, she too slumps over.

I planned to poison them with a drink, but this worked out better. Now, I can say they attacked me, and I acted out of self-defense. I take off one glove and call for the Death Stone.

"Back already," says the meek-voiced Spirit.

"I have your offering," I say.

"Don't you work quick," it replies. "Give me a moment."

A black light shines, and the Stone disappears from the table. I look for it, but it's gone. "What the—" But I don't finish the sentence because before me is a short girl with spiky dark brown hair and light brown skin.

"Let's see what you brought me today," she says in a meek voice that sounds oddly like the Death Stone.

"You're—"

"Lady Death," she says, "in the flesh." She giggles. "It's been so long since I could roam around. I'm only allowed to do this when someone uses my stone to complete their condition."

Her voice is innocent and races like she's talking a hundred miles per second.

"Is this a party? Oh my, you're killing party guests? Well, I guess it isn't something that I haven't seen before." She smiles. "Oh, what beautiful specimens. Which is which?"

I don't know what I expected, but the Death Stone transforming into a literal person was not on my bingo card.

"That one," I point to Edina, "is 135 pounds. She's the body I want to kill and preserve for transfer." I wait for a response. "Um, Lady Death?"

"Hmm, oh, right!" She looks at Edina. "So, this one is the one you have to kill?"

I nod. "He'll be dead in another ten seconds or so."

"Hmm... Well, let's make sure. I can't grant the death until I feel the other one, ya know?" She sits in one of the chairs in the room and kicks her legs. They're too short to reach the bottom. If I didn't know any better, I would think she was just someone's random kid.

I stare at her in wonderment.

"Three...two...one... Yep, he's dead as a doornail," she says. "Which means you've met my condition. Congratulations!" She sprinkles confetti from who-knows-where.

"Um, yeah, thanks." I sigh. "So, how does the rest work?"

"Old Soulen is next," she says. "I can only preserve the body for a few hours, so you have to fulfill Soul's conditions if you want to keep it. Otherwise, we'll have to do this over again." She looks around. "Wow, you're pretty loaded, aren't ya?"

I stare at her.

"Sorry, sorry, I told you, it's been a while. Remember, all conditions must be met by the original deadline, or you're, ya know, all mine." She smiles a toothy grin.

"I know," I say. I can't get a read on her. "Are you always like this?"

"Hyperactive, inquisitive, and generally all over the place?" She shrugs. "Yeah, it's why the others don't like me."

"But...you were so meek in the stone."

She shrugs again. "Not everything is as it seems. Are we done here?"

"Y-yes," I say. "Thanks."

"No problem. And remember, 20th of March!" And just like that, she turns back into a stone. I put the glove back on and pick it up.

One condition down, one to go. And I have to hurry if I want to finish before any switching occurs.

When I walk out the room, it's like no time has passed.

I find Angelo. "What time is it?" I ask him.

"Huh?" His face is stuffed with food.

I hold back a laugh. "The time?"

"Oh, oh, the time." He looks at his watch. "It's only 10:30. Why?"

"No reason."

"Well, you were gone for like, ten minutes. Is everything all right?"

"Yeah," I say. *At least, it will be.* "Where are Idabelle and Anton?"

He swallows and looks at me, surprised. "You're asking about my parents? The in-laws you hate?"

"Yeah, well, today I love them," I say. *Because of what they're going to do for me.*

Angelo scans the room and points to a corner. "Over there." He scarfs down some petit fours.

"Great," I say. "Hey, save me some of those, will you? I'll be right back."

"I make no promises," he calls to me as I walk toward my in-laws.

Anton is smart, so getting him to fall in line with my plan will be more difficult. But it's crucial if I'm going to make my dream a reality. This entire time, the moves on the board were all his—Liz and I were just playing right into his hands. Now, I have my own strategy. And I will not lose.

Chapter Twenty-Eight

I walk toward Anton and Idabelle, reminding myself I'm playing for keeps. I can't afford to misstep on this portion of the plan, and I only have one chance. I can't bring up Edina and Brax until I get to the end of the conversation, and I can't do that until we get past the small talk and on to the thing they want most. I take a deep breath, and when I reach them, I give them the biggest—and fakest—smile I can muster.

At least, that's my plan.

When I reach them, they're talking to Mother and Father. I want to bang my head against the wall. I need them alone for this plan to work. Except, maybe I don't.

The gears in my head begin to shift, and a new plan formulates immediately. *Yes*, I say to myself, *this can still work.*

I try to reach Lizzy in my subconscious, but she's still ignoring me. At least now I can feel her. The sense of loneliness and hopelessness she has begins to leak out, but I can't afford to have those negative emotions right now. So, I do to her what she's been doing to me all week. I shut it down and ignore her, but not before reminding her that it's all for her.

Father is glaring at Anton, Anton's eyes are filled with mischievous glee, and Mother and Idabelle seem to be in some weirdly polite staring competition where they compliment each other.

"Hello," I say, "Idabelle, Anton." I turn to my parents, "Mother, Father." They all look at me expectantly, but I haven't quite figured out how to bring up the topic of conversation that I wanted to discuss with them.

"Look," Mother says, "it's my daughter. The one who promised us a divorce," she says, sipping her drink. She winks at me.

Does she know about my ruse? I don't have time to process what she's saying or doing because Anton speaks next.

"A divorce that allows you to marry that man," Anton points toward Father.

"She should have married me from the beginning," Father tells him.

Idabelle quietly sips her drink and looks away from the scene.

"Actually," I say, "that's why I came over."

The four of them close their mouths and give me their full attention.

"Was it something I said?" I ask.

"I'm just surprised," Idabelle says. "We were friends, and then all this, but you're willing to do it?" Usually her joy would be infectious, but no one else is smiling.

"Angelo and I thought it over," I say. "We agree it's what's best." Except Angelo knows nothing about this plan.

"Then why isn't he over here," Anton says, looking for his son in the crowd.

"He is attending to the guests."

Anton eyes me suspiciously, but his distrust melts. "Great," he says. "When?"

"How about now?"

"Now?" Mother asks. "Are you sure that's wise? After all, he did—"

I hold up a hand. "I'm doing this for you," I tell her. "And for you." I turn toward Father. "Don't get me wrong, you're both awful parents. But," I pause for a moment to let my words sink in, "not terrible enough that I would let you succumb to the whims of this man." I nod toward Anton. If there's anything my parents and I do agree on, it's that Anton is literally the worst.

This wasn't how I hoped to get him and Idabelle alone, but now that I've gone down this path, it's the only option available. I sift through my thoughts of meeting Anton for the first time, of reconnecting with Idabelle, on how Anton must have set all of it up.

A part of my heart goes out to Idabelle. She might think she loves him, but I'm certain Anton manipulated her the same way he manipulated the rest of us. Too bad she'll have to suffer the same consequence as him.

And Anton...he thinks he's ahead of me, that he's won. But the Blood Pact said that I couldn't kill him. It didn't say that I couldn't trap him. I know what reneging on the Blood Stone means, and I know what will happen if I'm not able to go through with this plan, which is why the next few words exchanged in this conversation will make or break the rest of this night, the rest of my life, the rest of Lizzy's life, the rest of all our lives.

"Can't bygones be bygones?" Anton asks. "We're all here together, aren't we?" His voice is silver and smooth, like he's weaving a lie.

"Yes," I say, hoping I'm making the right decision. "Let's let bygones be bygones. Beginning with my gesture of kindness."

Anton and Father raise their brows at me, but I smile in contentment. "I've read up on how to achieve the breaking of a Marriage Pact. It's all rather simple. But I do need the help of a witch. Idabelle?"

"Of course," she says. "I've been waiting to help you with this."

I nod. It doesn't surprise me that she would want a hand in making her marriage happen. After all, breaking the Marriage Pact between Mother and Anton helps all of us. Mother and Father would be free to do as they please; Idabelle will get to spend an eternity with Anton—she just doesn't know it yet; and, well, I'm not sure what Anton gets out of this deal, but it won't matter because I'll be the one who gets the satisfaction of besting and trapping him.

"I've already prepared a room," I tell them. I'd split up the stones before the night began and placed them under an enchantment so that only I can see and touch them. I don't need the wrong person to go snooping around and messing with things they don't understand. I check the clock. 11:00 p.m. Lady Death said the spell could only be held for a few hours, but she didn't specify what that meant. If she meant two, she would have said a couple, and if she meant seven or more, she would have said several or given me a specific amount of time. But she said a few, which is three to six hours, and with my luck, it's on the lower end.

She preserved the body around ten, which means I must hurry. If I'm correct, there are about two hours before Edina's body is no longer eligible and I'd have to sacrifice something, or someone, else. Maybe I should have made Angelo purchase the rats after all.

I lead the four of them to the room with the Soul Stone and pray that Anton's senses aren't keen enough to pick up on it. I've had the servants lace his drinks all night, and I'm hoping he's in a somewhat weakened state compared to his usual limit.

"It's all ready," I tell them. "Everyone, please take a seat."

They do as I say. My heart beats so hard I hear it in my ears. I try to avoid my nervous gestures, tapping my hands or feet, blinking too much. If I fuck up here, if Anton suspects anything, it's all over.

But the first step is going well. Now that everyone is sitting, and thanks to the binding enchantment I placed at the beginning of the night, everyone except me is unable to leave from this spot.

Anton looks at the floor and narrows his green eyes at me. "You can't kill me," he says. "Remember the Blood Pact?"

If he's asking if I remember, that means that Angelo didn't tell him that he thought that it was broken. This bodes well for me. It means that I can trust Angelo and that sparing his life for his father's will be worth it.

"I wouldn't dream of it," I tell him, continuing with the steps for the ceremony.

Next, I pour wine into the two goblets on the table and sprinkle salt around them. Anton lifts them up and smells them. "Interesting," he says.

"Is something wrong?" I ask him.

"Nothing at all," he says.

"Why are you asking so many questions?" Mother says. "I'm not."

"Because you're not of the mind to," Anton says.

Mother doesn't reply.

"Hush now, y'all," Idabelle says. "You see that Lizzy Bear is trying to get everything set up." She smiles at me.

I try not to glare at her. "Liz," I remind her.

"That's right. I guess I should be calling you Liz Bear." Idabelle laughs giddily.

"Uh-huh," I say.

I prick my finger and put a drop of my blood in each wine glass. And then gesture to Idabelle to do the same. I look between Anton and Mother. "It calls for the blood of someone who is in a union and has connections to both parties."

Anton looks at Idabelle.

"She's right," Idabelle says, looking at the spell book. "But why do you need mine?"

Anton looks from her to me.

I exhale. "Because if you read the fine print, it says it works better if a witch adds her blood into the spell as well."

Idabelle holds the book closer to her face. She finds the part of the spell I'm referring to and lets out an audible sigh. "Right again," she says, looking at Anton.

"Are you running every step of this ritual by her?" I point the question toward Anton.

Anton chuckles and clasps his hands to look at me. "You can never be too sure. After all, this was all a bit... How do I say it? Ah, yes. Convenient."

"I did say this was a celebration when I invited you, did I not?" I ask him.

He smiles. "That you did. But you didn't say of what."

"Because there are so many things. Including this—if you'll let me finish."

He crosses his arms and leans back in his chair. "Very well."

What Anton and Idabelle don't know is that using my blood in this particular ritual serves a secondary purpose. It will bind my will to theirs, leaving them powerless when I'm ready to proceed with the true purpose of this meeting.

"Now," I say, "Idabelle and I will chant the words in the book. While we chant, you and Mother will drink from the goblets. Once every drop has been consumed—"

"And it does say every drop," Idabelle chimes in.

I clear my throat.

"Sorry," she whispers.

"Like I was saying. Once every drop is consumed, you and Mother will kiss."

Mother stares at me like I've gone crazy.

"It's just a quick peck on the lips," I assure her. "The kiss signifies the end of your relationship and the end of your marriage."

"Why couldn't Latina do this before," Idabelle asks.

I look at her.

Idabelle shrugs. "It's been bugging me all this time."

Anton takes a deep breath. "Because she doesn't have ties to me, as clearly stated in the spell."

"Oh," Idabelle says, "right."

"Can we get on with it?" I ask.

Everyone nods.

Idabelle and I begin chanting. Mother and Anton look at each other, pick up their goblets, and toast.

My palms begin to sweat, but I try my best not to show it. The goblets are laced with heavy magical herbs that I picked up from Moira when I checked on Arch a few days ago. She said they should be strong enough to knock Anton out, but that I should be careful anyway. Since I wasn't sure if Anton would switch the goblets, I had to make sure they were both laced.

I do have the antidote, and I will give it to Mother. But only after I take care of Anton.

Idabelle and I chant louder and louder as Mother and Anton drink from the seemingly never-ending chalices until finally they finish and set them down. I check both goblets. Every drop is gone.

I want to sigh in relief, but it's too early for that because the real battle begins after they kiss.

A few seconds pass, and then they both stand.

"Goodbye, Anton," Mother says.

Anton smiles, "Goodbye," he says. Then, he gives Mother a full-on kiss on the lips. It's not what we talked about, but it's happening.

It's only then that I see the knife in his hand.

It happens in slow motion.

Anton stabs Mother.

She falls to the ground.

Father circles around toward her.

Idabelle looks frazzled.

Anton grins, but then he crumples over.

Mother, Anton, and Idabelle lose consciousness.

Father looks to me for help, but I don't have time. I have to choose. Liz or Mother.

I make my choice.
I hope it's the right one.

Chapter Twenty-Nine

I thought I was prepared for life. I thought nothing else could surprise me. But I was wrong. The events of last month were intense, to say the least. There was so much confusion when it happened. Many of the guests were sent home early, and the servants had to work double-time. And now, this is the result.

Is this what it means to be successful? I started out on this mission with one goal, so how did it turn out like this?

Dmitri kisses me everywhere, making me forget what I was thinking about. For now, I am absorbed in the idea that I am alive in a body of my own and can drink in the bliss of the man I love.

"Lizzy," Dmitri breathes into my ear, "I've missed you so much."

"And I, you," I say.

He smiles gently and kisses my ear. Then he trails his fingers across every inch of my body as he drinks me in with his eyes.

It has been so long, so he takes it slow. Making sure every moment is precious and that the sensation of his body against mine will be burned into my memory for years to come.

He picks me up from the bed and guides me to the wall, hoisting my body up so that all I feel is the cold plaster against my back.

He enters me slowly, taking one of my breasts into his mouth while supporting my body with his hands. When he finishes with one, he moves on to the other.

I hold back a moan. It has been so long since I could enjoy his touch that I want to hold on for as long as possible.

He releases my breast, then gently puts me down.

I am about to protest, but he is not finished yet.

He sits me on a chair, spreads my legs, and uses his tongue to pleasure my core. He licks and rolls and sucks until a squeak leaves my lips.

He laughs at me, and then we're moving again.

This time, we are on the floor.

"I will take you on every surface of this room until we are both satisfied," he tells me.

And I do not know if it is the way he says it or if it is the way he is looking at me, but I believe every word. "It is important to keep your promises," I tell him, hiding a smile.

"That it is," he says.

And just like he said, we move from one part of the room to the next until we are back on the bed. We hold hands and make love until the sun comes up.

"LIZZY, LIZZY?" THE voice sounds like mine, but it is not mine. "Lizzy, come on, sit up."

"Five more minutes," I mutter sleepily. Dmitri left a few hours ago, and this is the only real sleep I have gotten since I have been back.

"We don't have five minutes. There are only two days left, and I don't know."

"We know," I say, wiping the sleep from my eyes. "But you want to check. How do we even check?"

Liz shrugs. "I don't know. I figured that I'd just, you know, ask."

I groan. "Fine, we will ask. But you want to do it now? In here?"

"Yes! Where else?"

"Fine, fine," I roll out of bed. "Tell Angelo he owes me one, though."

She squeals. "I will."

"Fine, we will do this."

She puts on the gloves and sets the Blood Stone on the altar. When it is in its place, she removes the glove.

"Are you ready," she asks.

I smile and look at my newfound sister, who is not my sister. "Are you?"

We touch the stone together, and the familiar darkness of the object appears.

"You're early," it says.

"And you're grumpy," Liz replies.

There's a warmth to its voice when it responds. "I have every reason to be. So," there's a whoosh near my ear, "to what do I owe this pleasure?"

"She has broken the Blood Pact," I say. "Or, at least we think she has."

"Of course. No one ever drops by just to say 'hi' to Bloodhaven."

"Is that your name?" Liz asks. "It's a little on the nose, isn't it?"

There's a sensation of movement before it says, "Well, that is the point. Lady Death for the Death Stone, Old Soulen for the Soul Stone, and Bloodhaven for Blood Stone."

"But you are all spirits," I say.

"Yes, but as you know, we each have corporeal forms."

He is talking about the moment Liz had to implant my soul into a preserved body. She released Old Soulen, or the Spirit of the Soul Stone, to complete the transfer. If she had not done that, then I would not be here right now. Or, perhaps, she would not be here. The night is still muddled in my mind.

All I can recall is Anton stabbing Mother, Father crying, and Idabelle shrieking her head off. And then, there was silence, a beating heart, Father cradling Mother by his side, and Liz holding me.

"Yes," Liz says, "we do. Now, on to this visit."

"Right," Bloodhaven says.

It moves throughout our consciousness, exploring the ins and outs of our minds, trying to determine whether—

"Ah," he says, "there it is."

"There what is?" I ask just as Lizzy blurts, "What did you find?"

Bloodhaven chuckles. It is the first time I have heard it make a sound like that. "I found two," it says.

"Two?" I ask.

"Two?" Liz repeats.

"Two," Bloodhaven says. "Two children. Two young ones. Two unborn—"

"We get it," Liz says. "I'm having two?" She turns to me. "You told me you only saw one soul. You lied."

"No," I say. "There is only one. Unless I'm wrong?" It comes out as a question. I am a bit out of practice. Is it possible I have forgotten how to identify the number of souls? I ponder this for a moment. No. I did not forget. There was only one soul in addition to hers. A small blue one without a scent. But if I am wrong... I whistle. Two children is a lot to take in. I feel the shake of a head interrupt my thoughts.

"No," Bloodhaven says.

"No?" I ask.

"No?" Liz repeats.

"No," Bloodhaven says. "Two children, one for each of you."

"One for—" I begin.

"Each of us," Liz finishes.

We look at each other. I am not sure if I want to laugh or cry. I do not know how to begin to process this information. I look at my newfound sister, the one who made me a queen to hijack my body but then executed the most ingenious plan in the world to make sure I could live a happy life—with or without her.

"Two," I say.

"Two," Liz repeats.

"Two," Bloodhaven says.

I gawk at them both before rounding on Liz. "You did not tell me that there was a child in me!"

She looks just as surprised as me. She shakes her head and puts up her hands. "That is not my expertise," she reminds me. "But still...isn't it great?" A huge grin begins to spread across her face.

This is not the worst news I have ever heard. But it is too early to celebrate. Bloodhaven has not answered our exact question, and I cannot be as excited as Liz until he does so. "Well," I ask him. I am certain he understands my inquiry.

We hold our breaths, waiting for him to say it.

"Fine," he says. "It is done."

"It's done?" Liz asks.

"It's done. Although you took some liberties," there's a sensation of a pointed look, "you did break the pact successfully. You married Angelo and bore his child as the Blood Pact mandated. And, although you reneged on killing Angelo, you did complete the Blood Pact before the day mentioned in my conditions. So, yes, you are free."

"That is the most he has ever said in a single breath," I tell Liz.

"Indeed." She grins.

And that is it. We are smiling and laughing and hugging in a shared mind space with the Spirit of the Blood Stone.

"Now," Bloodhaven says, "I must rest for another ten years."

"Is that a hard and fast rule?" Liz asks.

"Hmm," it responds. "Not exactly. Why?"

"We would like to see your corporeal form," I say.

"You know," Liz continues, "maybe at our wedding. Or the birth of our children."

Bloodhaven laughs. "I'll consider it." With that, he disappears, and we are sent back into the real world.

"Well," I say, "that was anticlimactic. We just get to live our lives now?"

"Not exactly," Liz says. "There's still at least one more thing to do."

"A week from now, right?" I ask.

"Yes."

"Great. Then tonight, we celebrate the good news."

"I'm with you on that," she says. "After all, it's been a good morning, the men will be excited, and we can end it on a high note."

"How long should we wait to tell them?"

"Let's make them sweat." She bumps my shoulder.

"For most of the day?"

She chuckles. "Yeah, it'll be a surprise. Let's go shopping for a cake or something."

"Okay, but after I shower."

She smells me, and her face blanches. "Yep, after your shower."

"Shut up," I tell her, laughing and giving her a playful push.

Her laugh is musical as she rubs my head, acting as if we were sisters since the beginning.

And in some ways, it feels like we were. I just did not know it.

I ALWAYS THOUGHT THAT a baby shower would be hell, but I failed to account for how much worse it would be with the people participating in mine. The games are okay, but the rest leaves a bit to be desired.

"Liz!" Lizzy shouts my name.

"What!" I shout back.

"Come on, Mother is doing it now."

"Now?" I ask. "During the shower?"

"Yes, so hurry up."

I rub my temples. I'm not sure whose idea it was to turn a baby shower into a baby shower/soul restoration party, but I've got some complaints.

I follow Lizzy past the living room filled with all the stuffed animals and toys that our children won't need and into the kitchen where Mother, Father, Dmitri, and Angelo are waiting for us.

"You came," Father says.

"We did," I reply. I can't say I'm completely on board with being the reason that he and Mother are together, especially knowing everything I know, but I figure it's worth giving it a shot. The worst-case scenario is that it backfires on me and I end up regretting everything. The best case is standing in front of me.

"So, how does this work?" Angelo asks. "Do you just, you know, pop it in like we did for Lizzy?"

"Not exactly," Mother says. "This is a bit more nuanced."

We watch in awe as Mother coaxes Father's soul from inside her. It's smaller than I thought it would be, but I guess that's what happens when it spends millennia in a stone and then another month or so in the body of a Sluagh.

When I traded Anton's and Idabelle's souls for Lizzy's and Father's to be placed in their respective bodies, Old Soulen said that he couldn't do Father's because of the way it had been given to him. All he could do was release it.

So, we went back to Plan A: Have Mother Restore It.

She gently caresses his soul before molding it into the shape of a small person. Then, she gently pushes it into his chest.

Father's amber eyes light up in a way that neither Lizzy nor I have ever seen. It's like a breath of fresh air has taken over.

Everything about his demeanor changes. His posture, his eyes, the way he's smiling. It's like he's a whole new person. And, in a way, he is.

"How long have you been without a soul?" I ask. It slips out before I can stop myself.

"Shortly before you mother left me." Father looks at her and strokes her face. "It's like I am seeing you, truly seeing you, for the first time in a while," he says. "And what is this feeling? I cannot recall it."

Dmitri is looking at Lizzy the same way Angelo is looking at me, and it is the same way Father is looking at Mother right this instance.

"It's called love," I tell him.

"That it is," he says.

And we all just sit at the table, feeling the joy that is love.

But it's short-lived because, moments later, there's a knock on the door.

"I'll get it," I say, getting up to open it. Like before, Regin stands in front of me, looking like he's just stepped out of a photo shoot. "How can I help you, Regin?" I step outside and close the door. "This is a family-only event."

"That it is," he says. "I trust everything went well?"

"Everything? You mean the stones?"

"Yes."

"Yes, they did."

"Wonderful. Then you may return them."

"Return them? I thought they were mine."

"The Blood Stone, yes. But the other two were loans. You understand, right?"

Something in the way he looks at me tells me not to cross him. "Yes," I say, more reverently than I would like to. "I...understand."

"Excellent. Hand them to me, along with my payment, and I will be on my way."

I open the door and get ready to go inside to fetch the Soul and Death Stones.

"What was that about?" Lizzy asks me.

"Nothing, just a...friend, coming to pick something up."

"A friend," she says skeptically. "You have friends?"

I nod.

"Why not invite them in then?"

"No," I say. "They're really busy. Maybe next time."

She gives me the side-eye, like she doesn't believe me. "Okay," she says, "well, try not to take too long or the cake will be gone."

"Right," I say. "Right." I nod at her, go to the altar, put on the gloves, and grab the stones and the four thousand five hundred dollars in cash. Then, I meet Regin outside.

He counts the money and checks that the Stones are what I say they are before placing them in the black box.

"Hey," I say, gesturing to the box. "The other two, they're gone."

He smiles, showing his sharp teeth. "Why, yes," he says, placing them just so. "They are." He closes the box, places it and his gloves in his suit pocket, and turns to me. "Now then," he says, "things to do, places to go. I'll see you at the club." He steps off the porch, but before he walks off, he grins at me. "And don't forget our deal. I'm not Anton or the Spirits. You don't want to fuck with me."

I don't have any words.

"Tallyho." He waves and disappears.

A chill goes up my spine. Did I make another bad deal?

Acknowledgements

I would first like to thank my family and friends for their support in this journey. Mom and Dashè, thank you for your financial and emotional support throughout this process. Dewand, Jane, and Lakita, thank you for cheering me on from the sidelines. Aaron and Athena, thank you for being here for my journey in spirit. A huge thanks to my close friends and beta readers: Derek Lane, Michelle Haynie, Kylin Hunter, and Vernon Scott. I wouldn't have gotten this far without you. I would also like to thank my editor, Michelle Rascon, for putting up with me through the entire revision process. Your help was invaluable and you made the editing process super enjoyable. A thank you Alejandro Smith and Giulia Calligola for working with me to create a book cover that captures the essence of my book and the characters. Alejandro's concept photos were beautiful and Giulia worked hard to turn them into the best cover I could have hoped for. I would also like to thank Monique D. Mensah from Make Your Mark Publishing for the 5 day The Biggest Book Launch Course, Audience Builder Blueprint Course, and all the free information on your socials. I learned so much from you. I would also like to thank my Street Team Members for their ongoing support. Last, but definitely not least, I want to thank my readers, both past and present for your continued support. You all are the best!

About the Author

J.S. Living has an MFA in Writing from the Savannah College of Art and Design. She enjoys binge watching television, spending time with her cat, and, of course, writing like her life depends on it.

Scan the QR code below for a special treat. Don't forget to follow the blood trail by subscribing to J.S. Living's email list and social media.

Twitter: thejsliving
IG: @thejsliving
FB: The JSliving
Website: www.thejsliving.com